"Get your weapon."

Tripp turned back to the closet, pulling out his service revolver before reaching deeper inside. He pulled out an extra gun and handed it over. "You still know how to use one of these?" he screamed.

She avoided the eye roll—and was well aware it would be barely visible through the smoke anyway—and took the gun. "I'm all set."

It was only then that the lights in the house flickered before going fully out.

Tripp's hand on her wrist shifted, his fingers lacing with hers. "Get on the floor and stay close to me."

In the thick, dark smoke they began to crawl for the interior of the house. It was the exact opposite choice of every instinct she possessed to get outside.

But deep down Sadie knew it was their only shot at survival.

* * *

Colton 911: Grand Rapids

Where there's danger—and true love—around every corner...

* * *

If you're on Twitter, tell us what you think of Harlequin Romantic Suspense!
#harlequ

I0836025

Dear Reader,

Welcome back to Grand Rapids and the intense adventure and suspense to be found with the Colton family. The Colton siblings are still reeling from their sister Sadie's kidnapping and the hunt is on to find the CSI expert. But no one is more determined to get her back than GRPD lieutenant Tripp McKellar.

Sadie is still dealing with the fallout from a very personal discovery. She's had a lot of time to think, spending the past month in a police safe house for protection, and she can't stop the self-recrimination and embarrassment from sinking in. A fact that is only made worse when her ex discovers her location and kidnaps her. It's only Tripp's quick thinking that ultimately saves her and puts the two of them in very close proximity.

Sadie's had feelings for the emotionally battered lieutenant for years. She's always pushed those feelings aside, well aware Tripp's tragic past has caused him to believe he'll never love anyone again. But she never expects that he's had secret feelings for her in return.

With Sadie's kidnapping, Tripp is convinced there's no one else who can protect her from her escalating ex-fiancé. Tripp knows he can remain professional and see to her safety, but he never counted on the deep, emotional pull of his feelings as he and Sadie spend time together.

I hope you're enjoying Colton 911: Grand Rapids. I've had such fun being a part of this series and hope you enjoy Tripp and Sadie's love story.

Best,

Addison Fox

COLTON 911: ULTIMATE SHOWDOWN

Addison Fox

HARLEQUIN
ROMANTIC SUSPENSE

Special thanks and acknowledgment are given to Addison Fox
for her contribution to the Colton 911: Grand Rapids miniseries.

Recycling programs
for this product may
not exist in your area.

ISBN-13: 978-1-335-62680-6

Colton 911: Ultimate Showdown

Harlequin Enterprises ULC
22 Adelaide St. West, 40th Floor
Toronto, Ontario M5H 4E3, Canada
www.Harlequin.com

Printed in U.S.A.

Addison Fox is a lifelong romance reader, addicted to happy-ever-afters. After discovering she found as much joy writing about romance as she did reading it, she's never looked back. Addison lives in New York with an apartment full of books, a laptop that's rarely out of sight and a wily beagle who keeps her running. You can find her at her home on the web at www.addisonfox.com or on Facebook (www.Facebook.com/addisonfoxauthor) and Twitter (@addisonfox).

Books by Addison Fox

Harlequin Romantic Suspense

Colton 911: Grand Rapids
Colton 911: Ultimate Showdown

The Coltons of Mustang Valley
Deadly Colton Search

The Coltons of Roaring Springs
The Colton Sheriff

Midnight Pass, Texas
The Cowboy's Deadly Mission
Special Ops Cowboy

The Coltons of Red Ridge
Colton's Deadly Engagement

The Coltons of Shadow Creek
Cold Case Colton

The Coltons of Texas
Colton's Surprise Heir

Visit the Author Profile page at Harlequin.com for more titles.

For April, Carley, Christine and Roxane.

Sisters of the heart. Always.

Prologue

It's called a safe house for a reason.

Sadie Colton had told herself that endlessly and she was no closer to liking it or believing the seriousness of the words. And she was sick to death of being cooped up with nothing but her awful thoughts and even worse self-recriminations.

How could she have been so stupid?

And not just sort-of-flighty-edging-toward-stupid stupid. Oh no, she was in that special league of foolishness that bordered on too ridiculously stupid to live, nullified only by the whole safe house thing.

That meant she was stuck. Physically *and* emotionally.

She tossed a few paperbacks into a packing box. How could she not have known? Was she so desperate for a relationship that she'd ignored every single sign her fiancé was a piece of crap? Worse, that he was the head of an entire criminal empire, a loan sharking organization called Capital X.

And she'd had no idea.

Not. One. Single. Clue.

She was a freaking crime scene investigator, for heaven's sake. That—*hello?*—meant she hunted clues for a living. Clues she uncovered and then used to solve crimes with the most minimal of information...

But if she tried to solve for "X" in Capital X, all she got was *Capitally Duped.* Worse, she was obviously clue*less* about her own life.

The same scenes that had kept her company flooded her mind once more. The time she'd spent with Tate, so convinced he was the man she'd waited her whole life for. Followed by the stunning realization the man she'd been so close to binding her life with was not only a bad guy, but had only been with her to get close to the Grand Rapids PD and her family's business.

Colton Investigations was one of the premier private investigative firms in the country and did work for both the Grand Rapids PD as well as private citizens locally and nationally. It was painful to acknowledge, but she now knew her family name and connections had been the only things Tate Greer had seen when he'd looked at her. And he'd preyed on her deep-seated desire for love and a family of her own as his way in.

Only now it had all blown sky-high. One of Tate's top goons at Capital X, Gunther Johnson, had been pulled in by the GRPD a few months ago. And now the team was after Tate. Sadie had gone from dupe to target, as kidnapping her would give Tate a huge bargaining chip against her family. Both the biological one and the metaphorical one she shared with the GRPD.

So here she was, squirreled away in some hidey-hole while others were doing the real work of catching Tate and taking down his criminal empire.

Her mind drifted to what her colleagues in CSI as well as the broader GRPD might think of her. Men and women who worked so hard to keep the good citizens of Grand Rapids safe and who were, even now, dealing with a criminal enterprise that had roots that went deeper than anyone really knew.

What did Tripp think?

Although she'd avoided personal flights of fancy since the faint stirrings of attraction she'd tamped down on in her early days with the force, Lieutenant Tripp McKellar helped run a tight ship at the GRPD. He'd also always had the uncanny ability to make her pulse kick up a few notches when she was in his presence. Even once she'd fallen in love with Tate, she'd never been fully immune to the lieutenant's appeal. She'd never do anything, of course—Tripp fell firmly in the off-limits category and always had—but she couldn't fully ignore that little flutter she kept secret.

Now he likely thought she was a ridiculous fool, not to mention a drain on department resources. All while he'd been working overtime on the RevitaYou case. The very case that had brought Tate's shady dealings into the light.

What was supposed to be a virtual miracle worker of an antiaging supplement, turning the clock back ten years for anyone who took the product, had been exposed for its dirty underpinnings. RevitaYou not only *wasn't* a miracle, it was a dangerous one at that. Its "re-

storative" properties came with a nasty side effect—
death due to castor oil in the product that turned into
ricin. It gave RevitaYou its functional properties but had
horrifying side effects. The product inventor, Landon
Street, had already been caught, but the damage his
product had wrought was already extensive. Add dis-
tribution via a pyramid scheme masterminded by Capital X, and Tripp was dealing with an incredibly vile
business.

Her family had been helping however it could, but
the shady powerbrokers behind the scenes had been
running her eldest brother, Riley, ragged as he tried
to manage the investigation, help their foster brother,
Brody Higgins, who'd gotten mixed up in it all, *and* run
Colton Investigations.

And here she was, the proverbial princess in a tower,
locked away and unable to help anyone.

A princess who was about to go on the move.

Again.

Her family had decided she needed to relocate to a
new safe house and, having been out of the loop for the
past month, she'd agreed.

At least she got to see her twin, Vikki.

"You said you were thinking you'd re-up for another
five years." Sadie looked around the room, marveling
at how relieved she was to be leaving the small space.

Her twin was a JAG paralegal and had always taken
her military service seriously. But Vik juggled a lot and
Sadie was surprised to realize how much she hoped her
sister would slow down a bit and remain closer to home.

"I know I did. I've so loved the Army job, but it's time
for me to make a change. I want to focus exclusively on

CI. This way I can support Riley without always feeling so torn between my active duty time or working for CI."

"I never looked at it that way," Sadie said. "You really haven't had a break in a long time, have you?"

Sadie understood that battle. Riley was regularly trying to recruit her full time to the family cause. And while there were definitely appealing aspects to working for the family business, she loved her work in CSI and wasn't ready to give it up.

"No, but I get fun in where I can," Vikki said.

Fun.

Sadie remembered fun. Once upon a time. Before she'd fallen in love with Tate Greer and had believed a bright future still awaited her.

The low growl of her stomach had her glancing in the direction of the kitchen. She didn't skip meals.

A fact she'd worried over while engaged to Tate.

She actually *liked* her curves, but Tate had a way about him that had always left her a little intimidated. Like she should count herself lucky, somehow. Not lucky like how-great-is-it-I-found-the-love-of-my-life lucky, but more of a my-luck-is-going-to-run-out-if-I-do-something-wrong lucky.

And really, she admitted to herself, that wasn't any sort of lucky at all.

A fact that only added one *more* check in the box on the list of self-recriminations over why she'd ignored the small but insistent voice in the back of her mind.

Seeking a diversion from her low thoughts, Sadie pressed Vikki about the man she'd fallen in love with. "Speaking of fun, what have you heard from Flynn since last week's takedown?"

"I won't talk about it anymore, Sadie."

Sadie felt that small flash of anger that flared whenever she had an argument with her twin, but the misery that hovered deep in Vikki's gaze had Sadie holding her tongue.

Vikki and Flynn had been through a lot. The Revita-You case was personal to Flynn and she had to imagine the man was dealing with a lot. Especially the news that his family member was instrumental in the development of the drug. "I still think I'm right. Landon was his half brother, for heaven's sake. That's a huge family deal. I'm sure Flynn needs time to process, and to do all the Army paperwork for why he was involved in the apprehension while he was on leave. Then you'll hear from him. When he knows it's right for both of you."

Sadie didn't get the sense Vikki agreed with her but she let her twin talk it out a bit before shifting gears to more inane topics like how she was going to keep busy.

"Time to go, Sadie." Her brother Riley walked into the room, his impatient gaze scanning the luggage. "You sure have collected a lot of stuff for being locked down the past several weeks."

"We'll get it in the car ourselves, don't you worry," Vikki batted back at their brother.

Riley scanned the room. "I'd rather wait until the FBI gets here. Give it five minutes. I'm going to do a quick sweep of the house and use the restroom."

Sadie knew they needed to be careful. The threat was real, no matter how much she wanted to believe otherwise. But all this process…

Moving to a new safe house. Waiting for an FBI escort. She let out a small sigh as the sound of vehicles echoed from outside the door. It was all too much.

"That's our cue." Vikki picked up a box.

Whether it was the desire to taunt her brother or just the mindlessly boring stretch of time yawning in front of her, Sadie picked up another box and tilted her head toward the door. "I'd love to have the truck packed before Riley's out of the bathroom."

As usual, her twin was in sync and Vikki pushed through the door, propping the screen with her foot. Sadie juggled the box, walking through the door as a low growl registered from behind Vikki's shoulder.

"Don't move or your sister's dead, Vikki."

Sadie saw it happen. She heard the words and registered the press of a gun to Vikki's temple, all while the carefully packed box dropped with a thud on the front porch of the safe house.

The same man stared pointedly at Sadie. "Either of you make a sound, you're all dead."

"Take her. Now!"

Sadie felt big hands close over her shoulders but wasn't able to do anything but stare. She was shocked stone-cold still by the voice of her ex-fiancé, echoing in the cold December air. Her feet finally moved as she registered the hard press of a gun to her back, pushing her forward.

"Hi, honey." Tate Greer grinned at her from where he stood beside a large SUV. The menace lacing that smile was only matched by the equally threatening sight of the semiautomatic held high in his right hand. "You're coming home with me."

Chapter 1

Tripp McKellar rubbed a hand over his growling stomach, the only acknowledgment he gave to the long hours he'd put in these past two days.

Sadie Colton was missing.

He'd sworn to her family he'd find her, but the continuously ticking clock—one that came with no answers to her whereabouts—had him working overtime with no solution in sight.

And the increasing fear he wouldn't get to her in time.

As dark images flashed through his mind, Tripp pushed them aside, just as he had for the past few days. Just as he had pushed aside his attraction for Sadie these past several years. His full focus needed to be on finding her.

Despite the increasingly dark thoughts that clouded

his mind, he remained equally hopeful Tate Greer was playing a bigger game. Why kidnap her if the man wasn't going to use it to his advantage? Sadie was only a bargaining chip if she were alive, and Tripp held on tightly to the fact that Greer knew that.

Only, Greer hadn't reached out yet, outlining his demands. Nor had he given any indication he was going to.

That left Tripp right back at square one.

Sadie was missing, in the hands of a dangerous madman, and he was no closer to finding her than he had been thirty-six hours ago when she'd been first taken.

Her sister Vikki had fired the warning shot over the bow, convinced her twin was in trouble despite the repeated checks the GPRD had made on Sadie in that safe house. Although he trusted his team, he trusted the Colton family, as well, and Vikki Colton was known for her cool head and her love of her family. Tripp and his team had moved in the very night Vikki had sounded the alarm and were too late.

Too damn late. He uttered a dark curse before he stood and marched over to his office wall and the oversize map of Grand Rapids and the surrounding county. No matter how scared he was for Sadie's safety, he had to *think*. Really think, instead of giving in to the continued self-recrimination that had kept him company for two days.

He'd been working the RevitaYou case for several months now; the various marks on that map reflections of what he'd already learned. "Think, McKellar," he muttered to himself. "What do you know?"

His gaze scanned the map once more, following a radius around the safe house. He still hadn't figured out how Greer had found it, which would be his next

order of business once he got Sadie back. He'd already
dealt a few months ago with a corrupt cop in his department. Joe McRath's death had sent some serious
ripples through the GRPD, and they were still dealing
with the emotional fallout and loss of trust.

Corrupt cops had a way of doing that.

And now he had a problem with a department safe
house? How the hell were some of the worst criminals
in the county getting their hands on sensitive information like that?

It was an urgent problem, but one he had to depriori-
tize until he found Sadie. And while he'd like to bring
in help to uncover the mole, he didn't know whom he
could trust to ferret out the answer.

A problem for a different day, he reminded himself as the frustration threatened to swamp him. In the
meantime, he had to go on the information he had.

Several points on the map were marked with red
pushpins, representative of Capital X crimes. The thugs
rarely took out hits in public. Rather, they enjoyed preying on their victims then taking them to a secure location to rough them up. That was how the Coltons
had gotten involved in the first place. Brody Higgins,
a young man who'd been a part of their family after
moving through the foster care system, had gotten in
with the Capital X crowd. He hadn't known the depth
of Capital X's depravity until it was too late. What
started as a demand for money a mark had inevitably
borrowed with no ability to pay back, slowly morphed
into an exercise in torture and abject pain.

But it also meant there was very little creativity with
respect to where the bodies were dropped.

Thinking about their torture methods—and the immediate danger to Sadie, who had been engaged to their boss—had his stomach curling, but Tripp pushed it back. What was on this map he could use? With that foremost in his mind, he evaluated the red pushpin locations again. Once they'd narrowed in on Capital X as a crime organization, they'd begun to understand some of their patterns. With each layer of investigation, they'd added more pushpins to their map.

There were three clusters. One near the spot where Capital X henchman Gunther Johnson had been captured. One in a run-down public park on the outskirts of the city. And one at a large lake outside of Grand Rapids.

Was it possible?

Tripp quickly calculated the distance between the safe house and the lake, and estimated there couldn't be more than about fifteen miles between them.

Had Sadie been that close all along?

With an image of the lake and surrounding area filling his mind's eye, Tripp snagged his coat off the back of his chair and slipped it on, covering the holstered weapon strapped to his back. The clutch piece at his ankle was an additional weight of security as he headed for the door.

They still had one of Capital X's henchmen in custody. It looked like it was time to have a little talk with Gunther Johnson.

Sadie stared at the walls of the small room she'd been in for who knew how long and counted off what she knew in her head. Tate's unexpected arrival had been the start of this ordeal. She'd been fed three meals since then, and another two today, so two full days hadn't yet passed.

Nor had she seen Tate.

A tactic or something else? Was he out making misery on others? Worse, was he plotting and planning against her family? Against the GRPD?

Thoughts of her coworkers filled her mind's eye, from the dispatch staff to the detectives' squad to her fellow crime scene investigators. She meticulously cataloged each of them in her head, saving the best for last.

Tripp McKellar.

Whether it was the despair of the past few days or an inability to hold her mind back any longer, she'd finally given her thoughts of their tall, imposing lieutenant free reign in her mind.

She cared for him and always had. Perhaps he was unattainable, but that didn't make her feelings any less real. Or her attraction to him any less powerful. How funny that with Tate's true nature revealed, it only served to highlight even further what a good man Tripp McKellar was.

No flashy persona or bad-boy good looks like Tate. Instead, there was raw honesty, framed out in a square jaw, dark blond hair and blue eyes that had seen sadness yet had never become bitter. He was full of strength without being hard-edged. There was power in that, Sadie acknowledged to herself.

Real power.

It also left her with a very real, very tangible, counterpoint to Tate Greer. The pill of his betrayal had been terribly bitter to swallow, but she'd spent a lot of time thinking about their relationship during the long, lonely days in the safe house. She'd dissected it, forcing herself to really look deeply at what choices she'd made, voluntarily.

It had also given her time to think about the things she'd overlooked.

"You couldn't have known, Sadie. No one could have." Vikki's voice was gentle but the grim set of her face carried the same conviction Sadie had felt since the moment Tate's true nature had come to light.

"I'm a trained cop. I should have known," Sadie shot back.

"How? Is clairvoyance in the job description for either role?"

"No, but I do know how to consider the angles. How to evaluate data and pull clues from it, no matter how little evidence I have to go on. Yet I allowed Tate Greer into my life—" Sadie flung a hand wide "—into all our lives. And for what? Because I was so damn happy to finally have a man?"

That look of fierce protection on her twin's face shifted, remolding itself into a mask of pure and utter fury.

"Don't talk about yourself that way. I won't hear of it or tolerate it. You're a good person, Sadie. You've got the biggest heart of anyone I know. More, I know you. Know who you are and how you see the world. Do not let some jerk like Tate Greer, a man who has proved himself to prey on others, taint that. Or make you question yourself."

The remembered conversation winked out of her mind, replaced by the breath-stealing fear she'd never see her sister again. Although their conversation at the safe house suggested Vikki and Flynn had a lot to figure out, her twin had fallen for Flynn Cruz-Street, the US MP who worked on the same Army base as Vikki did. After he was attacked on base by his captain, who had discharged his weapon, Vikki had been immersed in the case as the JAG paralegal.

All because of RevitaYou…

Sadie considered that, turning it over in her mind.

Some wonder drug. A supposed miracle pill that was killing people.

A shady operation helmed by her ex-fiancé, masterminding it all.

And all of it unraveling, right here in the hands of Colton Investigations and the Grand Rapids PD.

Sadie let out a hard sigh.

How had they missed it for so long? A question Tripp was no doubt asking himself. They didn't know each other well, but she had no doubt this case was causing him lost sleep and a level of personal heartache only someone who demanded so much from himself professionally could manage.

Even now, she could picture the hard set of his jaw as he worked through the problem. She'd talked to him a few times since the RevitaYou case had broken, her own family deeply integrated in the investigation. Her oldest brother, Riley, the head of Colton Investigations, had been working the case since former foster kid Brody Higgins had come to them for help.

The Coltons had taken the misguided eighteen-year-old in after he'd aged out of the foster system but wasn't quite ready to be on his own. Her father had believed in Brody's innocence of a deadly crime, but had been murdered before he could prove it. Even with Graham

Colton's pull as the district attorney, it had been a hard fight to see Brody proven innocent. It had been a tough road, but it had made them all appreciate their father's life's work that much more.

And, whether by accident or fate, it had led to the formation of Colton Investigations.

It might now be her brother's life's work, but all of the children of Graham and Katherine Colton took part. The fight for justice, instilled in them by their father, ran deep in the blood.

So when Brody had come to Riley back in July, confessing his part in the RevitaYou scheme, their collective, underlying desire was to berate the young man they'd all come to see as a brother. But as the case wore on, and Brody had disappeared after being attacked by Capital X—*Tate's*—goons, Sadie had come to realize it was something else entirely.

RevitaYou was not only a pyramid scheme, it was killing people. Good people, like Teri Joseph, the wife of Flynn's former captain. And several other victims whose names had been linked to the drug and whose photos, even now, she was sure were pinned to Tripp's crime board at the police station.

Brody had found out about the negative aspects of RevitaYou far too late. He'd fallen for the sales pitch and the mind-bending results the drug produced in the first few weeks of use. Because of it, Brody had rushed to invest, taking funding from Capital X to support his "investment." Only there wasn't any investment to be had, only a pyramid scheme and a violent organization waiting at the other end to collect. One that used the darkest corners of the internet to do its work.

Sadie shuddered, the image of Brody being brutalized at the hands of Tate's men spearing through her.

He was still alive—it was hard to get money out of a dead mark—but Capital X sure loved making life miserable for those who couldn't pay. Since that was the essence of their business model—either pay back a loan at exorbitant rates or get your fingers broken, one by one—their operation was never at a loss for capital.

Or, apparently, marks to do their bidding.

And she'd missed it all. Missed Tate's romancing her to get close to Colton Investigations as well as the GRPD.

Missed the fact that he'd disappeared for stretches at a time that she'd chalked up to a businessman needing the space to run his business.

And she'd sure as hell missed every single sign that suggested he was a violent sociopath whose need to control everything and everyone around him went bone deep.

Now she was here, and her family knew she was missing, and Tripp was trying to solve the case, and it was all a raging mess. One with violent undertones that—as the hours passed—she convinced herself had no pathway to a good end.

"Way to be a defeatist, Colton," she muttered to herself. And just as tears threatened, she heard her father's voice in her head.

What do you know, Sadie Pie? Not what you think, but what you know...

With her father's reassuring voice still ringing in her head, Sadie pushed down—*hard*—on the idea that she'd never see her twin sister or her family or anyone else she cared about. Instead, she forced herself to go through what she *knew*.

Because she might not be guaranteed a happy ending but she sure as hell wasn't going to willingly proceed even further into a nightmare.

That meant she had to think. She had to be smart. And she had to quit worrying about all the reasons she was in this mess and start thinking of ways to get herself out of it.

Although Tate and his henchmen had subdued her the other night at the safe house, they hadn't drugged her. That had given her a rough estimate in her mind of how long it had taken them to arrive at wherever she was now. She wasn't any more than fifteen or twenty minutes from the safe house.

With a map of the county spreading out in her mind, she worked it through, the safe house the epicenter of her mental images. Fifteen to twenty minutes one direction took her to downtown Grand Rapids, but it had been too quiet outside for her to think they were in the city. With one direction checked off, she analyzed the others. As she worked it slowly in her mind, a vague memory of the drive to summer camp shot up to surprise her.

She hadn't wanted to go that first year and the drive to Sand Springs Lake had seemed over before it had barely begun. Her mother had assured her that not only would Sadie have an amazing time at camp, but if she needed anything, her parents were only twenty minutes away.

Twenty minutes away…

Was it that easy? Was she really that close?

Willing her pounding heart to slow, she ran the map

through her mind's eye once more, following the various directions to the land formations that stretched out. And came up with the same conclusion the second time around.

She remained absolutely certain she wasn't downtown. And she'd bet anything she was nowhere near the suburbs that speared off in another direction from the safe house. That only left Sand Springs Lake or more distant suburbs broken up by farmland in the final direction. A secluded lake in December made a heck of a lot of sense.

Sadie searched her memory for any conversation she and Tate might have had about the area surrounding Grand Rapids, her summer camp experiences, holiday vacation cottages, or anything else that might have been said in passing conversation. In retrospect, that should have been another clue—that she and Tate really hadn't *talked* about anything. As the urge to berate herself welled up again, the tiniest fraction of a memory hit her full-on.

"My loathing for the great outdoors started early in life. Summer camp to be exact."

Tate smiled before running the tip of his finger over her hip. "Not a nature girl?"

"So not a nature girl."

"Like I couldn't have guessed that."

Sadie heard the slight sharpness through the joke but pushed it down. Did she have to take everything so seriously? Ignoring the prick of discomfort, she laid a hand over his, lacing their fingers. "Well, you can thank Sand Springs Lake for beating any sense of natural adventure out of me. From archery to rowing, I hated it all. I can still imagine all the creepy things floating on the bottom of that lake, just waiting for me if we accidentally tipped our canoe."

"There's not much in that lake. A few secrets, maybe." He leaned in then, pressing a kiss to her neck and distracting her from the conversation.

He'd done that a lot, she'd realized in her month-long, mental, deep-dive dissection into the sad, tragic tale of Sadie Colton's engagement to Tate Greer. If he hadn't been asking her questions, he'd been distracting her with sex. And in her naïveté she hadn't even been aware it was happening.

She'd had a lot of time to think about that, too. It was uncomfortable emotional work, but she'd made herself look at her responses to Tate—and her willingness to ignore signs—assuming it was due to her lack of prior relationships. While it had become comforting—and way too comfortable—to wallow in those memories, she had to acknowledge this one paid dividends. Not only had they discussed Sand Springs Lake and Tate had made that weird comment about secrets, he had swung back around to that discussion after sex. And he'd mentioned loving the lake and spending time there as a kid.

If he'd loved it then, it stood to reason he'd love it as an adult. And he'd equally recognize that a lake used by summer camps didn't have a lot of need for the area once the weather turned cold.

A secluded lake would be highly beneficial for his purposes. It kept him close enough to Grand Rapids to get in and out of the city for business, and it kept him secluded enough to manage his dirty deeds far away from the notice of law enforcement.

A heavy thud echoed through the walls and Sadie heard the harsh laughter of Tate's goons. She still hadn't gotten names for either of them so had dubbed them Fred and Barney for lack of anything better. The names had fit if for no other reason than one was big and brutish-looking and the other was spark-plug short, with a round barrel chest and empty eyes.

She'd filed away other details, too. They spent minimal time with her, bringing in her food and ignoring any question she asked. It was eerie how they were able to be present yet completely absent.

As if they'd been brainwashed by Tate to do nothing but carry out his orders.

For all her upset at how Tate had played her, there was a bigger part of Sadie that recognized those same lifeless eyes and automatous countenance could have been her if she'd ended up with Tate Greer. Much as it pained her to imagine it, the thought also gave her strength.

And much needed purpose.

The door swung open and Barney walked in. He barely glanced at her as he crossed the room to set a plate of food on a small table. Sadie could see the outer room beyond the door, and wasn't sure if it was an accident that Barney had left the door open or a small offering from the universe, but decided worrying about it only wasted time.

She had to move.

So with speed born of desperate purpose, she did.

Tripp raced toward Sand Springs Lake, located on the outskirts of Grand Rapids. It was known around the state as a summer destination, with a variety of kids' camps populating the perimeter as well as a canoeing outfit that had become quite a draw in recent years. Despite a swelling population when the weather warmed, the entire area remained fairly isolated in the winter.

As each mile ticked past, Tripp vacillated between the satisfaction that he was right, and he'd get Sadie back, and the horror that if he was wrong he'd only add more time to the hours she'd been missing without discovery.

Just like Lila.

Tripp shook his head.

It was nothing like Lila.

Nothing at all like knowing someone he'd cared for had been gunned down in cold blood by someone with a vendetta. Not against the pregnant woman at the end of the bullet, but against the man she'd loved, cared for, and had chosen to spend her life with.

Tripp scrubbed a hand over his face, the two-day-old beard scratching against the tips of his fingers.

Focus. Don't let the memories come. Don't listen to the lies they weave beneath the truth you know.

Wasn't that what his therapist had told him? The professional he'd finally given in and gone to see at the urging of his chief, Andrew Fox. He'd given it an honest shot, despite his skepticism, but in the end, other than a few coping mechanisms for times of extreme stress, Tripp could hardly call the sessions time well spent.

What could a therapist do, really? A criminal Tripp had put away, but whom the justice system had set free on a technicality, had gunned down his pregnant fiancée. Instead of coming after Tripp to settle the score, the bastard had found another way.

One far more meaningful and destructive.

Other than coping day to day through life, there wasn't anything else to do.

That was why he had to help Sadie. He'd made a promise to her family. Moreover, he'd made a promise to her and each and every member of the GRPD when he'd sworn he'd fight to protect them.

And if there was that small matter of how he'd always noticed her, a small shot of attraction he refused to act on simmering just beneath the surface, well, he'd accept it. Use it, really, to keep himself focused.

Because damn it, he was getting her back.

His cell rang, penetrating the urgent thoughts. He hit the Bluetooth button on his steering wheel just as he made the last turn onto the two-lane road that led to Sand Springs Lake. "McKellar."

"Where the hell are you?" Detective Emmanuel Iglesias's voice shot through the car's speaker. "Michaela just told me you put out a call for backup."

Although playing a hunch, Tripp hadn't been foolish enough to go in alone and had called Dispatch before leaving. But he had refused to wait around for anyone to join him. Every second was precious and Sadie didn't have any to waste.

"I did."

"Out to Sand Springs Lake? You think that's where Sadie is?"

Tripp had endless respect for the detective, but also knew he was on sensitive ground. With Emmanuel planning a wedding to Sadie's sister Pippa, he wanted to give them hope without overpromising.

Even if he felt this hunch clear down to his marrow.

"It's a hunch, but it's a good one. I triangulated all of

Capital X's victim drops over the past five years. And there's a lot to be said for an isolated lake in winter."

"Damn it." Emmanuel swore again, harsher this time. "She's been under our damn nose for two days?"

"That's what I'm betting on." Tripp slowed and cut his lights. He'd get out and walk if he thought it would help, but the area around the lake was big enough he'd waste precious time on foot versus risking the possibility of someone seeing or hearing a random car.

"Listen. I need you to work with Michaela on the coordination with the team. She's working on it but we need more cops on the perimeter if these jerks cut and run."

"There are three entrances to the lake area."

"Then let's get going and put teams on all three."

Tripp cut the call, his sole focus on what was visible through his front window.

The hollow husk of a summer camp came up on his left. The main building came first; a long, nondescript structure silhouetted by the moon. Small cabins were also discernible in the distance beyond the main outbuilding. Although the location was private, Tripp ruled it out for now. Based on Capital X's former crimes, he figured they'd need a private place of their own to shake down their victims. Squatting in an existing structure— even in the off-season—would risk unwanted attention.

He rolled down his window as he drove on, the dirt path going a long way toward muffling his approach. Despite the temperature, he wanted a shot at hearing anything that might carry on the cold night air. The path took him on a curving route around the perimeter of the lake and he passed the turnoff for one of the entrances Emmanuel had mentioned. GRPD didn't have men in place yet, but he had confidence in Iglesias that they'd be there.

For now, all Tripp could do was focus on Sadie.

Unbidden, a memory of coming upon her one evening came to mind. He'd run down to CSI himself to check on some ballistics results he needed and she'd been dancing around the room, oblivious to anyone else. He'd been captivated, happiness seeming to flow from her as she bopped along to whatever noise filled her earbuds.

He'd backed away, wanting her to have her privacy instead of possible embarrassment at being discovered by the boss, but the memory had stuck with him.

And the feeling of standing, for the briefest moment, in all that bright, vivid sunlight.

Willing that she'd find that happiness again, Tripp pressed on, the leafless trees allowing him to navigate easily with only the moon. A blast of frigid December air blew through the window but he ignored it. Chill was a small price to pay if it got him to Sadie.

It was only as he navigated another bend in the road that he heard it.

The unmistakable sound of a gunshot ricocheting through the clear night air.

Chapter 2

Sadie screamed as she caught sight of Tate, standing over Fred's body. The grisly scene had her stomach leaping into her throat and she sent up a silent prayer of thanks for her crime scene training. It couldn't erase the fact that her ex-fiancé was standing over the body of a man he'd just killed, but it did go a long way toward helping her keep a steady head.

A fact that nearly vanished when Tate swung the gun toward her. "Going somewhere?"

"You surprised?"

She had the slightest moment of triumph as she saw genuine shock cross his face before it winked out. Just like any bit of decency or goodness he might have once possessed.

With the shock gone, it left room for that cold sneer she resented with everything she was. "When did you grow a spine?"

How had she missed this?

And in what world was there a human who thought Sadie Colton lacked a spine? Yet even as the thought flashed in her mind, she had an answer ready to rise up and meet it.

She'd done that. She'd been so enamored of finally having her "true love" that she'd sublimated everything about herself for him.

It was such a useless, circular path, yet she found she couldn't stop treading over it again and again. How had she been so incredibly blind to who this man was?

A liar. A cheat. And now confirming what she'd already suspected, a killer.

"I've had one. You've just been too busy crushing me beneath your boot that you never took the time to look."

Tate's sneer—and the slow, lascivious slide of his gaze down her body and right back up—had her skin prickling in disgust. "I looked plenty, baby. And I never heard you complaining."

"Why did you kill him?"

That sneer turned even darker, twisting the face she'd once found bad-boy handsome into something downright devilish. "He's useless. And he let himself be followed here. I just got word disp—" he broke off, saying no more. Only Sadie didn't need more.

"We're not exactly hard to find. You think you're the only person who knows about Sand Springs Lake?" Her gamble was rewarded with Tate's near growl as he stared down at Fred.

"The bastard give you that information, too?"

"I figured it out all on my own. You didn't take me that far. Where else is this secluded this time of year? And who's working inside the GRPD for you?"

For the second time in a space of minutes, Tate's gaze flashed with that mix of surprise and something just a tad bit more. She wouldn't go as far as to say respect— he clearly wasn't capable of feeling that for anyone— but there was something there.

And Sadie took heart that maybe Tate might have the slightest indication he'd underestimated her.

Well aware she had little to lose, Sadie kept on pushing. "How do you manage to find people to work with you if you go around shooting them for telling you the truth?"

"I shot him for incompetence. The truth was just an inconvenience." That subtle sense he saw something new in her seemed to hover between them once more before he added, "And with the right tech, baby, you don't need to find squealers anymore."

Sadie eyed the gun still leveled at her chest, even as she filed away that tidbit for the GRPD. "Would you mind putting that down?"

"I very much mind."

Any shred of smug satisfaction she might have felt evaporated, faced with the very real knowledge Tate cared as little for her as he had for Fred. Up to now, she'd believed she was an asset to him, but she might have been overestimating the degree to which their former relationship might influence his decision to keep her alive.

"It dawns on me that you're uniquely positioned to help me out, despite Fred's incompetence," he said.

That gun never moved, nor did Tate's gaze.

"And how would I do that?"

"What does the GRPD know about Capital X?

And—" Tate leaned in closer "—what does your brother know?"

She knew he meant Riley and his role running Colton Investigations. Riley had earned a place of respect from the GRPD, his willingness to work with them and support their efforts going a long way toward fostering a good working relationship between the two.

Because she'd let him into her life, Tate knew that, too.

And the fact that he was asking meant his "all seeing" tech wasn't quite as mighty as he'd want it to be.

An aggressive bark from another part of the house drew her attention and was enough to remove Tate's scrutiny. He swore before moving toward the other room in the direction of the dog. "I'll be right back."

Although her instinct was to stay as far away from the gun and that ominous sound as possible, after two days, Sadie still didn't have a good sense of the house. The chance to learn a bit more of the layout wasn't something she could pass up.

Besides, she'd prefer to avoid staying anywhere near Fred's body.

So she followed Tate, not caring if it pissed him off. She needed as much information as she could get and sitting around like a wilting flower was not that way.

Tate had moved into a larger combined kitchen and living area, his attention momentarily focused on the dog. The German shepherd was gorgeous but dangerous-looking. A reality that only heightened when the dog caught sight of her, his ears perking as his lips quivered with clear threat.

Sadie was so shocked to see the dog holding still at

Tate's command, the words were out before she could stop them. "Since when do you have a pet?"

Tate kept the dog in place, but shifted his attention to her. "One more thing you don't know about me because you weren't meant to know. But Snake and I go back a long way."

"You named your dog Snake?"

Tate's flat expression wasn't amused. "What does the GRPD know about Capital X?"

Sadie considered how to play this. While she wasn't proud of her time with Tate, she had learned how to handle him. She could only hope that she knew enough tactics to buy herself a bit more time.

"You've been tracking them for months, securing intel off your informants. You likely know more than they do."

He hesitated for the briefest moment and Sadie sensed her compliment had hit the mark. Tate wasn't going to back off, but the subtle distraction was a help.

Every moment counted.

And she made the most of this one. Through the kitchen, visible beyond the dog, was a door. The heavy wood had a glass-paneled top half. She could see no bars or trappings through the panes to suggest it was further blocked by an outer door.

That door had to be her goal.

"I want to know what you know." Tate had dropped the gun during the interaction with the dog but he quickly lifted it again. "Now!"

"I don't know anything."

The gun never wavered as Tate moved closer. "You were never straight with me. Always hiding behind your family and their connections and the big bad badges at the GRPD."

"I wasn't the one who spent our entire relationship lying."

"Oh no?"

His audacity—the fact that he could stand there and suggest she hadn't been honest with him—was a joke. "You got with me for no other reason than to ferret out information you could use for your criminal activities. I never meant anything to you."

"Not like you ever gave me anything. You and your brothers and sisters are so tight. Colton Investigations." He nearly spat the name. "You're thick as thieves, only you're all so damn pure you'd never put a hand on a piece of anyone's gold."

"While I'd hardly apologize for that to anyone, I'm sure as hell not going to apologize to you."

Sadie had no idea where it was coming from—especially with that gun still in dangerous range—but she simply couldn't stand there and take it any longer. Maybe a month in a safe house, with nothing to do but ponder all the ways she'd lost part of herself to Tate Greer, was finally finding its due.

And maybe she might even get a few of those pieces she'd given away back.

"What the hell do you know, Sadie!" The harsh shout spilled out of Tate like a violent waterfall. The dog never moved, but she sensed the tense set of his body—ready to leap at the slightest signal—even as Tate stepped closer.

Sadie knew she should keep her gaze on the gun but she was unable to look away from the veneer of sheer hate that covered Tate's face. The dog whined beside him, a small growl that affirmed all she suspected about the animal's training. And still, that gun remained leveled at the center of her chest.

A hard slam echoed through the house along with a rush of winter air as the door in the kitchen flew open. Despite the gun, her gaze shifted to the door and the possibility of a new threat, only to find Barney stomping into the kitchen.

"Cops found us."

Tate swung around to face his other goon as Sadie saw another man tromp into the kitchen. He was as big as Fred had been, with hulking shoulders and a lethal-looking semiautomatic hanging from one meaty hand. Although Sadie had minimal exposure to the black market weapons trade in Michigan, she'd reviewed enough crime scenes and studied enough wounds to know what that type of weapon did to the human body.

An involuntary shiver skated down her spine as she weighed what she had to do.

Tate was shouting at Barney over the announcement there were cops, and the new henchman was adding his perspective, suggesting how to handle the threat. All three men were *right there*—along with their weapons— but so was the open door.

While she knew it was a suicide mission to try to run, it was still a better option than staying put.

With one final glance at the door, Sadie focused on the dog. He'd stayed in the position Tate had put him in, his training so absolute he hadn't moved. Sadie hoped that rigid training would be enough to give her the head start she needed.

Without giving herself one more moment to think, she bolted, her unerring focus on the door and the freedom just beyond.

* * *

Tripp held his position, the small copse of trees about fifty yards from the house his hiding place. The crystalline air had aided his listening in on the argument being waged inside the house, while also giving him time to assess their firepower and position.

He knew Sadie was in there.

He might not be able to see her, but he knew she was there. He'd heard her, her sweet voice floating through that cold night air. She'd been kidnapped and locked away by a madman, but what he'd been able to make out had held steady and solid. Tripp fought that sense of helplessness—the one that kept threatening to drag him under like a massive wave at the beach, complete with deadly undertow—and kept his attention on the house. This wasn't the same as losing Lila, he reminded himself over and over.

It. Wasn't. The. Same.

Instead, he needed to find a way in. But based on the two goons he'd already seen enter, he knew he was outnumbered.

Damn it, how had they missed this? An organization like Capital X, operating right under their noses. He was well aware organized crime was a consistent bane of police squads the world over, but the fact that Capital X had managed to stay under the radar for so long was a concern.

And Sadie Colton had somehow landed right in the middle of it all.

His mobile phone buzzed at his hip and Tripp picked it up, hoping for news that backup was on the way. Iglesias hadn't disappointed.

Team in place. Lake surrounded. Waiting for your Go.

Tripp tapped a message quickly in return to update the detective on his status.

Confirmed location. Sadie inside house on southwest corner of lake. I've got eyes, 50 yards out.

He typed a few more commands, until they ultimately agreed to surround the house from all angles. In under ninety seconds, Tripp felt the sensation of movement from behind him.

"Right where you said you'd be, McKellar."

"Took you long enough," Tripp muttered as Iglesias's tall form came into view.

The detective held up his hands. "You just put together a major op in less than an hour. Not all of us are superhuman, McKellar."

Tripp took grim satisfaction in the compliment. "The only goal is to get her out."

"I know, man." Iglesias patted Tripp's back. "I know. Pippa is beside herself. And since I already promised my fiancée I'd bring her sister home, you know I've got your back."

It would be little comfort until they had Sadie back, but it was a solid reminder that the entire department was invested in getting her home safe and sound. Iglesias had an added personal connection in his engagement to Sadie's sister, but he was as committed as the rest of the GRPD.

Sadie was one of their own.

Tripp pointed to the house. "Two guys went in a few minutes ago, armed to the teeth. Semiautomatics strapped to their sides and firmly in hand. Assumption is that Sadie is in the house, along with Greer. Gunshots echoed from inside, but I've heard her fighting with Greer, which suggests he targeted a different victim."

Iglesias shook his head. "He is one nasty bastard. Pippa said she and her sisters all got a bad vibe on him from the jump, but this goes way beyond not liking your sister's boyfriend."

Tripp wasn't sure why the word *boyfriend* chafed so badly—especially since he already knew the bastard in question had been Sadie's fiancé—so he ignored it. He needed his full focus on the mission. "We all get played from time to time."

"Yeah, I suppose we do," Iglesias said.

Tripp quickly outlined his observations from the past half hour.

"How many gunshots did you hear?"

Tripp fought to keep his voice clinical, with minimal inflection despite the personal nature of the op. "Just the one, and then I heard Sadie's scream. Then I heard the fighting."

"What does he want with her?"

"What he wanted before—access."

Tripp knew it for the truth. Sadie Colton was in a prime position to help Greer. Between her CSI role in the GRPD as well as being a member of the Colton family, and therefore connected to Colton Investigations, she had a lot of information a criminal could glean.

And Tate Greer knew it, too.

"Greer saw her as the way in." Tripp continued his assessment.

"Damn it." Iglesias shook his head. "Pippa was afraid this might be the reason he got close to her so fast."

"She thought Greer was trying to infiltrate?"

"No, nothing like that. But she was concerned with how quickly Sadie had fallen for the guy. As Pippa told me, it was like one day he just sort of showed up and within a matter of weeks her sister was smitten and talking of love and marriage."

While Tripp had never personally bought into it, he knew that people did fall in love quickly. In an instant, some said. If he was honest with himself, he had felt a spark of attraction for Sadie from the very first day they'd met.

He could still see her, the eager recruit joining the GRPD, determined to make her mark. She had done well enough and he had been impressed by her hard work, her dedication, and her unwillingness to rest on the laurels of the Colton name. But in the end, she'd really found her calling with crime scene investigation. She had showed an early knack, identifying some key evidence in a case she had worked her rookie season. She'd finished out that first year, giving her all to the force, but after her full commitment, it hadn't taken her long to ask for a transfer into CSI.

And she'd thrived there.

Although he no longer saw her every day, as a lieutenant in the department, he got regular updates from her division. Sadie was well respected and that work ethic they'd all recognized from the start proved itself over and over. She had uncovered a major piece of evidence that had put a large drug ring away within a matter of months after her joining CSI. She'd followed that up with some careful tech work that had put away a child predator. And just this past spring she'd worked round-the-clock to help uncover evidence to catch a serial killer.

Sadie Colton had found her calling in CSI. Their department, and more broadly, the entire city of Grand Rapids, was better for it.

"Rest of the team is in position." Iglesias interrupted Tripp's wandering thoughts.

"Tell everyone to hold the perimeter. You and I are moving in."

Iglesias relayed the information and Tripp heard a series of affirmatives through the detective's comm device.

The low level of persistent adrenaline that had haunted Tripp's system since the discovery Sadie had been taken spiked sharply as they moved from their hiding place. With determined steps toward the house, his sole focus was on getting her out safely.

"You ready for what's on the other side of the door?" he said softly to Iglesias.

"Damn straight."

Tripp figured there weren't many more on the team who would be as committed and he was glad Iglesias had his back.

Tripp pointed to the entrance to the cabin still about twenty yards away. "They both went through that door, but the gunshot came from the back of the house. Assume we're entering the kitchen and need to push through into a living room or great room of some sort."

"Got it."

They had closed the distance, the door nearly in sight, when loud barking echoed from inside the house. It wasn't the excitement of a chase or a game of fetch, but the harsh, violent bark of a dog on the scent of its quarry.

Tripp braced for that new dimension as he anticipated a large, aggressive attacker prepared to take them down at all costs.

And that's when he saw her.

Hair that he knew was just a shade darker than strawberry blond streamed behind her as she ran hell-for-leather out the door that had held their full focus. She was headed straight for the dock at the edge of the lake. Two hulking men were just behind her, oblivious to Tripp and Emmanuel's presence, struggling to catch up. Moonlight illuminated the deadly glint of waving weapons in each of their hands.

Tripp went into motion, racing toward her pursuers as he ignored the very real threat of that barking dog or the additional risk there might be more goons exiting the house. He ignored it all; his only focus on getting her back. All with the element of surprise in his favor.

But even he couldn't hold back a shout when Sadie jumped into the ice-edged water that surrounded the end of the dock.

Shocking cold pierced her skin with all the finesse of a thousand ice picks. She knew it would be cold. Had braced for the loss of breath as she'd plunged into the water.

But hell, damn, and all the really good curse words she and her sisters practiced behind her brothers' backs, was it cold.

The ice picks quickly gave way to sledgehammers and Sadie wondered how it was possible to even think let alone find a way to survive in this.

Only she did. She would.

Somewhere between the leap into the lake and the impossible cold, her mind went on autopilot. She'd gotten the jump on Tate and his henchmen and taken it as a small stroke of luck that they'd been so absorbed with their infighting it gave her a head start. It wasn't much, but the few precious seconds was all she'd needed to get a move on the footrace. But it had been a split-second decision to head for the lake.

If her memory served—and the trauma of going to summer camp had haunted her far longer than she wanted to own—there was a large dock at the edge of the lake. She'd also remembered the way the water eddied around the base, creating a small pocket of air between the wooden planks and the water.

That air pocket was her goal. If she could get in there, she could continue to breathe and hide until Tate, his henchman and the dog moved on. If…

Damn, it was cold, those icy sledgehammers doing their job. She could see the wooden dock. Could feel the water lapping around her, only instead of it feeling gentle as it did in summer, it felt like thick, heavy sludge as she fought her way across the lake.

Focus, Colton.

The order snapped through her mind, her own voice threading with that of her father. And her brothers.

Focus.

Battling the cold, she pushed herself on. She had no choice.

In a battle between hypothermia or her psycho ex-fiancé, she'd take the cold all day and twice on Sunday.

Assuming, of course, her body would cooperate.

She ignored the heavy pull in her limbs and forced herself forward.

The dock is your goal. The dock is your goal. Over and over, she kept that thought in place as she pushed on. The icy water dragged at her limbs, making her lethargic, while the drag of her wet clothes added to the thick pressure against her skin.

She would make it.

She *had* to make it.

Snake's frantic barking seemed to waver, growing dimmer as her full focus remained on propelling herself forward.

Her arms were so heavy. And she was going so slow.

The water was black around her, the bright moonlight that had illuminated her run toward the lake falling behind the clouds.

Was she even going in the right direction? Confusion had her stopping for a moment, her arms thrashing as she fought to catch her breath. Why was it so hard to draw air?

For the first time since jumping on impulse, something hit her chest with a swift fist.

What if she didn't make it?

What if…

"Sadie." The deep voice drifted toward her, bouncing off the water with a weird echo. "Sadie!"

Why did it sound like Tripp?

Sadie flailed her arms once more, shocked when she felt the hard edge of a dock pylon.

Did I make it?

She willed herself to focus, her gaze sharpening as her hand fought for purchase against the base of the dock.

And that's when she heard her name again.

"Sadie!"

As she looked up, large hands came around her upper arms, dragging her from the water. "Are you okay?"

I wasn't wrong. That thought dimly registered in the back of her mind as Sadie took in the broad, reassuring form of Tripp McKellar. His chiseled features and firm jaw were the last things she saw before her body convulsed in a hard shiver.

And then she felt nothing except the strong arms that came around her and the tight press of his body against hers.

Chapter 3

She's safe.

Tripp held tight to Sadie's small, shivering form and ignored the oppressive wetness that soaked his jacket. He'd survive. And, damn it, so would she. They hadn't come this far to accept any other outcome.

But she was so cold. And the shivers racking her body were nearly convulsive, she was shaking so hard. He had to get her out of her clothes and into something warmer.

The rest of Tripp's team had moved in on the cabin and grounds, the shouts of Greer's men still littering the air. All fought loudly against the bonds GRPD officers had already put on them. The two goons Tripp had seen going in had been captured as well as two lookouts discovered on the back side of the property.

But nowhere in the melee near the cabin could he see Tate Greer.

There was no way Tripp could have come this far and missed his quarry. Yet to go after him meant he would have to leave Sadie, and that was unacceptable.

When another hard shudder had her shaking against his chest, he knew the decision was made. With determined steps toward the cabin, his only goal was to get her somewhere warm. It was only the hard clutch of her hands against his forearms that had him stopping. "No."

He glanced down, the blue tingeing that heartbreaking face more than evident in the unclouded light of the moon. "We have to get you warm, Sadie."

"I... I-I'm n-not going b-back in there." Although it was a struggle to get the words out, her desperate desire to stay out of that cabin was clear in the stiffness of her body.

"We need to get you out of those clothes."

"No c-cabin." Her grip tightened on his forearm. "Car. Y-your car is f-fine."

The battle to take her someplace warm might be his goal, but there was no way he could ignore her distress. Knowing an ambulance would be there soon weighed even more in her favor. With quick movements, he swept her up in his arms. He thought there might have been a slight protest on her lips but it died as he carried her toward his vehicle.

"Where?" she finally asked, the lone word seemingly stuck in her throat.

"We'll go to my SUV until the ambulance gets here."

"Th...thank y-you." She whispered the words before laying her head against his shoulder.

All the adrenaline that had carried him for the past

two days shifted somewhere deep inside him. That insistent, driving need to save morphed into something new: the desperate, fervent desire to protect.

He knew that feeling. He'd had it once—so long ago he'd forgotten the sensation until Sadie's head had come to rest against his shoulder. The desire to keep those he cared for safe and secure.

Until he'd failed at both.

Those long hours of therapy his chief had suggested had ultimately helped Tripp find closure and acceptance in one part of the truth: he and Lila had only gotten engaged because of the baby. He'd still loved her, in his way, and he'd been wildly happy about their child. But in the long run, they'd likely not have made the most stable environment for a kid.

A truth he could accept now but couldn't go back and change no matter how often he beat himself up over it. He'd been committed to seeing things through, determined to make a life with Lila once they welcomed their baby. What he still had never fully worked through was the reality that Lila and their unborn child had died because of *his* life's work.

Yet he still chose to do it day after day.

And he'd never fully reconciled what that said about him.

The department-issued SUV he drove was just where he'd left it, and Tripp set Sadie gently on her feet as he opened the driver's-side door. He quickly turned on the engine, blasting the heat before he swung around to the rear door to retrieve his first-aid kit. He also had spare clothes in the back, but the first step was to get her out of the wet ones she wore.

"I'm going to help you with these," Tripp said,

moving to her side where she leaned against the open driver's-side door, tossing the first-aid kit onto the seat behind her. He kept his tone careful—neutral, even— but knew that to help her he had to strip her of every article of wet clothing.

Her soft grunt was all he heard in return as she fumbled with the hem of her sweater. The thick wool clung to her and flopped against her fingers where she struggled to grab hold.

Tripp took her hands in his. They were ice against his palms and he fought to keep his voice steady against the rising panic he still might have been too late, even with Dispatch's call into 911. "Let me."

With careful movements, he lifted the sweater up and over her head. Her skin had that same bluish tinge as her face, visible in the dome light, but he kept going.

Next he reached for the waistband of her jeans. The denim was thick and heavy, and he ignored the brush of soft skin beneath his fingers as he undid the button and released the zipper. He worked the material down her hips and held each calf as he removed the denim from her legs. It was only then he realized she wasn't wearing shoes, just a thin layer of socks.

Everywhere he touched, her skin was that horrible, clammy cold. He removed the socks then shifted to her underwear. His job was to help people no matter the circumstance. He could, and more importantly he *would*, do that.

But he was also acutely aware that he was going to see Sadie naked, which set off something strange deep and low in his gut. Something that reminded him when this was all over, and she was warm and well, he wanted to see her again.

Ignoring the flash of need that welled at the thought, Tripp put his arm around her and focused instead on reassuring her. "Hang on. I have a blanket in the kit."

He reached around her to the first-aid kit he'd tossed onto the seat. The thin solar blanket in his extensive supplies was right where it should be and he ripped the packaging off to unfold the thin yet effective material. Moving to stand in front of her, he wrapped the material around her shoulders. "I'm going to remove your underwear now. Okay?"

She stared up at him, her grip tight on the edges of the blanket, and nodded. "Okay."

With deft fingers, he reached behind her and unclasped her bra, making sure to keep his gaze on hers. Once the material sprang free, he reached down and removed her water-soaked panties. Leaving all her clothes in a pile beside the SUV, he opened the back door and set her against the seat. "I'm going to go around the other side, then pull you onto my lap. We need to get you warm."

Once more, she nodded, but it concerned him she didn't even put voice to an "Okay" or a "Yes." Hurrying around to the opposite side, he slid into the rear passenger seat then reached across the space for her shoulders. The small figure huddled beneath that wash of silver material tugged at his heart, but he willed it aside.

His only goal was to keep her warm until the ambulance arrived to take over.

Tripp gently pulled her onto the backseat so that she settled on his lap. His shirt and coat were still wet from where he'd held her, but the solar blanket ensured she wasn't touched by any of it. He gently tugged her long hair out from where it lay against her neck, determined to remove any bit of wet or cold from her skin.

Just like when he'd carried her, she settled against his chest. Heat blew heavy out of the SUV's front console and he positioned her so that she was in the direct line of the vent. He then settled his chin on the top of her head and rubbed his hands over her shoulders and down her arms, willing circulation and much needed heat to return to her body.

Then it was time to wait.

And hope like hell he'd acted fast enough.

The uncontrollable chattering that had gripped her since emerging from the lake finally subsided. She still felt bone-deep cold, but that sense of her body turning on her, taking on a mind of its own, finally faded.

With each stroke of Tripp's firm, flat palm against her body, Sadie felt a bit of herself return.

And with it, the dawning sense that she was basically naked in Tripp McKellar's lap. A fact that was mostly immaterial to her situation—he was the consummate professional—but was still one that had burrowed deep and decided to unfurl with heat.

And need.

It was amazing, really, how she could even think of that in this moment, yet if she were honest with herself, it was there.

Her attraction to Tripp had always been there. Yes, it had been muted and, basically, ignored when she'd become engaged to Tate, but it had never really died. Now that she'd distanced herself from Tate's influence, she'd had plenty of time to acknowledge that the allure of the GRPD lieutenant had never really gone away.

And what was to be done about that?

The large male body that fitted around hers was the epitome of safety and protection. Even more, there was a gentle, caring quality to his ministrations that pulled at her. Tripp McKellar was a good man. She'd always known that, but to actually be on the receiving end of that tender gentleness was impossibly wonderful.

Even as it felt impossibly right.

"I'm getting you wet." Sadie was surprised by how small and croaky her voice sounded.

Tripp shifted, his arms tightening around her. "I'm fine. Are you starting to feel warmer?"

"A little bit." Although she was still chilled to the bone, sensation was coming back into her limbs.

"The ambulance should be here soon. We'll get you fixed up and make sure that dip in the lake didn't do any damage. Iglesias is with me and by now he'll have called your family, too."

"I wasn't in there that long."

"It's December. Any amount of time is too long."

He was right, of course, but she still wouldn't have changed the decision. The chance to break away from Tate had been too good to pass up and she'd taken her shot when she'd had it. She was just thankful that Tripp and his backup had been waiting for her.

"How did you know where to find me?"

"I think a better question is why did it take me so long."

Sadie didn't miss his use of the word *me*, despite the fact that he had an entire department working behind him.

"No, I think my question is the right one. How did you figure out it was Sand Springs Lake?"

"I triangulated all of the offenses that we could identify as Capital X over the past several years. I've done some more work and I have realized that the crimes seem to fit into three distinct clusters in the county."

"And this was the most isolated of the three?" Sadie asked.

"Exactly."

Sadie considered it, struck anew when Tripp mentioned Capital X's crime*s*—as in plural—that her ex was behind it all. Would she ever get over this feeling of how badly she'd been played?

Stupid much, Sadie?

Yes, she'd had a month to think about it, to digest it, and try to come to some bit of reason for it all. But it remained nearly impossible to hear anything over the constant pounding of self-blame she couldn't seem to shake off.

Or drown out.

Or ignore.

Her entire family had been leery of Tate from the start, her twin sister, Victoria, most of all. Vikki had been kind about it at first, pressing Sadie often to know how the relationship was coming along and if it made her happy.

Since she and her sister had *always* known what the other was feeling, the continued questioning had finally taken its toll. No matter how large a smile Vikki had pasted on or how innocent her tone, Sadie had known the truth. It had all been an act. All designed to try to figure out what Sadie had seen in Tate.

And she *was* happy. Or had been.

For a few precious months, at the start of the relationship, she'd been practically giddy. Falling in love with a man she'd never expected to meet. Tate had the sexy, bad-boy look she'd always found appealing in movies yet had never imagined for herself. And as she'd gotten to know him, she'd seen that the sexy façade was only the beginning. They'd talked of so many things and, after every conversation, she'd been certain there was so much more to him than what was visible on the surface.

And she'd equated each of those conversations to herself and the woman no one seemed to see beneath her surface.

Yes, she was good, sweet, hardworking Sadie Colton. She was the baby of the family, her birth minutes after Vikki's ensuring she was the youngest Colton. Whether it was her status as youngest or her eagerness at work or her relatively upbeat personality, everyone saw her as the sweet, cheerful, girl next door. But no one seemed to see her as a woman. One with needs and desires and ambitions of her own.

But Tate had.

Only instead of falling in love with those qualities, he'd twisted them and used them to his own ends.

"Hey there. You okay?" Tripp's voice whispered over her ear, the light tickle sensation enough to pull her from the dour direction of her thoughts.

"Yeah."

He shifted until he could tilt his head just so to look directly at her. And in his vivid blue gaze Sadie saw a flash of redemption from the ugly direction of her thoughts. It was quick and fleeting, but it was there all the same.

Maybe—*maybe?*—this man saw her as a woman, too. The flash was gone in less than a heartbeat, but that lingering idea took root somewhere deep, helping to warm her from the inside out.

"You sure about that?"

"I am. I'm starting to warm up. The heat helps." She swallowed hard, once again aware of the fact that nothing but a thin layer of blanket separated her naked butt from his lap. And with it, the heat that had slowly worked its way back into her body crept up her neck. "Thank you for taking care of me."

The edges of those compelling eyes crinkled with his gentle smile. "All in a day's work."

In that moment, Sadie realized she could stay there forever. Right there, wrapped in his arms, warm and secure. Whatever emotional damage Tate had done, it would never be enough for her to believe that Tripp McKellar was anything but a good and decent man. There was no pretense here, no false front.

Only goodness and truth.

Sure, he had a past. She knew about the woman he'd been engaged to shortly before Sadie had started on the force. Knew the sadder end that had seen her gunned down by a criminal let out of the prison system too early.

She'd watched from a distance as Tripp had dealt with it all. The pain that came from survival and the will a person needed to move on, day by day.

But he'd done it. He'd moved on, focused on his work, the city of Grand Rapids and ensuring his team had all it needed to do the job.

It was how he'd known how to find her.

Suddenly tired, Sadie laid her head back against his shoulder and closed her eyes. She could never be with this man romantically, but she could admire who and what he was. And she could quietly, without anyone knowing, use him as her own personal lodestone, showing her the way to true north. There *were* good men in the world. Good, decent men who didn't use others or betray them.

If that was all Tripp McKellar could be to her, then she'd take it. Because it was a hell of a lot more than she'd ever had before.

Tripp held tight to Sadie and wondered over the mix of emotions he'd seen in her eyes. Despite the jump in the lake and the harrowing ordeal of the past few days, there was something so resilient about her. Something so warm and open.

Even as he clearly saw the pain she lived with.

Was it due to the stark truth that her former fiancé was a scumbag?

Tripp suspected that was part of it, yet not all. He'd watched her for a long time, quietly observing her at work or out in the field, and there was something else buried deep below that compelling green gaze. It was like a river of solitude flowing beneath the woman who always seemed to be in the thick of things. She was the first to arrange an impromptu, interdepartment pickup game of soccer in the park or an after-work round of drinks.

Yet through it all, he'd always sensed there was something she held back. Some inner longing that no one except him seemed to see.

Not like he could talk to anyone about it. Even if he wasn't so maniacal about privacy, determined to give others theirs even as he fiercely guarded his own, it wasn't exactly coffee conversation with his coworkers.

Did you notice that Sadie Colton looked sad today after the soccer game?

Did you see Sadie Colton, head bowed down over her lab desk, earlier this afternoon?

Sadie Colton's big smile never quite seems to reach her eyes, does it?

So instead he'd filed all those questions away, keeping them to himself almost like a warning. He had no right to dig into her business and even less to pry into her personal life. That meant his questions went unanswered and his observations were nothing more than a curious pastime.

Lost in thought, it was a surprise when Sadie suddenly struggled in his arms, shifting hard against his lap. He ignored the sudden jolt of discomfort as her body came into intimate contact with his and instead fought to steady her. "What's wrong?"

"Tate. He's gone."

He briefly considered downplaying it, waiting until he had a full report—and full confirmation—from his team that Greer had gotten away. But he couldn't do it. Regardless of his need to protect her, she was a cop and she deserved the truth.

"I think he is."

Sadie's focus remained on the activities taking place beyond the SUV's window. "I can see some of what's going on over there and it struck me that I can't see Snake." Tripp nearly asked who or what Snake was before she added, "The dog."

"Greer has a dog?"

"'Pet monster' is a more apt term. He's huge, ruthlessly trained and clearly lethal."

It was new information on Greer that was helpful,

but it also made what Sadie had endured that much worse. He'd envisioned Greer's tactics would be harsh and unyielding once he took anyone prisoner. Adding the power of a trained animal into the mix only further supported that assessment.

"Did he turn the animal on you?" Tripp asked. He hadn't seen any evidence of abuse when he'd removed her clothes, but that didn't mean she hadn't been intimidated or taunted. A fact that had his vision hazing as the image formed in his mind's eye.

"Tate's been gone since the night they kidnapped me. I've only seen his goons at mealtime since they stuffed me in that cabin."

The anger faded slightly at the news she'd been largely ignored since her capture. "And he came back today?"

"Tonight. That was the first time I'd seen him since he arrived at the safe house. The first time I'd seen the dog, too." She shook her head, a small, rueful laugh filling the space between them. "I had no idea he even liked animals."

From her description of Snake, Tripp wasn't sure he'd lay "animal lover" at Greer's feet, but he kept the observation to himself. They had to focus on what they knew and that empty sense of remorse in her tone wouldn't benefit from him piling on more questions she obviously didn't have answers to.

Nor would this overwhelming sense of anger he couldn't quite rein in. There would be time for it all later. Right now, he had to concentrate on getting Sadie safely to the hospital and on the road to recovery. As if to punctuate that thought, the lights of the ambulance suddenly filled the night, flashing red and blue as the vehicle pulled up into the clearing beyond the house.

In those flashing lights, Tripp knew something else with terrifying clarity.

Every minute they didn't have Tate Greer in custody was another moment Sadie was in danger. Because after tonight, there was no way Greer would be willing to let her live—and no way that Tripp would let him get to her.

Chapter 4

Sadie kept her gaze on the cabin in the distance as the medics prepared to strap her onto the gurney. She knew Gus and Gage, the two medics who treated her now, and appreciated their attention to her modesty as they covered her with more blankets before helping her onto the flat bed.

There were things to say to Tripp, starting with a thank-you for saving her life, but they'd have to wait. For now, she had to think.

Where had Tate gone?

If he'd gotten away so quickly, there had to have been another hidey-hole nearby. That meant once again they'd underestimated just how well set up he was and the depths of his network.

He obviously ran a successful business. It might be

a criminal enterprise, but she'd do well to start thinking of it through a new lens: as a business enterprise.

And corporations, she knew. After watching her brother build an incredibly successful business, she had firsthand knowledge and a strong sense for how a solid enterprise ran.

Well funded. *Check.*

Well resourced, with provisions for any number of scenarios. *Check.*

Well led. *Check.*

While she hated to think of Tate as a leader in the traditional sense, she needed to view him that way. It was yet another facet of his talents and personal charisma, and it was something she was uniquely qualified to assess.

"You doing okay, Sadie?" Gus's smile was gentle as he settled her into place. He had a blood pressure cuff in hand and was already gently shifting the thick blankets to get to her arm.

"Getting there."

"You're lucky Lieutenant McKellar was there. He did everything right, getting you out of those wet clothes and into the warmth of the SUV."

"He did." It was a memory that would live with her forever, the tender way he'd cared for her, with no thought to his own comfort. One she'd take out at quiet moments and remember with fondness.

It was only as Gus went to work in tandem with Gage, checking all her vitals and directing her to follow the movements of his finger or to stick out her tongue, that Sadie forced herself back to the problem at hand.

She had no doubt Tate's henchmen would remain silent and uncooperative with the GRPD. If Tate didn't already have them quaking in fear, Fred's death would provide added incentive. The PD needed to shift gears and approach the problem from a new angle.

The bright lights of the ambulance as well as Gage and Gus's conversation faded into the background as Sadie let the idea of Tate-as-leader into the forefront of her thoughts. It was a talent she'd had since she was a small child—the ability to shut out the world as she worked through a problem—and she took full advantage of it now.

Her body still ached, a fact that was increasingly clear as her circulation and warmth returned, so she'd let her mind go somewhere else. Somewhere useful. A place she hadn't been in far too long.

With that driving sense of purpose filling her thoughts, Sadie barely felt the shift as the ambulance began to move, headed for the hospital.

Tate watched the flashing ambulance lights fade away into the darkness and considered his next move. The one that would take his meddlesome, irritating ex-fiancée down a few more pegs.

He'd initially thought to just kill her, removing her as nothing more than an irritating nuisance. Quick. Effective. Easy.

But that was too good for her now.

For all she'd just pulled and the trouble she'd caused him, she deserved a lot worse. And he was hell-bent to be the man to give it to her.

Sadie had been the perfect mark, he thought as he ordered Snake into the large kennel he kept at his personal safe house. Sweet and innocent, those big cow eyes lighting up with interest and affection and—just as he'd planned—love in short order. It was just too bad she was such a damn goody-goody, his expected access to both the GRPD databases as well as Colton Investigations severely limited by her by-the-book personality.

She kept her work files on serious lockdown—an IT director's dream employee. She changed her password regularly and she made the damn thing impossible to figure out. No "Tate1234" for her. No way. She hadn't even used his name once in her password updates.

Nor had she given many details about her family. Oh, he'd heard the sob story about how her brother Riley, in lockstep with his siblings, had started Colton Investigations after the tragic deaths of their parents. How they'd banded together to help Brody Higgins, an innocent foster kid her late father had taken a special interest in.

It had been particularly sweet to know that same dumb kid was one of Tate's biggest dupes in the entire RevitaYou/Capital X scam. A scam that had been going smoother than silk before the Coltons had gotten involved.

Now it was all upside down. His number two, Gunther Johnson, was sitting in a jail cell, the cops had figured out how deadly RevitaYou was and Tate's cover had been blown.

He had contingency plans, of course, but there was no foolproof plan that could make up for how quickly it had all collapsed. That was why he was going to make sure Sadie went down with him. He'd given her the perfect role. Loving fiancée to one of the city's most successful businessmen. And she'd betrayed him.

It was unforgivable. And because of it, she was going to pay.

Tripp glanced around the waiting room at the county hospital and wondered how the Coltons had seemingly managed to multiply overnight.

The eldest, Riley Colton, had been the first to arrive with his pregnant fiancée, Charlize. He had been quickly followed by the rest of Sadie's siblings, each with their own significant others. They were all there except for Sadie's sister Kiely, who apparently couldn't get a babysitter on short notice. The entire Colton family seemed to have coupled up lately, and while Tripp wouldn't consider himself on the pulse of local gossip, it had been impossible to ignore the heavy strikes of Cupid's arrow on this one family.

Working with Emmanuel, he'd seen firsthand the man's relationship—and hard fall into love—with Pippa Colton. And Sadie's twin, JAG paralegal sergeant Vikki, had recently fallen in love with Army Sergeant Flynn Cruz-Street.

They were all there, concerned about their sister and equally concerned at the news Tate Greer had gotten away yet again.

Tripp was already expecting the quiet outreach when Riley approached him. The family had settled in, anxious for news of Sadie's condition. Coltons were scattered across the waiting room, and the moment he left to get a cup of coffee, Riley followed.

"Can I buy you a cup?" Tripp gestured toward the large machine.

"Yeah, thanks." Riley seemed to hesitate for a moment before diving in. "I know she's going to be okay. She's young, and strong, and I know that all works in her favor. But I also need to know what happened to her."

Tripp knew that need, understood it intimately, and so he would play it straight with Riley. "She's fine, physically. Greer didn't get a hand on her, and for that we can all be grateful."

"Why do I hear a 'but' in there?"

"Because the psychological is going to be a lot harder. She spent a month in the safe house, mostly alone, and even that wasn't safe enough." That same raw anger and fury-fueled frustration welled up once more. "And that's on me."

Riley took the cup Tripp handed to him, his eyes wide. "On you?"

"Damn straight. I put her there, and it's my responsibility to make sure she stays safe."

"I could say that right back at you. She's my sister. My family. It's my responsibility to make sure she stays safe, too."

"In a government safe house?" Tripp shook his head, no intention of getting into a pissing match with Riley. "Greer found her on my watch. I need to get underneath the why and the how."

"You can count on me to help, however I can. This isn't on you, man. Greer and Capital X's tentacles run far deeper than we know. And they've been burrowing in for a lot longer than any of us realized."

The comment might have been meant to make him feel better, but Tripp took minimal comfort. Nothing could change the fact that Sadie had been kidnapped from an environment he'd controlled. And he was going to make it his personal mission to find out who had facilitated that access.

After, of course, he put that bastard Tate Greer behind bars.

"I do want to talk to you about some ideas we've been working up for RevitaYou," Riley added. "I think we may have a way to get Wes Matthews back on US soil."

Tripp's mind flashed to the crime board in his office. If Tate Greer was the man behind Capital X funding RevitaYou, banker Wes Matthews was the linchpin in the operation. He was the centerpiece of their investigation. Get him and they had a chance to get to the bottom of it all—and they'd get Tate, too. "That's gotta take some doing. Matthews doesn't have a lot of incentive to come back."

"That's where my new soon-to-be sister-in-law, Matthews's daughter Abigail, has been a tremendous help." Riley tilted his head in the direction of the waiting room. "She talked to Griffin about trying to help, and he convinced her to bring her ideas to all of us. She and her father have always been estranged and I get the feeling she'd have been just fine ignoring him for the rest of her life. She has helped us immensely."

Tripp considered what he knew of Sadie's siblings, and the news that Griffin was cooperating so closely was something of a novel development. Falling in love with Abigail and her foster daughter, Maya, had changed him. Clearly for the better. "I'm glad to hear it, man. But I guess I'm a little surprised to hear Griffin is helping out the family business."

"It's amazing, actually." Riley clearly warmed to his subject. "I feel like I have my brother back. I know it was hard for him, an adopted child in the midst of five more kids, but we love him. We've always loved him. All of us. And now it feels like we might have him back.

"I guess it's the beauty of having an amazing woman in his life."

At that comment, Tripp couldn't help but think of

Sadie. *She* was an amazing woman. Hadn't tonight proved that? Not just what she'd survived, but the gumption and the attitude that had carried her through it all.

Vikki poked her head in the door, her excitement palpable. "Riley. The doctor just came out to see us. We can go back and visit with her."

Tripp gave Riley a solid pat on the shoulder. "Go. Go see your sister. We can pick this up later."

Riley didn't wait, just headed for the door. It was Vikki who hesitated, calling after her brother as he passed through the door. "You go on. I'll be right there."

She moved forward, coming right up to Tripp and laying her hands over his. "Thank you. Thank you for finding and saving Sadie."

The steady need to protest that he'd nearly been the one responsible for losing her died in his throat. Vikki was so earnest—so determined—and for the first time he let himself slightly relax that Sadie was safe. He still wasn't convinced that Tate Greer wasn't going to try again, but for the moment, she was safe.

Now, all he had to do was make sure she stayed that way.

Sadie battled the mix of exhaustion and impatience that fought for purchase in the back of her mind. She was thrilled that her family was there and took deep comfort in the presence of all of them. But she also wanted to see Tripp.

She *needed* to see him.

It was the strangest thing, but ever since the doctor had given her the news that she was going to be okay, she'd wanted to see Tripp. To tell him herself.

It was because of *him* that she was going to be okay.

If left to her own devices and Tate's demented criminal activities, she could've drowned in the lake. And deep down inside, she recognized the truth of that.

Yes, if given the chance she would run from Tate Greer all over again.

But she also couldn't deny she'd made a narrow escape, all because of Tripp's quick thinking and amazing police work that had put him at the lake in the first place.

Vikki must've sensed her exhaustion, because she finally put an end to the fun. "Okay, loved ones. I think Sadie's had enough. We can come back tomorrow morning. And since Kiely couldn't get a babysitter on short notice, Flynn and I will swing by to see her and Cooper and let her know our girl's okay."

Her siblings hugged her, each in turn, Pippa hanging on an extra few beats before she let go with a promise. "I'll bring the donuts first thing tomorrow morning."

"I'm holding you to that." Sadie smiled. "And there'd better be chocolate-frosted ones."

"Why bother buying donuts if you don't buy chocolate-frosted?" Pippa shuddered in mock horror before moving to stand with her fiancé, Emmanuel.

"Clever girl." Abigail leaned in to give her a quick hug. "And it also ensures that your brother will be here bright and early, too. Assuming Maya doesn't wake up when we get home and pay the babysitter." Sadie's future sister-in-law said it all with a smile, before jokingly giving Griffin the lightest edge of her elbow to the middle of his stomach. Griffin used the shift in position to wrap his arms tightly around her, and it made Sadie's heart happy to see them together.

To see all her siblings, together with their significant others.

"Come on, come on. The donut mandate has been laid down. Now it's time Sadie got some rest." Vikki maneuvered them all out with a drill sergeant's precision, before walking back over to stand by her bedside.

"I'm so glad you're all right." The stern voice vanished as quickly as it had come, replaced with a quaver Sadie rarely heard coming from her twin. "I've been so worried."

"Vik, I'm okay. Really, I am."

It wasn't a lie, exactly, but Sadie wasn't silly enough to think there wouldn't be repercussions. But right here, right now, gathered up in the love of her family, she simply refused to focus on any of it. "Now get out of here and go kiss that hot guy of yours."

"You're my sister! You're my priority and I'm worried about you."

Sadie waved a hand. "Well, I'm fine now. And I'm ordering you to go kiss Flynn. If I had a man like him, that's what I'd be doing."

The tease was enough to bring a smile to Vikki's face, removing that crestfallen, ashen look that had been there only moments before. While there would be plenty more to say, for now, Sadie knew that had to be enough.

She kept her smile bright until Vikki was out of sight and then let it fall. She was happy for her brothers and sisters. Deeply happy, and so pleased that they had found such wonderful men and women to share their lives with.

But it did hold up a mirror to all she didn't have.

She *hated* thinking that way. It was so against her nature to begrudge anybody anything, especially those she loved as much as Riley, Griffin, Pippa, Kiely and Vikki.

Yet, try as she might, their happiness was also a counterweight to all the pain she was dealing with over Tate. She'd believed herself happy, as well, preparing for an upcoming wedding, only to find it all had vanished. And in the worst, most embarrassing—and dangerous—way.

She felt the first tear well up as a light knock came on the door.

"Hey. You up for a little bit of company?"

Tripp McKellar stood in the doorway, tall, broad, and exactly what she needed. "Hi. Yes, that would be nice."

She quickly brushed away that last tear, refusing to let him see such an embarrassing bit of selfish emotion, before meeting his gaze across the room. "What are you still doing here?"

"I wanted to see how you were. I didn't want to interrupt when your family was here."

"So you've been waiting this whole time?" It was absurdly touching, the idea that he'd hung around, waiting to see her.

"I just needed to see you for myself."

"That's funny, because you were the person I wanted to see, too. The doctor gave me a clean bill of health. And it's all because of you."

Those compelling blue eyes shot to the floor and with it his face settled in harsh lines before he seemed to compose himself. "You saved yourself. Don't forget that, Sadie."

"As nice a thought as that might be, I think we both know it's not true. If you hadn't been there, my jump into the lake would likely have ended very differently."

It was strange to say it—that knowledge that a split-second decision could have had such a horribly different outcome—but that didn't make it any less true.

"I'm just glad you're okay."

Sadie wasn't quite sure where the impulse came from, because it was probably better just to let him leave, but she waved him forward. "Why don't you stay a few minutes?"

He didn't hesitate, just nodded as he walked into the room and took the seat beside her bed.

"I'd like to ask you a question, but I need you to promise that you're going to tell me the truth."

"Of course I'll tell you the truth."

"You haven't heard my question yet," she said with a smile.

He answered that with a smile of his own, one of those rare ones that lit the depths of his eyes. "Okay. Fair. What do you want to ask me?"

"I need you to tell me everything you know about Tate Greer."

"Sadie, come on. What good is going to come from that?"

It was basically the answer she had expected, which was why she'd pressed for honesty. "The good is that I'll finally know. The good is that I'll finally understand what I got myself into." She reached over and took his hand in hers. "I need to know."

"You're still a member of the GRPD. This case isn't exactly a secret."

"Not something out of a case file, but in your own words, Tripp. Please."

Whether it was the urgency in her voice, or the personal nature of her touch, she wasn't sure. But Sadie knew the moment she got through to him. Resignation painted his face before he took a deep breath. "He's not a good guy, Sadie. But I suspect you already know that."

"Yes, I do." It was only as her eyes shot down that she realized she still had her hand over his. She pulled it back, even as she couldn't deny how nice it had been to touch him.

"From all we've been able to figure out based on the most recent evidence, Tate has been revealed to be the head of the Capital X organization. Likely its founder, too. They engage in some really nasty loan-sharking and do whatever they have to to enforce their rules."

"And murder?"

"When it serves their purposes."

Just like Fred, she thought. "I'm sure your team has already found him, but Tate shot one of his henchmen when I was there."

"I'm sorry you had to see that. We did find him, but we didn't yet know the reason why he was dead."

"Tate claimed Fred had been followed and that the cabin was being closed in on. Tate shot him for sharing the news."

The memory sent a shudder through her and those earlier tears she had managed to hold back welled up once more.

"I called him and the other guy who was looking after me Fred and Barney. He was the big one, Barney was the little one, and they seemed to be a duo, you know?" She sniffed hard, even as a few more tears dropped silently down her cheeks. "I have no particular affinity for either of them and I know they chose their paths. But the man I was going to marry, to bind my life with, shot one of them in cold blood. I don't know how to reconcile that in my mind."

All the tears she had been so determined to hold back finally fell with all the finesse of a dam overflowing in spring. It felt like she kept traveling the same ground—endlessly—yet all she could ask herself was how she could've been so stupid. How she could've missed it all.

She was so wrapped up in her emotions that it took a minute before she realized Tripp had shifted some of the wires and her IV to settle in beside her on the bed. His big arms came around her, just as they had in his SUV, and he pulled her close.

"Shh. It's okay."

"It's definitely not okay. I'm a cop. And CSI. I should've known better."

"I'll let you in on a little secret. It's something I don't tell anybody."

She twisted a bit in his arms so she could look at him, curious about what he was going to say. "What secret?"

"Much as we try to be, no one in this job is omniscient. No one's a mind reader. And no one can anticipate another human being's every move. It's just the way of things, as hard as it is to accept."

"I should have known."

He pressed a light kiss to her forehead. "Someday, I promise you, you'll understand and accept why you didn't."

It didn't make sense, and Sadie wasn't even quite sure she believed him, but sitting there in his arms she felt better. For the first time in weeks, she could see the real possibility that, someday, she might feel like herself again.

And she had Tripp McKellar to thank for it.

Chapter 5

Tripp held tight to Sadie, for the second time in less than twelve hours, and marveled at how good she felt nestled in his arms. He'd only meant to comfort and care, yet somewhere between pulling her from Sand Springs Lake and pressing a kiss to her forehead, something inside him had broken wide open.

And the balance between his rigid self-control and the interest he'd had in her for years had decidedly shifted.

Attraction or not, he was still a leader in the Grand Rapids PD and she was not. Her CSI role meant she didn't directly report to him, but he was still her superior as far as departments went.

It was time he remembered that.

He carefully disengaged himself from the wires, gently settling her back against the pillow. "I think it's probably time for you to get some rest."

Those pretty green eyes were dazed, her brow knitted in confusion, before she nodded. "I probably should."

"I want you to think about what I said. You don't need to keep beating yourself up, Sadie. You couldn't have known. Really, you couldn't."

He sensed her protest, her lips opening, before she closed them. "Thank you for saying that."

"Now, get some rest. I'll come back and visit in the morning. I've even heard a rumor there might be donuts."

The mention was enough to get a smile out of her. "Oh, there will be donuts. If I know Pippa, there will be enough to feed the entire hospital."

"Well then, I'll definitely be back for that."

"Oh!" Her sleepy eyes went wide. "I did get something else."

"Got what?"

"Tate believed Fred was followed because he heard it on GRPD dispatch. When I pressed if he had someone inside he mentioned how good his tech was." She yawned, her sweet face scrunching up at the involuntary motion. "And that's all I got."

All?

That was huge and it went a long way toward answering how Greer might know about the safe house, too. But looking down at Sadie Colton's sleepy countenance, Tripp knew now wasn't the time to get into it all.

He patted her foot underneath the blankets, the move silly and awkward after what they had just shared, and figured that was his cue to leave. He'd nearly made it to the doorway when she spoke behind him. "Thank you, Tripp. For everything."

He turned at the doorway, surprised to see how small

she looked amid the sheets and the big bed and all the monitors. It was such a counterbalance to a woman who always seemed so alive. So robust. "Sleep. Feel better. I'll be back in the morning."

When her eyes drifted shut as she nodded, Tripp took it as a good sign. She needed to sleep. To heal. Even with the doctor's excellent prognosis, she had been through a traumatic ordeal. Escaping from it all into sleep would do wonders.

He walked down the hall, nodding to the cop placed at the entrance to the ward. He recognized the man, an eager second-year who continually impressed everyone with his hard work and dedication to the job.

Sadie was in good hands.

Even if the fact they'd needed to post a guard at all was a bigger problem. As she'd accurately assessed even before they'd put her into the ambulance, Tate Greer was still out there. And for as long as he was, Sadie wasn't safe.

Making his way along the corridor, Tripp glanced into the waiting room. It was now empty of Coltons, but had turned over with a few new families, all as equally anxious to see their loved ones as the Coltons had been to see Sadie.

Tripp considered them all and couldn't help but remember his own time in one of those waiting rooms. He had sat in one of those seats once. The night Lila had been brought in, he had waited, like those families were waiting, only the news at the other end had been the worst of his life.

We're sorry, Lieutenant McKellar. We did all we could...

Sustained blood loss from the severity of her gun-shot wounds...

At only fifteen weeks of gestation... We were unable to save the baby...

It played through his mind on a loop, the memories shockingly easy to rise to the surface, even so many years later.

The real surprise: how hard they hit and the fact that he needed to take one of those seats now for a few minutes to gather himself. Tripp stared down at his shaking hands, unable to believe he could still be so affected by the memories. Hadn't he worked on this? Hadn't he believed himself past this?

Would the grief and the guilt ever fade?

Taking slow, deep breaths, he willed the air in and out of his lungs, calming himself the only way he knew how. As he slowly came back to himself, Tripp had to admit that this was only partially about Lila and the baby.

It was also about Sadie.

He cared for her. Had cared for her for a long time. No matter how many times he told himself he shouldn't, he *did* care for her. And tonight he had almost lost her. That shook a man down to his core.

Was it finally time to tell her how he felt?

It all felt so futile, yet at the same time his ability to deny his attraction was rapidly fading. Because even beyond basic attraction, he had deep feelings for her.

That was the most dangerous thing in the world.

Hadn't he made a vow to himself? He'd never risk someone's life again because of his job. He'd cared for Lila and it had been hard enough to lose her. But even without spending any real time together, he knew his feelings for Sadie ran far deeper than they ever had for Lila.

And he had no idea what the hell he was supposed to do about it.

Rubbing a hand over his face, feeling the scratch of a day's worth of beard, he got up and headed for the vending machines. He didn't need any more coffee, but the jolt it provided would be enough for the drive home. Besides, what would a little caffeine hurt? He didn't sleep very well anyway, so what did it matter?

He walked down the hall, following the same path he had taken with Riley Colton earlier. Step by step, he willed the old hospital memories away until they were locked in that quiet place he kept them. He dug out some coins and pressed the directions on the coffee machine, then shoved his hands in his pockets to wait.

It was only as he turned, an oh-so-brief matter of a split second of overlap, that he saw a big frame pass by the alcove for the vending machines. There were still people in the hospital, coming and going. Yet there was something in that slithering form that captured his full attention.

Coffee forgotten, Tripp moved.

And feared that Tate Greer had come back to finish the job.

Sadie shifted and tried to get comfortable, but between the wires and the lightly beeping machines and the lingering troublesome thoughts, she wasn't having a lot of luck with sleep. She knew she could ring her call bell and a nurse would give her something to sleep, but she never cared for medicine of any kind. Something about artificially induced sleep just felt wrong.

Off-putting, somehow. It worked for some, but she was just afraid it was one more way to lose control over her situation.

She'd had enough of that lately, thank you very much.

And then there was Tripp.

Had she been imagining things?

It was sweet that he had stayed to check on her to see how she was. If that had been all, she would tell herself she *had* just been imagining things. But the way he'd settled next to her on the bed and held her close…

Well, it was everything.

Did she dare hope that he had feelings for her, too?

Damn it, Sadie Colton, dream much?

It was silly. *This* was silly.

And still, she couldn't help feeling…*something*.

On a heavy sigh, she readjusted and tried to get comfortable. "I will sleep," she whispered. "I *will* sleep."

She had nearly done it, too, the world going dark around her, when something she couldn't identify made her eyes pop wide open.

The lighting was set to dim, but it was still easy to make out any and all movement. And the large, hulking form that had just slipped into her room was definitely moving. A scream crept up her throat, nearly spilling out when Tate's firm, unyielding hand came over her mouth.

"Shut up or I'll kill you now."

She struggled against his hand, but the dark, dangerous look in his eyes brooked little argument.

"Now, we are going to finish what we started back at the cabin. I want to know what you know. And I want to know what the GRPD knows."

She kept her gaze on his, calculating as quickly as

she could what to do about the situation. If he'd gotten this far, it meant he'd quickly—and silently—dealt with the guard positioned outside. Tripp hadn't made a big deal about it, but Riley had, stressing there was police presence on-site to watch out for her.

So what had happened? She might have been drifting off to sleep but she'd have heard something if there had been a fight. She even knew the officer they'd put in the hallway, remembering him when he'd come in to introduce himself.

"Nod once if you understand me," Tate snarled.

She nodded, still trying to buy herself time. He'd see it if she tried to buzz the nurse, and she'd prefer to avoid dragging any innocents into this if she could.

He removed his hand but it meant little when he lifted his other hand and a gun glinted in the dim lighting. Brandishing it to make his point crystal clear, he hovered even closer, like the brute he really was. "Now tell me what the cops know."

The gun seemed to dance before her eyes, but she refused to cower in the face of this relentless evidence that he was a horrible human being. "They know the same as I do. That you're a monster."

The hard slam from the butt of the gun against her jaw was swift and immediate punishment, the contact enough to make her bones rattle and stars cloud her vision.

"Bull. I know you know more than you're telling me. Unlike all the time you spent with me when you knew nothing. You didn't even know who I was, Little Miss Crime Scene Investigator. What a top-notch worker bee you must be."

Since the words matched a bit too closely to what

she'd already berated herself for—endlessly—over the past month, she forced herself to ignore them. She also ignored the pain coursing through her jaw, refusing to show him anything but disdain. "Believe me, I've caught up."

Tate leaned in even closer and Sadie scrambled frantically for something to do. While she didn't want to endanger a nurse, she needed some way to issue a panic alert. Her hand fumbled along the inside of the bed, desperately trying to find the small red button they'd told her about earlier when suddenly Tate went flying.

Shock morphed quickly into a desperate desire to help when another person bodily removed Tate from her bedside. It was Tripp. Even now, the two men lay on the floor, struggling in a death grip for the gun in Tate's hand. She scrambled for the call button by touch, hitting the small panic alert before she sat up.

With an eye to the rolling stand that held her IV fluids, she figured she could use it as a weapon if she needed to. Only Tate gave her an easier opening. As he and Tripp rolled on the floor, Tate managed to maneuver himself on top. Sadie watched in horror as he lifted his gun. She didn't think, only acted. With a hard push to the heavy wheeled tray beside her bed, she shoved it as hard as she could into Tate's back.

It was awkward and not nearly heavy enough to do damage, but the recently filled pitcher on top added some advantage. Aside from spewing water over both men, the entire pitcher also hit Tate in the back of the head as the tray fell on him.

Tripp didn't waste time, using the shift in momentum to slam the gun from Tate's hand. The weapon clattered to the floor and both men grunted as they continued their physical battle before Tripp reached out blindly, trying to drag the fallen table to hit Tate once more.

Sadie screamed as she struggled to put her feet on the floor. She would be of minimal help in a fight, but she'd already begun looking around the room for something to strategically up the stakes in Tripp's favor. The vase of flowers her sister had set earlier looked like a good option and she walked toward the small desk that held the arrangement.

Pain swam in her head from Tate's pistol whip to the jaw, but she kept moving. Tripp needed her. So did the cop Tate had gotten past in the hall.

Shouts echoed from outside the room and she knew help was coming, but still she pushed on. With the vase in hand, she moved back to the struggling, wrestling men on the floor and waited for a clean shot to drop the vase on Tate's head. When an opportunity presented itself, she didn't wait, slamming the heavy vase into the back of Tate's skull.

It made a satisfying thud but barely slowed him down as her ex suddenly struggled off Tripp, rolled away and headed for the door. The sudden shift in direction was so abrupt, it took Tripp a minute to react. By the time he'd reached the door, he collided with two incoming nurses.

"Ms. Colton!" one exclaimed as the other nurse took firm hold of Tripp's shoulders.

"Let him go." Sadie waved at them, but the second nurse wasn't having any of it.

The throng of shouts finally died down enough for Tripp to point toward his hip. "My badge is in my pocket. I'm a lieutenant with the GRPD." His teeth were nearly clamped shut as he continued to grind out directives. "And you're letting the perpetrator against Ms. Colton get away."

The nurse finally stood down, releasing him, but Sadie knew it was too late. With a resigned sigh, she nodded at Tripp. "Go. I'll explain what happened here."

He ran off and she turned to face the two surprised women.

"There should be an officer in the hallway. We need to get him immediate help."

For the third time in less than twenty-four hours, Tripp cursed himself for the unrelenting danger that continued to find Sadie. It had been bad enough that she'd been taken from the safe house. Worse, that she'd nearly died in the lake. But *this*? To be nearly snatched right out from under him?

There was no way he was willing to trust her safety to anyone else. Not anymore.

He'd given chase after leaving Sadie's room but Greer had a significant head start.

And Greer was crafty, he'd give him that. The bastard had felled the cop on the ward with a quick pressure syringe and basically kept on moving. Straight into Sadie's room. If Tripp hadn't stopped for that cup of coffee…

If he hadn't had that moment of quiet remorse in the waiting room…

He didn't want to think about it.

Just like that moment she'd jumped in the lake to escape, Tripp knew the vision of that hulking form hovering over Sadie, alone and vulnerable in her hospital bed, would stay with him forever.

He slammed back into Sadie's room, his badge now visible high on his jacket. Backup was on its way and he'd already spoken to security for the hospital. The nurses had taken his officer into an exam room and had assured Tripp he'd be all right after they woke him from the sedative.

Now he just needed to convince Sadie that there was no way she was staying here.

Tripp came to a halt as he crossed the threshold. She was no longer huddled on her hospital bed in her hospital gown. Instead she was sitting on the bedside chair, having changed into a fresh set of clothes. One of her sisters must have brought them to her, because they certainly weren't the wet ones he had removed from her a few hours ago.

"Going somewhere?"

"I'm not staying here." She dragged a boot onto her right foot. "I'm not sure why I've remained this long."

"You can't go home."

"Then I'll go to Vikki's. Or to one of my other siblings'. But I'm not staying here. I already had one of the nurses remove my IV."

The lights were fully on in her room and underneath the harsh fluorescence, he could see the dark bruise on her jaw. "What happened?"

"Tate decided to introduce me to the butt end of his pistol."

Once more, Tripp shook at the evidence of what could've happened to her. Hell, based on that dark bruise, what *had* happened to her... It was too much.

"You're coming home with me."

She stopped as she slipped on the other boot and stared up at him. "What?"

"You'll stay with me. I know how to keep you safe and I have my place well outfitted."

"What is that supposed to mean?"

"I know how to take care of myself. I'm a lieutenant in a major city's police department. Believe me."

He did know how, and he had also gotten better since Lila's death. Between extra security on his home and his own rigorous self-training, he felt certain he'd do a better job caring for Sadie than one of her siblings.

"Tripp, this is crazy talk. I can't stay at your house."

"Why not?"

"Because—" She stopped before standing to her full height. "Because I'm not your responsibility. I'm a grown woman. I'm also a cop, or I *was* one, before I shifted into my field. I know how to take care of myself."

Although the past month had seemingly suggested otherwise, she did know how to take care of herself. And to her larger point, she was trained. She knew how to handle a weapon, she knew self-defense and, most of all, she wasn't required to accept his help.

But he didn't know how he could live with himself if something happened to her.

"I know all those things. And I believe them, too. The last month has been anything but normal, but your situation isn't indicative of your ability to defend yourself."

"Thank you."

"But I would feel better if you were with me."

"Why?"

"Because I don't want to see anything happen to you." *Because I care about you. Because I've always cared about you.*

He didn't say those things. He *couldn't* say those

things. But somewhere way down deep inside, that was all he wanted to say to try to convince her.

"I don't want to be a burden to you." She pressed on, but he could see her conviction wavering ever so slightly.

"You're not a burden. More than that, you have more knowledge of this case than anyone else. Even if you didn't, I would help you. But, selfishly, I'm going to ask for your help. I need all I can get right now."

"You want my help?"

"Of course I do. You know Greer better than anyone. I bet if we sit and think about it, you can point to certain times when you may have picked up information. Windows, or gaps in our knowledge, you may be able to fill in. If he was in or out of town… If he told you he was traveling… Or even casual conversation that didn't mean anything at the time but might be beneficial to us if you look at it now."

And if it meant Tripp had to listen to details about the quiet, intimate evenings she'd spent with her former fiancé, then so be it. He needed the help and, more importantly, he needed her safe. If it took a few uncomfortable conversations to ensure that, he'd deal.

"I was thinking about it before." She sat on the edge of the bed. "Maybe we've been considering him and Capital X all wrong."

Immediately intrigued, Tripp prodded her. "How do you mean?"

"Well, it's easy to think of him as just a criminal. But he's a businessman, too. Heck, that's what I thought he was up until the big reveal."

He almost laughed at her description of finding out who Tate really was, but decided it wasn't quite the right moment. So he went with honesty instead. "That's what I'm talking about. That kind of thinking. That's what I need right now."

"And I'm not going to be a burden?"

"No."

"And you're not just saying that?"

"No."

A small grin edged the corner of her lips before she winced, laying a hand on her jaw. "Ow. Don't make me smile like that."

He knew she was trying to lighten the mood, but at the sign of her pain, he made one more internal vow.

Whether he liked it or not, the RevitaYou case had become personal. And when he finally got his hands on Tate Greer, there was no way he was going to give the man any mercy.

No way in hell.

Chapter 6

Sadie yawned and ignored the shooting pain in her jaw as she tried to remember the last time she'd been this exhausted. She'd pulled some all-nighters when she was in the police academy. She'd studied overtime and in every free moment she could find when she was learning the ropes for CSI. But none of it had felt so all-consuming.

And so emotionally draining.

Neither had it come with that bone-deep chill that still lingered from her dive into the lake.

"We're almost there," Tripp said. "The turnoff for my neighborhood is in two more lights."

"Sorry. I guess I yawned out loud."

He grinned, the smile visible in the light of the streetlamps. "It was hard to miss."

She had always wondered about where he lived. Now

that she had the chance to see his home, she could admit to some excitement. Tripp had always been a mystery at work. He was kind, a hard worker and a true champion for his people, but he kept himself aloof.

Separate.

It made him mysterious and, she admitted to herself, even a little bit sexier than he already was. Which was silly, because not knowing about people didn't necessarily mean that lack of knowledge was a good thing. Look at all she didn't know about Tate, for example.

"What's the frown for?"

"Nothing." Goodness, she needed to stop this train of thought. Not only was it frustrating and repetitive, but clearly those negative feelings were stamped all over her face.

"Look, I know we don't know each other incredibly well, but I'm a good ear. I don't really talk to others, and I certainly don't share confidences."

He made the turn at that second light he had referenced, pulling into a nice older neighborhood on the outskirts of Grand Rapids. Sadie had been here before, she realized. A friend of hers from high school had lived nearby and she'd visited often when she was younger. Although the trees were bare now, the neighborhood boasted huge oaks and the most gorgeous fall foliage when October came around.

It suited him well, she thought. There was something solid and sturdy about the neighborhood. Just like Tripp.

"It's not that I don't want to tell you, or anyone, really." Sadie started in, stopping as she tried to think of the right words. "I mean, I have my sisters, and we talk about pretty much everything pretty much all the time."

"I'm not trying to pry into the sisterhood."

She smiled at that and his sweet attempt at lightening the mood. "I promise I won't make you pinky swear on anything, nor will I make you do my hair. But that's not actually what I meant."

"I can do a mean braid, if I do say so myself."

"I'll remember that."

She hesitated and wondered if she dared to say what was on her mind.

Oh, what the hell.

"It's just that I can't stop thinking about what a bad decision I made. And how horribly duped I was. It's embarrassing, you know? Like, really embarrassing. Like, I-jumped-into-a-freezing-cold-lake-to-escape-the-jerk-I-thought-I-was-going-to-marry embarrassing."

Now that she'd gotten into it, the words wouldn't stop.

"I realize I should be incredibly upset because he tried to kill me. And I am. Don't get me wrong, I *really* am. But it's like one more example of how shortsighted I was. How stupid I was. And all that keeps going through my mind, over and over, is one question."

"What's that?"

"Was I so happy to finally have a relationship and someone who wanted to marry me that I didn't pay any attention to what was actually going on?"

Tripp navigated the neighborhood streets until they reached his driveway and he hit the opener for the garage door. He pulled in, his attention on the rearview mirror until the door closed fully behind them. It was only then that he turned off the ignition and turned to face her.

"I don't know how you feel. I haven't been in that situation and I won't insult you with some dumb platitudes designed to make me feel better, not you. But I will tell you something and I hope you take it to heart."

When she'd started in on her tirade, she'd expected he'd do nothing more than politely listen to the pressure cooker he'd unknowingly unleashed.

But the serious look in his eyes, visible in the dome lighting, told another story.

"What's that?"

"You're a remarkable woman, Sadie Colton. I've thought it since the first time I saw you at the academy and I've thought it every day since. You're sharp and smart and you care about people. You believe in people. And because of it, you're one of the finest members of our department. You do right by others and you want to see justice brought for all who deserve it.

"I can't tell you how to feel, but I can tell you how others see you. And I can tell you how I see you. And it's not as some helpless damsel in distress or some silly duped woman. Tate Greer is a criminal and he behaves like a criminal. And you, unfortunately, were collateral damage. That's his fault, not yours."

He flipped off the dome light and reached for his car door handle, admonishing her before he got out. "Stay where you are. I'm going to come around and help you."

The normal urge to argue or to tell him she was fine never made it past her lips. Because she was still so shell-shocked over his speech.

He thought she was remarkable.

Her.

She was still trying to make sense of those words when he came around and opened her door.

Tripp wasn't sure what had gotten into him, but now that the rush of words was out, he wasn't sure if he should be embarrassed or pleased by Sadie's response.

Or lack thereof, if the fact that she hadn't moved from her seat was any indication.

"Once you're ready, step down carefully. If you place your foot on the running board, I'll help you from there."

Sadie did as he asked, planting her feet as she shifted herself out of the passenger side. Her movements were slow, but he was pleased to see she seemed to have full range of motion as well as some pink color back in her cheeks.

Even if that rosy glow competed with the purple bruise lining her jaw.

Ignoring the hot rush of anger, Tripp took hold of her hands and helped her step down. Just like earlier, the gesture was simple and meant to help, but Tripp couldn't help but feel there was something more to it. Something monumental.

That was a train of thought he definitely needed to pull off the tracks if she was going to be living with him for the next few days.

"There are just two steps up to the garage door. If you wait, I'll help you up them and into the house."

He went around to the back of the vehicle to pull out a few of his work items as well as the small bag her sister had brought to the hospital. But by the time he closed the rear door to his SUV, Sadie was already at the steps.

"Hey there. I told you to wait for me."

She turned to him, perched on the second stair. It basically made them eye level, but she had the slightest advantage in height. From her perspective, she looked down on him, a small smile at her lips.

"I want to do this, before I lose my nerve."

Before he could even register her words, she leaned in and pressed her lips to his. It was a quick kiss, and rather chaste, but something inside him imploded.

Unable to stop himself, his free arm wrapped around her, holding her in place. Without questioning if he should, or even if she'd welcome the gesture, he returned his mouth to hers. She hesitated for the briefest moment and he nearly pulled back, but her arms came around his neck, her lips opening beneath his.

Desire and a delicious sort of shock rippled through him as the kiss spun out. Heat, need and the culmination of what felt like endless years of wanting combined to create something he had never felt before. A soul-deep desire that made all the principles he held on to so tightly seem almost silly.

He didn't need or want a relationship in his life… right?

Somewhere a small voice inside kept trying to remind him of that, but Tripp disregarded its steady drumbeat. And then he ignored it completely as he dropped the bags from his one hand, lifting that arm to join the other at her waist. With the additional leverage, he pulled her closer, reveling in the way she seemed to melt into his arms.

Her lips were playing over his, pulling sensation after sensation. Like that runaway train he had worried about, the emotion sparking between them was electric.

And wildly raging out of control.

It was Sadie who finally broke the kiss, her pretty green eyes hazed with passion. "I guess that means you didn't mind."

"No, I didn't."

She reached behind her for the doorknob. "I should probably go in now."

As she still fumbled for it, Tripp reached past her, his forearm brushing her waist, to turn the knob. "You should. I can help you, if you need it."

She shook her head, sudden shyness taking over her normally ebullient personality. "I'm good. A friend of mine from high school used to live in this neighborhood, and I think your house has the same layout. I can find my way."

He bent to pick up her bag, handing it over. "The bed in the spare room is all made up. And there are towels in the attached bathroom."

"Thanks."

She turned then and slipped into the house. While he hated to see her go, Tripp was strangely relieved. In the cooling aftereffects of their kiss, reality was rapidly coming back.

He'd kissed Sadie.

Well, she'd kissed him, but then he'd kissed her.

The dangerous swings of emotion he had carried for the last several days had erupted at the touch of her lips. It was a distraction he didn't need. More, with the threat to her well-being still out there, it was a distraction that could prove lethal.

Yet no matter how hard he admonished himself, he couldn't deny how good it felt to touch her. To kiss her.

He gave her one more minute and then followed her into the house, setting the alarm behind him.

As he heard the light creak of someone walking over the floors above his head, Tripp acknowledged he couldn't deny how he felt at all.

It was good to have Sadie here with him.

Even if having her here, close enough to touch, would be the hardest test of his life.

Sadie came awake the next morning in a rush, the same way she had woken up every other day of her life. Only this day, she was different. Wildly different. Because last night she'd kissed Tripp. More, she had *initiated* the kiss with Tripp.

Although he had caught up quickly, she thought, unable to hold back a smile.

She hadn't intended for things to go quite so far and, if she hadn't been so exhausted, likely wouldn't have worked up the courage to kiss him at all. But her guard had been down and he had said those lovely things in the SUV, so she'd gone for it.

And then been beyond surprised to find such a willing partner in the kiss.

Oh, could he kiss. Whatever she'd imagined, the strong lips with their gentle-but-firm pressure and the warm, secure feel of his arms around her had been beyond anything she'd imagined. And over the past several weeks, she'd imagined plenty.

Only to find that reality had been so much better.

Sitting up, Sadie tested her body, curious how many aches she would find. She was lightly sore all over. Yet, all things considered, she felt pretty good. But oh, her face. She raised a hand to lay it against her cheek and felt the tender, warm-verging-on-hot skin beneath.

Damn it, Tate had done a number on her. She could

only imagine what her face looked like and was dreading her first glance into the mirror. If it appeared half as bad as it felt, she was prepared to look pretty awful.

Hitting her had been a nasty move, designed to make her feel small. And it had worked. Only now, with the bright sunlight of a winter morning streaming through the windows, it made her angry. She meant what she had said to Tripp the night before. She *did* want to help him. And in light of what he had suggested, working together through a timeline of the past several months in the investigation into Capital X, she likely did have something to contribute.

Tate had thought he was so clever, concealing everything he did from her, but there had been some cracks. They had spoken of travel and he'd mentioned a lot of the places he had been to. He had almost bragged about it, really, talking about the things he had done and seen.

She could use that. If they could triangulate some of the locations, they might have a better chance of tracking where Capital X's interests might lie.

Regardless of what they turned up from her memory, she was also a pretty decent whiz with the computer. She could dig as much as the next person, and she was determined to help Tripp find what he needed. They would put Tate away. And she was first in line to be part of the team to do it.

With that resolution keeping her company, she got out of bed and crossed to the bathroom. Flipping on the light, she moved before the mirror, offering up a small prayer as she went.

"May it not be too bad," she whispered before opening her eyes. And watched them widen in her reflection as she took in the purple and blue that ran down the edge of her jaw.

Wow. She breathed out, shocked to realize that it actually looked *worse* than it felt. That was saying something.

Determined to find the silver lining—and realizing it was rooted in the fact that her jaw wasn't broken—Sadie quickly washed up and headed back into the bedroom. She put on a fresh change of clothes then headed for the kitchen. Coffee would make it better.

Then she'd hunt up a pad of paper and start writing down what she knew.

It was only as she came into the kitchen that she found Tripp at the table a few steps ahead of her. He had his laptop open and a series of photographs laid out on the kitchen table. He was also scribbling notes on a legal pad beside his computer.

"You're up early."

He glanced up from his notepad. "I could say the same about you. Have you had enough sleep?"

"I'll probably crash again later, but right now I'm good." She pointed to the coffee maker on the counter. "Can I get you a refill?"

Tripp stood at that, snagging his mug from the table. "You don't have to wait on me."

"It's coffee. I think it's okay."

He'd left a mug out for her on the counter and she filled it before turning with the pot to replenish his. It was only as she turned, morning light streaming through the window, that she caught his dark glare.

"What?"

"That bruise on your cheek." Tripp came closer, ignoring the outstretched carafe in her hands and instead setting his mug on the counter with a hard thud. He then reached for her, tilting her face so he had a better view in the light.

"How sore is it?"

"It hurts, but I'm fine."

He ran tender fingers over her jaw, from just beneath her ear all the way down to her chin. The light touch sent shivers down her spine and Sadie had the abstract thought that if given the chance she'd happily stand there with him every morning for the rest of her life.

Oblivious to her thoughts, Tripp gestured with his mouth, his movements reminiscent of the Tin Man after a dose of oil. "Can you move it back and forth?"

Sadie followed suit, nearly laughing out loud at the image.

"What's so funny?"

"I'm waiting for you to pull out your oilcan, Dorothy."

It was enough to break the moment and he dropped his hand from her jawline. "Very funny."

"I'll be fine. Nothing's broken and, while it hurts, it'll heal."

"We should get some ice on it. I should have thought to do that last night."

Last night.

When they'd kissed.

If she'd been even half thinking when she'd come into the house, she'd have thought of it herself. She'd fallen into bed, so exhausted from the day, that it had never crossed her mind.

"I'll do it in a bit. Right now I want to enjoy my coffee and see what you're working on." She turned to refill his mug before setting the coffeepot back on the burner. "I've been out of the loop on everything for the past month. Fill me in."

He looked about to argue before grabbing his mug and following her to the table. "What has Vikki told you?"

"We communicated by burner phone when I was in the safe house, so I know a few things. But why don't you give it to me through a cop's eyes?"

She took a seat, reaching for one of the photos he'd placed on the table. A name was pinned to the bottom: Landon Street. Sadie turned the photo over, curious to the details. "This is Flynn's brother, right?"

"Half brother. He's the man who came up with RevitaYou."

That meant he would soon be Vikki's half brother-in-law.

"We've got him in custody," Tripp continued, "but he's not saying much."

"He probably knows what'll happen to him if he snitches on Tate's organization."

"Possibly. He's also likely biding his time in hopes he can work a deal. He's a scientist, after all. He probably doesn't see himself in the same criminal class as the group he went all-in with."

Sadie figured a deal was highly unlikely, but at this point, the entire RevitaYou case was like something out of another dimension anyway. The depths of depravity as well as the strange layered mess of it all was tough to navigate.

Sadie took a sip of her coffee, a new idea playing in her mind. "It's weird, you know. How intertwined my family has become with this case."

"How do you mean?"

"Well, the inventor of RevitaYou is Landon Street. And his half brother is now my twin sister's fiancé."

"Funny coincidence?"

"A happy one, too. But curious, don't you think?"

"People find their way to each other in any number of ways."

Sadie knew he was right, but even so, it struck her as odd. Her five siblings had all reached the age of maturity and none of them was married. And now here they all were; after just a matter of months working the RevitaYou case, all were coupled up with people intimately involved.

"It's still a bit odd. Vikki's engaged to Flynn, whose brother invented the product. And Griffin is engaged to Abigail, whose father was the banker behind the pyramid scheme. And even Kiely found her true love, Cooper, because they were working the case together at the FBI."

"They also dealt with the kidnapping of Cooper's son because of it."

Sadie thought of sweet little Alfie and how excited she was to see her soon-to-be nephew again. "They did. Which only adds to my point. My family is so deeply layered in this case and has been from the start."

"Riley told me about your family's relationship with Brody Higgins. That personal connection is why you're all involved. And things have progressed from there."

He was right. Trying to find some weird connection made little sense when it was clear how her siblings had met their significant others.

"Okay. So personal connections aside, things have been moving forward. And between you and the GRPD, Colton Investigations, the JAG investigation that solidified Landon Street's involvement, and the FBI, it stands to reason this would be locked up by now. Yet the sands keep shifting. Every time it feels like there's a lead that will wrap the whole thing up, a new dimension opens up."

"You're on point with that one, Colton."

"Thanks, McKellar. So what do we know and where are the gaps?"

Over the next hour, Tripp walked her through the case. Every detail he had, from what had actually happened all the way through to his personal theories. He showed her his notes and replayed a few of the interviews they'd done with both Landon Street as well as Tate's henchman, Gunther Johnson, in custody.

"Then Street and Johnson are where we need to begin today."

"We?" Tripp glanced up from where he'd scratched another note on his legal pad.

"Sure. You said you wanted my help. Gunther Johnson is our first stop."

"You're not going to talk to him."

"Sure I am." Sadie made a point to keep her voice light and breezy, even if steel had gathered in her gut.

The RevitaYou case had lingered too long. They needed answers and they were losing precious time before key criminals either cut bait and got away or more people died from the drug.

Or both.

"You know how deep Greer's tentacles go. Johnson only ratted him out to get out of Murder One charges. He's not going to give up anything else."

"Then we gently persuade him to."

"I'm not sure gentle and Gunther Johnson belong in the same sentence."

"I just want to ask him a few questions about who and what he knows. He's one of Tate's lead guys, which means he knows where the money is and where the bodies are buried."

Tripp reached for his mug, setting it back down when he realized it was empty. "Which amounts to further ratting out Greer. Sadie, this isn't going to work."

Sadie stood to get the pot of coffee, returning to the table to refill both their mugs. "Sure it will. I have an ace up my sleeve. Tate didn't tell me anything, but Johnson doesn't know that."

"You're going to play him."

Even with the pain in her jaw, she couldn't hold back the big, broad smile. For the first time in months, she began to feel like herself. "Like a well-tuned fiddle."

Chapter 7

Tripp unlocked the door to his office and wondered, not for the first time since waking up, when he'd lost his mind. Was it when Sadie had kissed him? Or before? Maybe when she'd huddled in his arms in the SUV after jumping in the lake? Or maybe it was those quiet moments in her hospital bed.

Or hell, maybe it had been that very first day he'd seen her, rookie-crisp in her uniform.

Whether or not he could pinpoint the moment, it really didn't seem to matter. The woman was in his blood and she made a damn fine argument to boot. And he was about to expose her to a one-on-one interview with Johnson. So far, the man had been a rock. Unchanging and absolutely unwilling to talk on almost anything related to Capital X.

Sadie followed in behind him and took a seat in one

of the chairs opposite his desk. "Run through it with me again, will you?"

Tripp closed his door then turned to her. "Shoot."

"Gunther thinks he's being loyal by not spilling on Tate's activities. And he's been here for—what?—about two months."

"About two and a half."

"So he's out of the loop."

"He is. Although…" Tripp stilled, a new thought taking root. "What if he's the one who got Tate access to the safe house?"

"You think he influenced somebody here?"

"Possibly. I've been racking my brain but I never once considered that Gunther could have been his way in."

"It's an interesting angle. Who here has access to him?"

Tripp mentally ran through the roster. Although he knew most members of the department, he didn't know everyone. And it was impossible to know everyone's personal situations, which were usually the key. He had long believed in the fundamental decency of his fellow cops. But if someone fell on bad times, it was not difficult to be taken advantage of by a persuasive criminal with nothing to lose.

"I need to look into it. Check anyone who has been with him."

"I can help you with that later. If you get the files, I'm happy to cross-reference them with the team."

"You don't have to do that."

"Sure I do. Gotta earn my keep. And we'll add in the tech angle Tate let slip to me, too. See if we can figure out what or maybe who he's hacked." She winked at him, the move positively cheeky. It was refreshing to see, especially after her confession in the SUV last night. Tate's betrayal had done a number on her and while Tripp didn't fully understand what she was going through, he was human. He could imagine how something like that would put a boulder through her self-confidence.

That made it all the nicer to see Sadie safe and excited about the case.

And while he might not fully understand, he meant what he'd said. He was impressed with her every day and knew how talented she was, as a cop and as a lead investigator for CSI. She had skills and smarts, and the GRPD was lucky to have her.

He wasn't crazy about putting her in front of Johnson, but maybe it was what she needed. An emotional shot in the arm to begin to heal some of the damage Greer had caused.

"You ready to do this?" Tripp asked.

"Let's do it."

"All right, then. Like we agreed, I want as few people as possible to see you."

She nodded. "I know. Head down all the way to the interrogation room."

"And you wait in the viewing room until you get my signal."

"That's the plan."

"Okay, Ms. Colton," Tripp said as he stood from his desk. "Get ready to lead the witness."

Tripp waited until Sadie was settled into the viewing room before he opened the door to Interrogation

Room One. Johnson was already in the room, having been brought up by one of Tripp's detectives.

"Mr. Johnson, Chief Fox told me you're waiving the right to counsel."

"Sure. Whatever."

Gunther sprawled in his chair with that special sort of disdain only a young man could truly manage. Tripp had read Johnson's file so many times, he had it memorized, but he'd still refreshed himself while briefing Sadie.

Johnson was only twenty-two and, by all accounts, had been working for Greer at least four years. He'd worked his way up to being one of Greer's deputies in that relatively short period of time. The only reason he'd even given Greer up was that he was facing a murder rap.

Tripp would do his job—he always did—but it killed him to see young men like this, their lives wasted before they'd even begun.

Sad situation or not, the kid was scary. His hulking frame had to be at least six-three and, for as big as he was now, he'd likely still fill out further over the next year or two. He was bald, with ice-blue eyes that seemed almost devoid of life.

Resigned to the fact that this one was likely beyond saving, Tripp got to work. "Your rights were read to you, but I will ask you again, do you understand them?"

"Yes."

"Do you continue to waive those rights?"

"Yes."

"All right. Let's begin. You've already shared with me and my team that you work for Tate Greer. That correct?"

"Sure is."

The minimalist answers were what Tripp had expected, so he pressed on. "In the course of doing your work for Mr. Greer, when did you learn about the product RevitaYou?"

"I didn't learn about it."

"You don't know anything about it?" Tripp prompted.

"No."

"Have you heard of it?"

"No."

Tripp recognized the blocking and the bravado for what it was, so he kept on. "Surely you had to know something. You're one of Tate's lead guys. If his pyramid scheme did well, didn't you stand to get a cut of it?"

For the first time, he saw the ire rise in Gunther's cold eyes. "I keep my head down and I do my job."

"Killing people?"

Gunther finally looked up, that ice flashing hot before the kid banked it. "Making sure Mr. Greer's business interests are seen to."

It was a new angle, but Tripp had to give the kid credit. He was hardly incriminating himself by making that claim. Taking the "I'm just a lowly employee, I keep my head down and do my job" angle was surprisingly smart.

Had he thought of it on his own? Or had he been coached?

"I think we've established that Mr. Greer's business interests aren't aboveboard."

"Guy runs a business, man. You got a problem with that?"

"Last time I checked," Tripp said, "most businesses don't require murder in order to be successful."

Gunther crossed his arms but didn't respond.

"You've been in here awhile, Gunther."

"Yep. Getting moldy."

"While that businessman you're so loyal to has been out running free and clear."

Once more, Tripp saw that little shot of heat frisson through Gunther's gaze. He didn't say anything, but Tripp took satisfaction he'd hit his mark with the image that Tate was still out while Gunther sat around. It was all the prep Tripp needed and he gestured at the two-way glass for Sadie.

Gunther's attention shifted toward the door as it opened. Tripp didn't miss the shot of appreciation that filled the young man's gaze when Sadie walked in.

"I've asked my colleague to join us, Mr. Johnson. May I introduce you to Sadie Colton."

Gunther lifted his hands as high as he could, the cuffs that encased his wrists limiting his movement as the chain slid through an anchor attached to the table. "Hey."

"It's nice to meet you, Mr. Johnson," Sadie said. She didn't say anything else, just settled herself beside Tripp at the table. As she did, she angled her head so that her bruised jaw was visible to Gunther.

It didn't take any time at all for the kid to comment. "Quite a bruise you got."

"Hurts like hell, too." Sadie added a fierce grin to punctuate the point.

"You run into a wall?"

"No. I took the butt end of your boss's gun."

Although Tripp hadn't pegged the kid for much compassion, he didn't miss the way those broad shoulders stiffened at Sadie's news.

"Do you know who I am, Mr. Johnson?"

"I just met you."

"And I, you. But that wasn't my question."

Just like with the comment on her face, she let her question hang there, more than willing to wait him out.

"Sure, I know who you are. You're the boss's fiancée."

"*Ex*-fiancée."

Once again, Gunther didn't respond and it gave Sadie the opening she was clearly waiting for.

"You know, it's funny how it all worked out. You ratted him out and then I was forced to realize what a nasty-ass criminal he really is. You know—" she leaned forward conspiratorially, getting into it "—my family tried to warn me about him, but I didn't listen."

"I don't rat people out."

"Right. You just happened to tell the Grand Rapids PD that Tate Greer is the head of Capital X."

The kid struggled to sit straight, that lazy slouch gone. "I didn't tell anybody anything they didn't already know."

"I'm not quite sure Tate would see it that way. In fact, based on my conversation with him just yesterday…you know—" she tapped her jaw "—the one where he gave me this? He's still pretty steamed about it all."

She kept up that low, steady conspiratorial tone. "Between you and me, I think he's starting to panic."

"Dude doesn't know how to panic."

"Oh, sweetheart, everybody knows how to panic."

Just as she had played the conversation from the start, Sadie let those words hang there. And like a fish swimming past a baited hook, Gunther took it. "You think you can touch him?"

"I think we already have. I think that's why he's panicked."

Tripp watched as Sadie spun her argument, her demeanor sweet as cotton candy yet layered with threads of steel.

"That's why he hit me. He knows the cops know something. And between you and me, he's right."

Although the rest of him might remain frustratingly stoic, Gunther's eyes said all they needed to know. "Cops don't know nothing."

"Sure." Sadie nodded. "You keep thinking that."

"If they do know something, why isn't Greer rotting away in here, too?"

"You've worked for Tate long enough to know that. He always has a hidey-hole or two set up. He'd never expected we'd find that one at Sand Springs Lake. I'm sure he thinks you gave him up on that, too."

The explosion came exactly on cue. Gunther slammed a hand down on top of the table. "I didn't do that!"

"You sure? It would be easy enough for Tate to think that."

"I didn't do it."

"He's a man of action, isn't he? Shoot first, ask questions later. That's what he did to one of his goons. The big guy was shot dead on the floor."

"Tommy's dead?" Like a balloon popping, the air flew out of Gunther's bravado. "Big guy? Dark hair? Always wears a suit."

"That's the one."

"He was identified as Thomas Brackett." Tripp took the opportunity to layer on the details of Tommy's death. The description drew Johnson's attention from

Sadie and gave her time to catch her breath. All while she waited like a patient tiger, ready to strike.

Sadie shrugged, the move deliberately casual. "He never gave me his name, so in my mind I named him Fred and the short guy who works with him I named Barney."

"Little guy's name is Rick." Gunther's words were flat. "They were a team. Worked for Greer for a long time, too."

"And clearly that loyalty was rewarded." Sadie's voice was low and quiet, and there was something beneath her words that had Tripp turning to look at her.

It was in that moment that he saw the truth. She had put on the casual charm and ready bravado for the meeting, but she wasn't unaffected.

Not his Sadie.

"What do you want from me? I don't know anything."

"Sure you do. But I respect the fact that a man needs time to think about things. Why don't you do that?"

With that, Sadie rose and walked out of the room.

It was inspired and Tripp had to give her a lot of credit. He had seen many an interrogator press too hard or go too long. Sadie had done neither. Instead, she was leaving Gunther with plenty to contemplate.

Tripp raised his hands. "I'm done, too."

When Gunther didn't respond, Tripp stood and walked to the door. He opened it and gestured one of the cops waiting outside into the room. With a last look at Gunther, he said, "You can take him back to his cell. We're done in here."

Sadie flipped through Gunther Johnson's file once more as she waited for Tripp in his office. Although she had read it already, after meeting the man face-to-face, she was hunting for any new perspective she could find.

How could someone's life be so ruined, so young?

It was a question that had haunted her since walking out of that interview room. One she hadn't been able to shake since.

Though she still considered herself young, not even yet thirty, she felt light-years away from Johnson. She had a job helping others. She had a family she cared about. And while things had certainly gone beyond sideways with Tate, her gaze had been firmly on her future.

Yet young men like Gunther traded their futures for violence and some sort of temporary accolade from an employer who couldn't care less about them. Worse, one who found him disposable. It was a strange sort of belonging, doing business in an organization like Capital X. It didn't make sense. And on a bigger level, she knew it would never make sense to her.

With that sobering thought, her mind drifted to Brody. For far too long, she'd only seen him not as a foster brother, but as the young man her father had been helping before her parents had been senselessly murdered. Although the cases weren't related, she'd conflated them in her mind in a sort of resentful stew that had taken her several years to get past.

A fact that shamed her now.

Especially because all her siblings had pretty much taken to Brody. He hadn't been ready for the pressures of real life, nor had he had any resources. Save one.

Her father, Graham Colton.

In his role as district attorney, her father had taken an interest in Brody's case, determined to prove his innocence in a murder trial. It was a crime her father had been convinced Brody hadn't committed. His tenacious work ethic had ultimately proved the young man innocent.

It was Graham's belief in Brody—and her siblings' desperate need to find some meaning after their parents' deaths—that they'd taken Brody in as their own.

And ensured that he would have a better shot at a future than being left to his own devices.

It had mostly worked. Brody had built himself a future, ultimately going to college and law school and working hard to make something of himself. He was only a year younger than she and Vikki, but he'd always seemed younger, somehow. And when she wasn't being stubborn, frustrated and—she'd own it—acting like the baby of the family, she knew he deserved better.

Something she'd come to understand since the RevitaYou case had been cracked wide open. Brody wanted more out of his life, but it was his investment in RevitaYou that had knocked him down.

Terribly.

And every step he'd worked for and pushed for over the past decade had seemingly vanished overnight.

She knew her feelings about Brody weren't simple—especially the quiet one that liked to sneak in and claim he'd taken precious hours of her parents' time in the months leading up to losing them—but she knew she needed to think differently.

Vikki's voice echoed in her head—just like it did every time Sadie mentally went down her Brody rabbit hole. *You can't live his life for him, Sadie. And you need to cut him a break every now and again.*

Although she had spent a lot of time working toward Vikki's approach to Brody, she couldn't deny he still had a future. And a rather bright one, in fact, once they got past this RevitaYou mess.

Something Gunther Johnson would never have.

Tripp closed his office door behind him, their continued secrecy at Sadie's presence in the office still in full effect. "Why the sad face?"

"Just a lot to think about."

"Gunther Johnson?"

"Yes, mostly."

"Mostly?"

"I was thinking about Brody, too."

Tripp's gaze narrowed. "Brody Higgins?"

"That's the one." She waved a hand. "It's complicated emotions."

"I know I said it before, but I'm a good listener."

He was, but in this case she wasn't quite ready to share. She wasn't proud of how she felt about Brody and wasn't quite sure how to put voice to those frustrations without her own biases coming out.

"Maybe some other time. What I was really thinking about was Gunther Johnson. And the fact that he's basically traded every bit of his future."

Tripp took the chair next to her, one of the two seats opposite his desk. "I was thinking along the same lines as we talked to him. He's set his future on a boss and an organization that see him as disposable."

"But he doesn't see it," Sadie said.

"No, I don't think he does."

"It puts one more check mark in the Tate-is-a-world-class-jerk column."

Tripp cocked his head, and she saw the thoughts playing through his mind. Curious, she pressed on. "You don't think so?"

"Oh, I won't argue the world-class jerk point. In fact, I've used a few more choice descriptions. But I'm not sure I would let Gunther off so easily, either."

"He's a kid."

"He *was* a kid when he started at Capital X. Now he's a young man. Let's not lose sight of the choices he has made and continues to make."

"You mean like not helping us?"

"That, yes. He's been in here for two and a half months and, other than seeing a shot at reducing a Murder One charge, he hasn't done a whole lot to help himself."

While she didn't want to give her bleeding heart too much credit, she couldn't ignore Tripp's counter-argument. And it would be highly perilous to give too much sympathy to a dangerous criminal like Johnson. "Something to think about."

"Yeah, it is. One of the unexpected bonuses that come with this job."

She heard his light chuckle, one without any trace of humor, before she continued. "Does it ever get to be too much?"

"Some days."

"What do you do about it? On those days when it gets to be too much."

It was something, Sadie realized, she really wanted to know. How did Tripp manage the pressures of his job? Both the dangers he put himself in, and the human depravity he saw on a regular basis.

"Believe it or not, a burger usually helps."

Whatever she was expecting him to say, that wasn't it. "Thinking of your stomach?"

"Always." He leaned back and patted his delectably

flat abs. "But, seriously, a beer on the back porch as I get the grill going? It usually helps."

They hadn't talked about their kiss the night before. In fact, they had both sort of silently agreed to ignore it. But in that quiet moment of camaraderie and solidarity, Sadie couldn't resist a bit more human touch.

Extending a hand between their chairs, she turned it palm up. "Want to go home and make a burger?"

He hesitated, and she thought he might be looking for a way to avoid making contact. Until his large hand came out, taking hers firmly in his own. "I think that's an outstanding idea. Let's go."

Gunther Johnson stared up at the ceiling of his jail cell and considered the conversation with Sadie Colton. He figured Tate was pissed about the whole Capital X thing, and the exposure Gunther had unleashed, but he'd done right by the boss, hadn't he?

He was the one who'd got Greer the address to the safe house. And he was also the one who'd kept his ears wide-open since he'd been inside this hellhole.

But killing Tommy?

It sent a shudder through him. And, damn it, it made a man think, too. Tommy had been a big man in the organization. Tate had always joked with him, making it seem like Tommy was indispensable.

Then he'd killed the guy?

Gunther'd had the briefest suspicion that Sadie had been lying about that, but her description of Tommy was spot-on. And there was no way she had made up that bruise on her jaw. While he didn't have sympathy for the cops, he'd never taken Greer for one to go around hitting women, either.

And *damn*, the boss had played her. Gunther had watched it all from afar and knew way more than he had let on to the cops. Tate had worked her and worked her, making her feel so special, telling her how important she was. And all the while he'd kept poking around in her files, trying to get more details on the GRPD and on her family.

Yeah, Gunther knew who the Coltons were. Everybody in this part of Michigan knew who the Coltons were. And that was what Tate had wanted when he'd gone after their precious baby girl. Information from the easiest in he could find.

Gunther had quietly listened when Tate would laugh about her, mentioning an upcoming "date" or weekend trip she was all excited about. Greer had laughed and laughed, like she was the dumbest mark he'd ever seen.

Only she hadn't seemed dumb today. In fact, if he had to guess, she was smart as hell and was now nursing a serious vendetta against Greer.

It made her dangerous. And, he wasn't ashamed to admit to himself, sort of hot. Those sexy green eyes had sized him up and he'd liked it. But he wasn't dumb enough to let his dick do the thinking. Sadie Colton was in that interview room today for a reason and he had to figure it out.

Before he ended up as dead as Tommy.

Chapter 8

Tripp took a long drag on his beer as he checked the temperature of the grill. He could already feel some of that relaxation and sense of calm returning, just like he'd told Sadie.

Even if the woman was driving him a little out of his mind.

He glanced down at his hand where it rested on the edge of a chair that went with his backyard dining set, and could feel the way her smaller one had fit so neatly in his earlier. He'd nearly held back when she'd stretched out her hand, but after the day they'd had and the underlying sadness of their conversation about wasted futures, he hadn't been able to resist.

A situation he continued to find himself in, more and more.

Determined not to dwell on the things he couldn't

have, Tripp considered the conversation with Johnson. Sadie had been impressive, her interview skills incredibly advanced. Whether it was her role as the youngest of six that had made her a good negotiator, he wasn't sure, but she'd hit all the right notes.

She had also left him something to think about when it came to whom Johnson had had ready access to.

Tripp had pulled the log files for the past month before they'd left his office and included anyone who had been on duty at the prison or had checked in for any reason. He wanted to settle into them after dinner.

Sadie came through the back door and out onto the porch. Even though it was December, he had set up heaters at both ends and it made for a cozy space outdoors.

"You've got quite a setup out here." She looked around. "Those space heaters are incredible. I never would've expected you could sit out here, no matter how many heat sources you put up."

"It's a bit of an oasis. Add that I like to grill and needed to find some way to do it year-round."

She slid a plate of uncooked burger patties beside the grill. "Nicely done. And proof that one should never underestimate a man's ingenuity when it comes to his ability to cook meat outside."

"You've made a study of it?"

"My brothers love it. Griffin, especially." Sadie smiled at that, and he saw the clear and genuine affection on her face. "Though I suspect he's grilling less now that he's got Abigail and baby Maya in his life. I've really missed seeing that little one for the past month. She's got to be changing every day. And I missed her first birthday."

Tripp saw the brief bit of sadness and tried to cheer

her up. "You've got two things in your favor on that count. First, she likely didn't realize it was her birthday. And second, a well-placed gift from a doting aunt is always a happy occasion."

"You're right." Sadie picked up the beer he'd left for her on the table and took a sip. "You're also surprisingly optimistic. I'm not sure I would've thought that about you."

"You think I'm a downer?"

"No." She seemed to consider her words. "But you are serious. And I think I'd likely misjudged that seriousness for negativity."

"I have my days."

"We all have our days. But here you are in the midst of a highly stressful case and yet you've still found numerous opportunities to make me feel better." She lifted her beer to his in a toast. "Thank you for that."

He clinked his bottle to hers. "You have to admit, you kinda make it easy. You are the sunshine of the Colton family."

She set her beer down, a look of horror on her face. "Oh no, that's what you really think of me?"

"What's wrong with that?"

"Sunshine? The next thing you'll tell me is that I'm cute like a baby kitten and should be patted on the head for my efforts."

"That's not what I meant. Although, what's wrong with being cute?"

"At the risk of borrowing too heavily from Susan Sarandon's rant in *Bull Durham*, let me tell you, a woman would far prefer to be called sexy than cute."

"Can't you be both?"

"In my experience, people tend to prefer to put you in one category and leave you there."

He suddenly realized they weren't talking about cute *or* sexy, but something that ran far deeper. Something that felt a lot like the lifelong expectations others carried for you.

"It's hard to be the youngest?"

"Probably no harder than being the oldest or the middle or anywhere in between. But when it's your life, it does have its challenges."

"Your family cares about you."

"Yes, they do." She smiled, with a benevolent sort of acceptance. "And I love them back. But it doesn't change the fact that we drive each other nuts on a regular basis."

"It's nice to have that."

"You don't?"

He didn't, and while it wasn't something he thought about often, faced with someone who had five siblings, it was interesting to compare. "No. I was a late-in-life baby and it was just me."

"I would imagine that has its challenges, too. We may have our fair share of sibling spats, but they're there for me. And I can't imagine life without them."

"Like you said, we know what we've lived. I don't think about it all that often. Mostly, in conversations like this one, when it's hard to really picture myself in your situation."

She studied him, keenly interested in what he was saying. Although he got that sort of ready acceptance at work, it was rare to have a personal conversation with someone so present, so thoroughly in the moment.

"What situation is that?" she asked.

"The assumption that because they dote on you, they don't see you as a fully capable person."

He wasn't sure where he was going with this, nor was he sure why he felt it was his business to butt in. But that hadn't seemed to stop him with any conversation they'd had so far. In fact, an odd intimacy had sprung up between them, where he didn't really feel the need to hold back the things he was thinking.

"It's not an assumption, to be honest. It also comes from their actions and the things they say."

"What do they say?"

"About what? My job? My personal life? Where I'm going to live? Who I'm going to live with? What my future looks like?" She stopped, a broad smile suffusing her face. "Gee, that's sort of whiny, isn't it?"

"I wouldn't use that term."

"Then your mother clearly raised you right. But even if I quit my bitching, I can't say I'm entirely in the wrong about them. My brother Riley had a really difficult time when I went out for the force. And Kiely and Pippa, as the older set of twins, love playing mother hen to Vikki and me."

"You don't do the same for them?"

Her eyes went wide at the suggestion. "Of course not. Like they would take that from me."

"Then you didn't see what I saw. Last night at the hospital, for instance. I was waiting out in the hallway and I could hear the way you maneuvered the end of the conversation. You were quick to shoo everybody on after they'd hovered too close. They listened to you."

She reached for her beer, her gaze fully focused on him. "There you go again, making me feel good. And seen."

"Because you are."

"So you say. But I think it's something else. *You* see a lot, Tripp McKellar. It's interesting and affirming, and a little unnerving."

There was that idea again, about being seen. He'd gotten the sense the night before that he'd touched her with his words in the SUV. Statements that he took as simple fact, about her competence and her capabilities. Yet she clearly saw it as so much more.

"That's probably because I'm prying again."

"No, I wouldn't put it that way. You see things, because you're an observer. Things that sometimes the person in the middle can't see very accurately or without being clouded by their own judgment."

"Only-child observer syndrome?"

"Maybe." She tilted her head, considering. "Maybe it's something more."

"Too many years on the force, being suspicious of anyone and everyone?"

"That one probably has a bit of merit. But it makes you a good detective."

He saw the split second of hesitation, curious as to what she held back. Every moment they had spent together over the past twenty-four hours had suggested Sadie hesitated over very little. Yet even with his curiosity, he couldn't quite reconcile that with the serious way she looked at him.

Ducking away from her close observation, he tilted his head toward the edge of the patio. "I should probably get the burgers on."

He moved to the grill but stopped when her hand reached out and settled on his forearm. "I do think it's something else, Tripp."

Without his even asking, she continued. "I think you're a good man. An all-the-way-down-deep good man. And I'm afraid there aren't nearly as many of you as I had believed there would be when I grew up."

"I don't know. I think your brothers are pretty good guys. I also know a few of the guys your sisters are marrying and they seem like fine men, too."

"I agree. I think there's good in all of them. But right now, I'm talking about you. And what I see."

Captivated, Tripp couldn't resist asking, "And what do you think you see?"

"I don't think. I know." Her hand fell away, but that serious gaze never left his. "You're the man who does right by others, no matter the cost to himself. It's heroic. And absolutely unusual."

Her words struck a chord and, while a very big part of him was grateful for the way she saw him, an even bigger part refused to believe her. It was sweet that Sadie saw him that way, but he knew the truth. If he truly was a hero, Lila would still be alive. His child would be alive and in kindergarten by now. And he wouldn't carry around this endless emptiness in his heart.

But he didn't say those things.

Even if, in that same place in his heart, Tripp knew he was right.

Sadie sensed that she'd overstepped but had no idea why. She'd meant what she'd said and had been as complimentary of Tripp as he'd been of her the night before.

Yet somehow she felt the genuine praise had fallen flat.

It was tempting to think the intimacy they had developed over the past twenty-four hours was a mirage.

It was something she might've let herself believe, even a few days ago in the safe house while berating herself over her failed relationship with Tate.

But Sadie refused to go there, allowing that self-defeating behavior to define her reaction.

She hadn't imagined the quiet moments that had passed between them, which meant Tripp's denial was steeped in something else. But what?

She knew he had something tragic in his past. Although she hadn't been on the force when it happened, personal details always had a way of coming out. Was he still mourning and grieving the loss of his fiancée? Because if that were the case, then she *had* overstepped.

And the intimacy she had pressed for had been ill placed.

She would do well to remember it and focus instead on the reason she was staying with Tripp. It was a protective measure, nothing more. Tate Greer was still out there and she still had a target on her chest.

With the excuse that she needed to go back in to set the table for dinner, Sadie headed inside. She puttered around in the kitchen, pouring them both drinks and hunting up some fixings for salad. By the time he came in ten minutes later with the cooked burgers, she had a big bowl on the counter and plates set out for them.

She kept her smile bright and her tone equally light and airy. "Those smell delicious."

"Making burgers is one of my few skills. I feel pretty confident in telling you that they will be."

"With a sales pitch like that, how can I resist?"

They settled in at the table and Sadie sank into small talk. It was a skill she had honed over the years with her family and she was pretty good at it, if she said so herself.

Although they had begun to find their way as adults, especially over the past year or so, there had been plenty of tension between the six Colton siblings after their parents died. Adopted as a child, Griffin had always battled feelings of being separate from the rest of them. And she and her sisters, while there was deep love between them, had the typical ups and downs that a group of four women could have for one another. From drama to secrets and back to drama again, often in the course of one conversation.

And then there was Riley.

The oldest, the head of Colton Investigations, and by default, their resident leader. There were times they loved him for it and there were times they resented him for it. Often, Sadie thought ruefully, at the same time.

But through it all, they'd each figured out a way to deal with one another. And for Sadie, that had meant lighthearted conversation and a way to navigate through all the emotional land mincs that lay beneath the surface of their family unit.

With that skill firmly in hand, she put it to good use over dinner.

For his part, Tripp seemed to take the conversation in stride. He laughed when she talked about various members of the CSI team. Who was overly serious and who was working on the side to become a stand-up comic. Even one who came in each Monday with a dating story that could make a person's hair stand on end.

Tripp listened to it all, laughing and offering his own version of events when they shifted gears to discuss other colleagues. But nowhere during dinner did they get back to that easy intimacy and layered conversation they'd shared before.

It was like a switch had flipped off, Sadie thought as she rinsed dishes before putting them into the dishwasher. And she had no idea how to get the old Tripp back.

"You don't have to do that."

"It's fine. I'm one of six kids, Tripp. Every one of us rotated through cleanup duty."

"Back to sibling politics again?"

She didn't miss the curiosity in his question. "It's been drilled into me since birth. I guess I never really realized, though, how much I depend on them. Or mention them, for that matter."

"It's nice."

Tripp's phone went off, putting a pause to their conversation, and Sadie finished loading the last few dishes as he answered the call.

"Riley. How are you?"

"Speak of the devil," Sadie muttered. What was her brother doing calling Tripp? The two men knew each other and worked well with one another when it was required, but, best she knew, Riley didn't make it a habit to call GRPD members after hours.

Was he checking up on her?

Although she didn't need anyone's permission to stay at Tripp's, she had given Pippa an early morning heads-up. Not only was she her calmest sister, but since Pippa was also on the hook for the morning donuts, Sadie had wanted to save her the trouble. Pippa had promised to spread the word about where Sadie was staying, especially since Sadie was still without a cell phone.

Complete the survey below and return it today to receive up to 4 FREE BOOKS and FREE GIFTS guaranteed!

FREE BOOKS GIVEAWAY
Reader Survey

1
Do you prefer stories with suspensful storylines?

◯ YES ◯ NO

2
Do you share your favorite books with friends?

◯ YES ◯ NO

3
Do you often choose to read instead of watching TV?

◯ YES ◯ NO

YES! Please send me my Free Rewards, consisting of **2 Free Books** from each series I select and **Free Mystery Gifts**. I understand that I am under no obligation to buy anything, as explained on the back of this card.

❑ **Harlequin® Romantic Suspense** (240/340 HDL GQ5G)
❑ **Harlequin Intrigue® Larger-Print** (199/399 HDL GQ5G)
❑ **Try Both** (240/340 & 199/399 HDL GQ5S)

FIRST NAME

LAST NAME

ADDRESS

APT.#

CITY

STATE/PROV.

ZIP/POSTAL CODE

EMAIL ❑ Please check this box if you would like to receive newsletters and promotional emails from Harlequin Enterprises ULC and its affiliates. You can unsubscribe anytime.

Your Privacy – Your information is being collected by Harlequin Enterprises ULC, operating as Harlequin Reader Service. For a complete summary of the information we collect, how we use this information and to whom it is disclosed, please visit our privacy notice located at https://corporate.harlequin.com/privacy-notice. From time to time we may also exchange your personal information with reputable third parties. If you wish to opt out of this sharing of your personal information, please visit www.readerservice.com/consumerschoice or call 1-800-873-8635. **Notice to California Residents** – Under California law, you have specific rights to control and access your data. For more information on these rights and how to exercise them, visit https://corporate.harlequin.com/california-privacy.

HI/HRS-520-JANFBG21

"Your brother's coming over, along with Ashanti Silver," Tripp said as he put his phone away.

"CI's tech expert?"

"Yep. They've got an idea for how to draw out Wes Matthews once and for all."

Although Sadie knew the players broadly in the RevitaYou mix, a month out of the loop had been a bit too long to go without new information. "I know Wes is the man behind the pyramid scheme. His daughter, Abigail, was embarrassed but honest about that from the get-go as she got to know Griffin. What's their idea?"

"It was suspected for a while that he was still in Michigan, but the FBI has officially debunked that. Latest intel suggests he's hiding out in the Bahamas."

Realistically, Sadie knew the man needed capture. But as she thought about Abigail and Griffin creating their new life with baby Maya, there was a part of her that wanted to spare them the upheaval. All while keeping Abigail's father at a distance.

"I hate what this must be doing to Abigail."

"Your brother has an idea and if it works, she will be able to put it behind her soon enough."

But would she?

It was a nice dream, to think that you found closure. And focusing on Maya's future would undoubtedly help Abigail in the healing. But looking to the future or not, the reality of her father's crimes would have their day. They'd have to.

Wasn't that the root of what she was experiencing over Tate? Realistically, Sadie knew she was better off without him. *Far* better off.

But the embarrassment of being so wrong, coupled

with the betrayal of genuine feelings, wasn't something that was so easily healed.

In the end, Sadie admitted to herself, it just hurt. More than she could ever have imagined.

Tripp settled Riley and Ashanti in his living room before returning to the kitchen to get drinks for everyone. Riley had already hugged Sadie and affirmed for himself that she was okay, insisting she sit with them and recount the events at the hospital.

The drinks had given Tripp a polite excuse to escape. And also think about Sadie.

Something had shifted during dinner, before taking a decided left turn over the dishes. He'd thought they were getting along, but something had clearly spooked her. Although he knew the events of the past day, as well as the entire month before, were likely catching up to her, it seemed like something else was bothering her.

So much more.

And he felt wholly responsible for whatever "that" was.

Tripp brought the requested drinks into the living room, passing them out when Riley spoke up.

"I realize my sister is probably downplaying what happened last night. Which is why I want you to know that this comes from me and all the rest of my siblings," Riley said. "Thank you for being prepared and for making sure that she's okay."

"I'm fine, Riley." Sadie laid a hand on his arm, in that way of hers that was so warm and natural. "Truly, I am."

"Because of Tripp."

Sadie looked about to argue before her jaw snapped closed. In fact, if he wasn't mistaken, it looked like she might be biting down on her back teeth. Although he hadn't ignored what she'd said earlier—*We may have our fair share of sibling spats, but they're there for me. And I can't imagine life without them*—watching the byplay between brother and sister gave Tripp a new appreciation for what she must deal with as the youngest in the family.

Anxious to change the subject and take the spotlight off her, Tripp shifted gears. "What is this idea you have to pull Wes Matthews out of hiding?"

"He fancies himself as something of a playboy," Ashanti started in, clearly as happy as Tripp to divert attention off the family politics. "We've been working with Cooper and the FBI, and we're going to use that weakness to catch him."

Sadie looked to Riley for confirmation. "We're talking about Abigail's father?"

"Yep." Riley nodded. "He's quite the ladies' man. Kiely learned that firsthand when one of his discarded women, Meghan Otis, kidnapped Alfie out of some weird need for revenge."

"Which only reinforces my point," Sadie said. "Is he really going to be dumb enough to risk extradition?"

"No extradition needed," Ashanti said. "I put a few feelers out and he's nibbled on every one of them. If he's so dumb to go diving into a honeypot while in the midst of fleeing, he deserves what he gets."

It was hard to argue with Ashanti's logic. And while a big part of him was determined they play every bit of this by the book, Tripp couldn't deny the fact that it made a lot of sense for Colton Investigations to handle this part of the work. As a private enterprise, CI could function in a way that neither the Grand Rapids PD nor the FBI could.

A little coloring outside the lines, as it were.

He was still glad to know the FBI was involved. Cooper Winston was one of the best agents the Bureau had. The man was solid, aboveboard and, as of recent events, also engaged to Sadie's sister, Kiely.

Even with his reassurance that Cooper was on the case, Tripp was concerned that the team followed all proper protocols. Especially if they didn't want Matthews getting off on a legal technicality later.

"You're not doing anything illegal to capture him, are you?"

Ashanti warmed to her subject. "I've done nothing to coerce return contact."

"What have you done?"

"I started with the suggestion I had a rather sizable fortune from my older late husband that I was looking to invest."

"And he bought it?"

Ashanti smiled as she took a sip of her soda, her warm brown eyes taking on a decidedly fierce quality. "At the risk of undervaluing my mad skills, he didn't just buy it, he swallowed the whole damn hook."

"Unbelievable," Tripp muttered. They'd spent the past three months trying to think of any number of ways to lure the bastard out and maybe they never really needed such schemes at all.

"Or highly believable," Sadie argued. "Looks like no matter how smart Wes Matthews thinks he is, he's still dumb enough to fall for the oldest trick in the book."

Ashanti tilted her soda toward Sadie's, clinking glasses. "Score another one for an old classic. Because once again, the honeypot does its job."

Chapter 9

Sadie sat beside her brother and willed her teeth to unclench. To her credit, she'd tried doing that all evening, but Riley was making it difficult. Since he was also oblivious to how much he was annoying her, she was seriously considering adding bodily harm to her to-do list.

That only made her feel guilty when Riley pulled her in close for a hug after Tripp and Ashanti left the room to go into the kitchen.

"Are you sure you're okay?"

"Riley, I'm fine." His hold remained as tight as a python's but, strangely, she didn't care. "I'd tell you if I wasn't."

He let go at that, pulling back to stare down at her. "Now you're just lying to me."

"No, I'm not."

"Sure you are. But since it's a family trait to keep one another in the dark about anything bad, I'll try to forgive you."

Sadie thought about that, especially in light of her earlier conversation on the back porch with Tripp. "Do you think we do that?"

"Of course."

"*Lie* is a rather harsh word choice."

Riley patted her knee. "I'll do you one better, then. How about 'gloss over the details'?"

Now that one she'd buy.

"It's the Colton love language. Make sure no one else knows just how bad the situation is."

Sadie laid her head on his shoulder and let out a small sigh. "How is Brody holding up in all this?"

"On the rare occasions we hear from him, not very well."

She lifted her head at that news. "What do you mean *when* we hear from him?"

Riley got that look on his face—the one that said he was about to gloss over details—and she put her foot down before he could go there. "Riley, come on. I know I've been out of the loop for the past month, but you have to tell me."

He let out a sigh, but based on his head nod and the serious look on his face, Sadie knew she was about to get the truth. "I think he's scared and I think his situation is pretty bad. We know he's hiding out."

"From?"

"Greer. And Wes Matthews. He put money into that pyramid scheme and because it's a big fat lie, he hasn't made a profit. Now they want their money back and made that abundantly clear with their usual starting point of broken fingers."

Once again, Tate's real job reared up and slapped her in the face. Capital X didn't take kindly to investors who couldn't pay them back. They were willing to make large loans, but they wanted payback in full, in a timely manner, and with serious interest.

In spite of her earlier, confused thoughts about Brody, she couldn't understand his reasons for staying away. "He came to us for help when this all blew up. Why won't he stay with one of us? We can help him and keep him safe."

"When any one of us has been able to talk to Brody, that's what we've tried to tell him. Vikki has got a couple of texts and Pippa got a phone call. But that's about it."

"I don't understand this." Sadie thought about the young man who'd been a presence in their life for nearly a decade. Despite her uncharitable moments, she loved him. They all did. Didn't Brody know how much they cared for him? And that they were his family? "Why won't he let us help him?"

"My money is on embarrassment, which, before you tell me I'm wrong, you know is true."

"I don't know any such thing." Sadie pushed back, surprised that was how Riley saw the situation. "Why should he be embarrassed?"

Riley stared at her dead-on but his voice was gentle when he spoke. "Why have you been embarrassed? About Greer?"

She sat back on the couch, that family urge to brush it off welling up sure and strong. "I'm not."

"Sadie—"

"Come on, Riley, it's not the same."

"How is it different? Greer is an ass and he took advantage of you. Why should you feel any embarrassment about that? At all?"

"You don't understand."

"I understand plenty. What I don't understand is why you seem to think you're responsible."

She didn't want to have this conversation. She certainly didn't want to have it *here*, with Tripp a room away. And she really *really* didn't want to have it with her brother. But Riley wasn't backing down and it seemed like Ashanti had Tripp occupied in the kitchen.

"Because it *is* embarrassing."

"The man is a criminal."

"And I almost married him!" Sadie caught herself and lowered her voice. "Do you have any idea how awful it is to think about that? To think that I had almost run off with him to Vegas and bound my life to a criminal. A man who murders people, Riley."

She felt the tears working their way up and did her best to swallow them back. "Where would I be right now if Vikki hadn't caught wind of it all?"

Riley pushed back, unwilling to back down. The paternal role was one he took often as the eldest sibling, but there was something different this time. He seemed *more* insistent. And even more determined than usual to make her see reason. "She did catch wind of it. And Kiely got Johnson to spill the details on Greer's involvement with Capital X. Disaster averted."

"Hardly. I still lost over a month of my life, stuck in a safe house because of him. And believe me, I had plenty of time to think about my poor judgment."

"He played everyone, Sadie. Why is that on you?"

"Because 'everyone'—" she made air quotes around the word "—wasn't desperate enough to rise to his bait. And *everyone* wasn't so freakishly eager to be married that they missed every sign that he's a horrible person."

"None of us knew the real Tate Greer."

"Yeah, but none of you liked him, either. Only, I refused to see it or even acknowledge it. That's all on me. Every time one of you tried to tell me that there was something off about him, I ignored it. And instead, I kept pushing forward, thinking how lucky I was and how in love I was. That I finally blossomed from that nerdy little kid who shoved her nose in books and had long stringy hair and now here I was, finally getting my man. My hot man who loved me. How wrong I was."

Tripp and Ashanti chose that moment to return to the living room. If either of them noticed the heated conversation, they were polite enough to ignore it. Sadie was grateful for that, but she couldn't deny her sense of social equilibrium had been badly blown off course.

Falling back on a polite excuse—she refused to use the word *lie*—Sadie stood, effectively ending the conversation with her brother. "I'm sorry to do this, but I think I'm going to wrap up for the night. I'm still a little tired."

"We should probably get going," Riley said, standing, as well. "But before I leave, let me give you your new cell phone."

Sadie made all the polite niceties, oohing and aahing over the phone her brother had procured for her, but all she really wanted was the quiet of her own room. She nearly had it, too.

She made it through an extra-long hug at the door with her brother, along with his promise to bring Charlize over to visit later in the week, and then he and his tech expert were off.

That left her and Tripp awkwardly standing together in the foyer as if they'd just waved off their guests, which they *had* just done. Only, there was no "they," nor were the two of them a couple, jointly entertaining visitors.

Seeking to break the awkward silence, Sadie returned to their earlier conversation. "What do you think about the plan to draw Matthews out?"

"I was skeptical when Riley first said CI was working on something, but it sounds like they're on to a plan that has a shot at working."

"There aren't many who are as good as Ashanti."

"The same can be said for your brother. He runs a good shop."

"That's high praise, coming from a cop."

"I mean it."

Sadie backed up a few steps, fumbling for something to say. "Riley said we're supposed to get snow tonight."

"News is calling for about six inches overnight."

Since she was dangerously close to fumbling her way through a conversation about the weather, Sadie opted to cut bait. "Okay...well then, I'm going to go up."

"Sure. Let me know if you need anything."

She nodded before heading up the stairs.

It didn't take a genius to know that she needed something. But she'd be damned if she was going to ask for it.

Tate stood out past the edge of Tripp McKellar's property and watched the headlights as the car pulled out of the driveway then vanished down the street.

Interesting.

What was Riley Colton doing visiting the good lieutenant?

Since running from the hospital the night before, Tate had spent his time trying to figure out where they'd moved Sadie. He knew hospital security would be looking for him if he showed his face there, but that hadn't stopped him from calling the main switchboard to talk to her, playing like he was a concerned friend.

The volunteer who'd answered the phone had seemed confused when he'd continued to insist that Sadie was a patient there. He'd used that confusion to his advantage. The woman finally gave in after he'd pressed and prevaricated, becoming more and more frantic when Sadie couldn't be found. The ploy had worked and the woman had finally told him that Sadie had been checked out.

That information had affirmed his belief that the GRPD was once again looking out for her.

He hadn't bothered going back to the safe house. Between the destruction he and his men had wrought as well as the fact the site had been compromised, there was no way they would take her back there. So he'd spent the rest of the day casing out Coltons, which hadn't produced Sadie, either.

It was only when he'd replayed the battle with McKellar over again in his mind, and all that had gone wrong in the hospital room, that it struck him.

The cop was watching out for Sadie.

Police officers might not normally list their personal information in the local telephone directory, but he had ways to find the information he needed. And getting an address hadn't been that hard.

Imagine his surprise at seeing his sweet little ex giving big, wide-eyed glances to the cop as they merrily cooked up dinner on the back porch.

Tate had no lingering feelings for her, but he sure as hell couldn't believe the little bitch had moved on so quickly. She'd barely known how to act on a date when he'd first started hitting on her. She'd been so nervous and awkward. She'd learned—quickly, too—but it wasn't like she was the soul of experience.

And here she was already with someone else?

Tate shook his head at the irony, laughing to himself before he muttered, "Once you get a taste for it, sweetheart, you just can't help yourself."

He'd done that.

Given her the taste for a real life and a real relationship, while giving her a taste for sex, too.

Sadie was cute enough—she'd even tried to be sexy and playful once she was comfortable with him—but in the end, none of it had been about her anyway. She'd been a sweet diversion while he'd gleaned the information he'd needed, and now he was done with her.

The practical part of him knew he'd be better off just taking her out. He knew her whereabouts and he really needed to just take his shot.

But something held him back.

His goals hadn't changed. He still wanted her to pay for the sheer trouble she'd caused him. But watching her tonight, out on the back patio with McKellar, he realized he wanted something else, too.

There was still something wholesome and honest about Sadie Colton and he had the strongest need to crush it. To obliterate it so that she didn't just die, but that she ended so badly no one would ever be able to talk of anything else.

She could have avoided it. If she'd only played along and done his bidding, she wouldn't be in this situation. But in the end, she'd been weak, listening to that damn meddlesome family of hers. And there was no way he'd let that insolence and disobedience pass without punishment.

Sadie had to pay.

And after she did, the rest of the Coltons would, too.

Every one of them would know, every single day for the rest of their lives, that their precious sister died because of them. It was the only way he'd walk away from Capital X a winner. And Tate Greer always won.

Always.

Tripp stared at his laptop, but the names blurred together on the screen.

He hated this. Hated thinking there was something going on with someone in his department. But there was no way around it. Someone had given Tate Greer the information to the safe house and Tripp was determined to find out who had put Sadie—hell, all of them—at risk.

"Are you still working on that?" Sadie padded into the kitchen, thick, fluffy socks on her feet. Her hair was pulled up on top of her head in a messy bun and Tripp admitted to himself that she had never looked more beautiful.

"What are you doing up? I thought you were going to sleep."

"I tried."

Tripp understood the ways a person's body could betray them under stress. "It's a difficult time. Even when you're exhausted, sleep doesn't always come easily."

"I suppose." A small smile drifted across her face.

"Even setting up my new phone didn't tire me out enough."

"Technology. The great distractor."

She shrugged. "Not this time. Anyway, I'm just going to get some water. Do you want anything?"

"I'm good."

Tripp tried to focus on his screen, but his gaze kept drifting to where she puttered around the kitchen. An oversize GRPD sweatshirt covered her to mid-thigh and underneath it she wore yoga pants. She looked like the girl next door.

Although he never considered himself someone with a type—and his limited dating life since Lila's death had been more about quietly seeking a mutually willing partner for an evening of comfort and sexual release— he had to admit the look worked for him.

That meant he needed to focus on his computer and off Sadie. He didn't need to be attracted to her. He needed to protect her.

Even if he was still curious about what she and Riley had talked about earlier, it hadn't escaped his notice that the conversation had been intense. Sadie had looked on the verge of tears. That, based on the stress she had experienced over the past month, and particularly the last few days, wasn't necessarily a surprise.

But still he wondered.

Sadie came over to the table and took a seat. "Are you finding anything?"

"No, which isn't necessarily a bad thing."

"It would be a really tough blow to think that someone in the department had given up the safe house address."

"Especially coming on the heels of Joe McRath."

Tripp knew he couldn't take McRath's betrayal solely on himself. He had a captain and an entire team of people to work with. But it was difficult to know that a man he had respected had been dirty.

"After it happened, Pippa said Emmanuel was struggling with it, too."

"It's hard enough knowing a cop you worked with and trusted wasn't who you thought he was. But the stakes are life and death in our business. McRath traded on the wrong side of that."

That same anger that had accompanied him for the past few months—ever since Emmanuel and Pippa had brought the situation with McRath to light—flared high and bright. It was like a hot coal he'd held on to for endless weeks now. He'd gotten used to the steady pain, but every once in a while something forced him to really think about it again.

To acknowledge the reality of what they'd dealt with as a department.

"You doing okay with it?" Sadie asked.

"I have to be."

"That wasn't my question."

"No, I'm not fine with it. Not at all. I hate looking at my fellow officers with questions. I hate thinking that one of them could have fallen on hard times and is even now making a bad decision. Just like Joe McRath."

"Don't forget good, old-fashioned greed. Sometimes a person doesn't need hard times as an incentive."

Based on when Sadie started as a rookie, Tripp had always pegged her about five or six years younger than his own thirty-three. But in her comment, he heard all the pain and suffering that had narrowed that gap far faster than the standard passage of years ever could.

"You're right." On a hard sigh, Tripp pointed to his computer. "This little exercise doesn't help. I need to trust the people I work with, and combing through names, considering each of them, doesn't instill one iota of belief or conviction."

"I'm sorry."

"You don't have to be sorry. And you know as well as I do that the world isn't black and white."

"No," she sighed. "It isn't."

Maybe it was because the world wasn't black and white. Or maybe it was just because he wanted to know...

"It looked like you and your brother were having a pretty serious conversation earlier."

It was curious that she didn't immediately stiffen or turn defensive. Though Tripp did hate that his question seemed to make her sad.

"It was pretty serious. I know he's worried about me, and I appreciate that. I worry about him, too. I worry for all my siblings. We look out for each other, because we're family. But none of us can walk the other's path. We can't take away the realities and the pain of living."

"I'm sure Riley understands that."

Sadie snorted. "Understanding and practice are two different things."

Tripp knew it wasn't his business. At all. Yet still, he nudged. "Is that all?"

Sadie stared down at her glass of water before that pretty green gaze settled squarely on him. "For someone who doesn't answer a lot of questions, you sure do ask quite a few of them."

"I can stop."

"I'm not asking you to stop. But I want to make sure you're ready and able to accept the answers."

He sensed he was standing on the edge of a very shallow ledge. But that didn't stop him from pushing for an answer.

"Try me."

Sadie knew this was her shot. On some level, she'd been waiting for it since her first day as a rookie at the GRPD. Even then, she'd been captivated and awed, and yes, attracted, to the impressive leader that was Tripp McKellar. As the years had passed, after she'd transferred out of the squad room and into CSI, she'd watched him.

And always, she'd harbored that little flame of attraction.

She'd believed herself unable to act on it. The nerdy kid image of herself that she'd carried into adulthood often did a number on her self-confidence. Add that they were both in their place of work *and* Tripp appeared to keep his personal life deeply private, and she'd never felt she even had a shot at a relationship with him.

So she'd kept her feelings to herself.

She'd waited, year after year, until Tate Greer had found her, alone and vulnerable and the perfect foil for his dirty deeds.

Tracing a finger along the rim of her glass, Sadie shared some of what was racing around in her mind. "The past month has given me a lot of time to think. To dig deep into who I am, what I want out of life, and how I see myself."

"You were dealt a tough blow with Greer's deception. I see what we're dealing with as a department, and it's not nearly as personal as what happened with your relationship."

"Maybe not," Sadie said, considering. "But just like you said, it's discouraging to think of our fellow officers as potentially not being who we think they are. It makes us question ourselves." She briefly hesitated, but knew it was up to her to finish. "Imagine how much deeper that goes when the subject is personal."

Sadie wasn't sure why she had started down this path, yet somehow, she knew it was the right one. Whatever these feelings were that she had for Tripp, she also trusted him. Saw him as a friend. More, saw him as a confidant.

"It's the things in our personal lives that have the power to cut us down at the knees. And when you have spent much of your life feeling awkward and unlovable, I can tell you, it cuts you off at the waist."

Whatever Sadie expected, Tripp's immediate protest wasn't it. "Unlovable? Sadie, that's not true. Not even close."

"It's completely true. I did have those feelings and I had them for a long time. I felt that way about myself and Tate was able to use that."

"But you're a beautiful, confident woman," he argued. "I don't see how this connects."

He had no idea how much those words meant, but Sadie refused to be diverted from her point. "While that's nice to hear, it doesn't change the way we see ourselves inside. I was the proverbial nerdy kid, with my nose always buried in a book. I wasn't athletic and, outside my family, I didn't have a lot of friends. You carry that with you, Tripp. It doesn't go away just because you pass a certain age."

"But you just said it, you were a kid. You're not one anymore. I've watched you since you were a rookie. You're one of the hardest working people I know. You're competent—*highly* competent—in your job. And you go after what you want. I'm not dismissing how you feel, but I'm also telling you what I see now. Here. Today."

Although her family, particularly her sisters, had tried to tell her the same, the words did have more impact coming from Tripp. But should they?

Yes, it was wonderful to have affirmation from a man. Particularly one she was attracted to. But hadn't that been what had happened with Tate? He had showed her a bit of positive reinforcement and she had mistaken it for love.

Tripp *was* different. She held on to that, even as she searched for the real lesson beneath all the heartache.

Because whatever emotional lessons she was supposed to take out of this experience, she knew for a fact that one of them was *not* comparing Tripp McKellar to Tate Greer.

Still, the thought had taken hold. It was wonderful to be told that she was competent. Confident. And beautiful. Especially by a man that she cared about. But *she* had to believe those words. She had to find those feelings within and believe them for herself. Not because they were said to her by someone else.

But because *she* really, truly believed them.

Chapter 10

Tripp was still thinking about Sadie's late-night confession the next morning as he put coffee on. She'd headed back up to bed shortly after their discussion, leaving him to his endlessly roiling thoughts once she was gone.

While that's nice to hear, it doesn't change the way we see ourselves inside... You carry that with you... It doesn't go away just because you pass a certain age.

He was well acquainted with emotional baggage. Admittedly, he'd never imaged Sadie Colton as having any. That was monumentally unfair, but true all the same.

Yet wasn't he the same? He still carried myriad feelings about Lila and their baby. But even before that, he'd had conflicted mindsets on his family and his upbringing. He'd been loved—he never questioned that—but they'd lived a quiet life. His parents had only been able to have him. Many families thrived with only one child, but he'd always felt his mother harbored a low-burning resentment she hadn't been able to have more kids. By the time he was old enough to understand it or to even ask her about it, she was gone.

That brought him back to Sadie. She was one of the brightest lights he knew. And he'd always thought that about her, regardless of his secret feelings for her. She seemed like someone who tackled life head-on and kept a cheery disposition all the while.

But now, in the cold light of their conversation, he was forced to wonder if he'd not only done her a disservice, but had also failed to see her as a whole, fully feeling person.

He knew the story of the Colton family. Her parents, Graham and Katherine, were killed in a story that had grabbed headlines for months. Her father's role as Michigan DA had ensured the story remained top of mind for everyone in Grand Rapids, from the point it happened all the way through to the trial that had put the murderer away for life.

The pain of losing a loved one was hard enough. He knew that and lived it every day. And he also knew that those feelings only grew more intense when the loss came from such senseless violence.

He still struggled with the reality of moving on. And yet he hadn't given Sadie the same consideration.

The woman who'd dominated his thoughts suddenly filled his kitchen and he watched, curious, as she padded into the room. She was freshly showered, her strawberry-blond hair in loose, damp waves around her head. She walked to the counter where the coffee was finishing the last few moments of its brew. She blew out a breath when it was evident she had to wait, before turning in a huff. "Do you sleep?"

"Of course I do."

"Because I've seen no evidence of it yet."

He wasn't sure what had brought on the rush of frustration but opted for humor to deal with it. "You're cheery in the morning."

"I'm horribly grumpy in the morning."

"You weren't yesterday."

"I was happy to be alive. Today I'm just irritated."

The coffee maker made its final gurgle, indicating it had finished, and Sadie turned back to the counter, reaching for the pot like a lifeline. To her credit, basic manners had her taking two mugs out of the cabinet and pouring him one, but he was still thinking over what she'd said.

I was happy to be alive.

In the midst of his musings, he'd set that one aside. And it was jarring to have it shot back at him, and so matter-of-factly.

"Doesn't that bother you?"

"Hmm?" She was busy doctoring her coffee, pouring in copious amounts of cream.

Suddenly frustrated, Tripp walked over and snatched his mug off the counter. She wasn't wrong, but the fact that she could say it so casually over a cup of coffee was a surprise.

"That yesterday you were just happy to have your life."

"What?" Genuine confusion marred a few subtle lines into her forehead, while a small furrow dug in between her eyebrows. Her reaction also seemed to magnify the purple and blue bruise that ran down the length of her jaw, a dark, lingering souvenir from her hospital stay. "What are you talking about?"

"You, Sadie!" The words were out like a shot, coffee sloshing over the rim of his mug as he slammed it on the counter. "You. And the fact that you almost died this week and you're casually assessing it like writing out a grocery list."

The coffee that spilled over was still piping hot and he moved to the sink to run cold water over his hand. The heat covering his knuckles had nothing on the rising ire that filled him.

"I'm not casually assessing anything."

"Could have fooled me." Tripp grabbed a kitchen towel to dry his hands before tossing it back on the counter.

"What's that supposed to mean?"

He whirled on her, well aware it wasn't the right moment for this conversation. But he was frustrated, and all of it had bubbled over, needing a place to land. "It means what it means."

"That I'm not taking this seriously? That I don't value my own life? That I'm not aware of what's going on around me like the clueless woman I've been for the past six months?"

Her voice rose with each question and Tripp had the first flicker of recognition that he might have an equal partner in the battle clearly brewing between them.

He knew he needed to stop. Knew it, down to his bones. Yet no matter how that thought beat in his mind, thrumming in time to his racing pulse, he couldn't pull back.

"We're back to that again? That you're some poor, clueless woman because your boyfriend was an ass?"

Shock waves rippled through the room, radiating out from where he stood. Only, this pulsating disturbance had a directed target, and he saw Sadie nearly stumble in place before something hard and stubborn seemed to lodge in her spine. She set her coffee cup down, oh so carefully, on the counter, before standing to her full height.

"I knew you were cold, Tripp. But I didn't know you were an ass." She turned to leave, the easy camaraderie they'd had for the past thirty-six hours vanishing with her, when Tripp moved.

Just like the words he hadn't been smart enough—or hell, capable enough—to hold back, he wasn't able to stop himself. His hand snaked out, grabbing her elbow to keep her from leaving the kitchen. His touch was light, meant to stop her versus hold her in place, but battle lit her green gaze as she turned to face him.

"Leave me alone, Tripp."

He let go immediately, even as those hard breaths continued to build in his chest.

He needed to back off.

He needed to take control of himself and the situation.

He needed...her.

The already heated air between them shifted instantaneously, the hum of battle transmuting into something so full of need his own knees nearly buckled.

And then they moved. Both of them in unison. United in the same goal.

Tripp wasn't sure if he pulled Sadie into his arms or she moved into them, but as his mouth came down on hers, he knew it didn't matter.

They were both exactly where they belonged.

* * *

Sadie fought to catch her breath, but the press of Tripp's shockingly impressive chest against hers, as his mouth kept up that delicious pressure, made steady breathing an impossibility.

And she didn't care.

All she wanted was *him*. And this sense of belonging that went beyond her deepest fears, straight toward something she hadn't felt in a long time.

Hope.

Somehow, some way, in the midst of some of the worst days of her life, Tripp had found a way to restore the one thing she'd never realized she'd been living without.

Only she knew it now.

And she was desperate to keep the feeling going.

Although she wasn't a short woman, his tall, muscular frame seemed to dwarf her where he wrapped her in his arms as he pressed her against the counter. Her hands had gone to his waist and it was with excitement she realized that their close proximity meant she could explore that impressive physique to her heart's content.

Never one to waste an opportunity, she did just that, her hands drifting over the thick sinews of his back before tracing the hard lines of his shoulders as his mouth continued to ply hers with long, sumptuous kisses that pulled at something deep inside her.

Something real and raw, and completely amazing.

Sadie opened herself up to him and, as she fervently drank him in, recognized something else.

She *needed* him.

It was a rogue thought that was just heady enough to pull her from the moment.

Tripp sensed the shift and lifted his head. "Sadie?"

"I—" The urge to sigh was strong but she held it back. "How did that happen?"

And how do we make it happen again? Not because we're fighting but because it's as natural to us as breathing.

"I'm not sure," he finally said, his gaze still stark and hungry with unmet need.

"But you were so angry."

"I wasn't—" He stopped himself before he nodded. "I was angry. But you just seemed so laid-back about everything. The current situation. And then you went right back to that place where somehow it's your fault."

Sadie stepped out of his arms and away from the counter, increasingly aware that thinking was difficult in such close proximity.

"Nothing about my life or how I feel is laid-back. Of all people, I thought you understood that. Clearly, I was wrong."

"Sadie. Don't walk away. You asked me why I was angry."

"And now I know."

His bright blue eyes clouded over, that crystalline gaze going cold. "You can be mad if you want, but I'm not wrong."

"You enjoy sitting on that high horse?"

The anger that had tinged his words before was nowhere in evidence. Instead she felt the chill slash through her with each syllable. "I'm not sitting anywhere. I'm staring at a woman who is bright and wonderful and who needs to quit feeling sorry for herself and start realizing that she's in danger."

"Your compassion absolutely spills over."

"You don't need compassion. You've got five brothers and sisters as well as a host of soon-to-be in-laws to give you that. It's my job to give you the truth. To keep you safe."

"Keep telling yourself that, Tripp. Say it as often as you like. In the end, you'll realize that they're just words. Safety. Security. Sanctuary. It's all an illusion anyway."

Before he could reply, she shot out of the kitchen and up to the spare bedroom. It was time she got to work on not needing him so much.

"He's so hot." Vikki's voice rang with authority and, since she'd said the same thing at least four other times in the past half hour, Sadie was getting close to kicking her twin. Lightly, of course, and only hard enough to push her off the double bed she sat at the end of.

"You're not listening, Vik." Kiely interrupted from her perch on the rolling desk chair in the corner of Tripp's spare bedroom. "Because attractive or not, Lieutenant Hottie can't be bothered to listen to Sadie."

Vikki waved a hand, seemingly unconcerned. "He jumped straight to doing, and that goes a long way in my book."

"There is something to be said for doing." Pippa's smile was dreamy, hearts and unicorns practically circling the air above her head where she sat on the floor. "All the doing."

"Fat lot of help you three are." Sadie added a satisfying harrumph before slamming back onto the pillows she'd propped against the headboard.

"We might be more helpful if you came up with

some argument other than 'Tripp McKellar is an ass,' baby sister."

"I'm the same age as you, Vikki," Sadie shot back. It was an argument as old as they were, but it never stopped Vikki from using it in times of discussion. Or family disagreements. Or, well, ever.

"She's a stickler for those extra minutes," Kiely said before adding, "A fun fact you can use when you turn forty."

"In twelve years. I'll be sure to wait with bated breath." *If I make it that long.*

Sadie fought off the terrible image that came to mind at the dismal thought. She was here now. She was with her family now. And Tripp—despite his ham-fisted way of dealing with whatever this thing was between them— was determined to see her stay that way.

Now.

If only her loved ones could see how crazy he made her…

"Much as I'm enjoying how readily we all feel we can and should—" Kiely eyed Vikki "—deliver love advice, we're here to game-plan."

Leave it to Kiely to get down to the heart of the matter, Sadie thought. Her sister had earned her stripes as a freelance private investigator, working with Colton Investigations, the FBI and any other qualified organization that could afford her. She had her finger on the pulse of just about everything and she had a way of subtly pulling everyone in line.

"Riley filled you in on how we're going to try to take down Matthews." Kiely directed the statement at Sadie, even as all her sisters nodded in unison.

"He was here last night with Ashanti."

"It's a good plan. But one that is going to take some really tight planning and flawless execution," Pippa added, her dreamy-eyed stare vanishing as that of a hard-nosed attorney took over.

Although Sadie had been somewhat skeptical of the idea last night, she was even more so in the cold light of a new day. "Do you all think it will work? Is Wes Matthews, mastermind behind RevitaYou, so dumb to fall for a honeypot?"

"Yes," all three of her sisters said in unison.

The unanimous agreement was swift, followed by all three of them talking at once.

"He's a total pig," Pippa said.

"Abigail's trying to hold up under all this, but even she agrees her father can't stay away from a beautiful woman," Kiely added. "That horrible Meghan Otis just one terrible example in apparently a long line of them."

"He's a man," Vikki scoffed in the loudest voice, as if her answer said everything, even as the gaze that landed on Kiely was clearly sympathetic. They'd all come to love Alfie in the short time Cooper Winston and his small son had been in their sister's life, and everyone knew how dangerous Meghan Otis had really been.

It was that last remark that Sadie keyed in on. "We know I'm no expert on men, so maybe you're right."

Sadie saw the judgment flash across Vikki's face before her sister firmly tamped it down. The urge to press her was strong, but Kiely had already launched in. "Cooper's on the FBI task force focused on bringing Matthews in. They missed him twice in the Bahamas, but they've got tabs on him. The outreaches Ashanti has made so far have worked. We've got him nibbling on a baited hook. And if Matthews behaves as he has in the past, it'll work again."

"What are the next steps?" Pippa asked.

"Ashanti's begun to make subtle outreaches on how to meet in person. She's added a few…ahem—" Kiely's normally indefatigable demeanor flagged a bit. "A few choice stock photos to sweeten the deal."

Although she'd had limited sexual experiences before Tate, Sadie was well aware men were visual creatures. Obviously the added incentive of suggestive photographs was needed to get Matthews to give up his hiding spot.

And still, it seemed like they were missing something.

"You still don't look convinced, Sadie," Pippa noted.

"It's not that I'm not convinced. Matthews is a pig and, if his own daughter believes this is his weak spot, it's well worth pressing the advantage. But it feels like we're missing something."

Alert, Kiely leaned forward from where she sat on the desk chair. "Go on."

"So, Brody got pulled into this relatively early on. The pyramid scheme had been active long enough that some people had a successful outcome, which was a plant to entice more investors. But it was also in place long enough to start tanking results for the next round of investors."

"Which was Brody," Pippa added.

"Exactly. And he got the loan from my scummy ex-fiancé to finance his way in."

"But we know all this, Sadie. That's why Brody came for help in the first place." Vikki blew out a hard breath. "Even if he refuses to take it now."

Brody's disappearance had been a sore point for Vikki from the start. Sadie knew that, but she'd already warmed to her point, her CSI training to look beneath every surface kicking in. "And we've got Landon Street, who made the product effective but highly deadly."

Her sisters nodded in unison, still seeming to follow where she was going.

"So in the planning of all this, who's supposed to get out of here with the big score? Matthews works up the pyramid scheme but Tate is the funding and the muscle? Yet now Matthews is gone? And despite Tate's sick focus on me, he has to be thinking about pulling up stakes. There's no way he can stay here any longer."

"That's true," Pippa agreed. "I hadn't thought about it like that, but you've got something here. It's like Wes is off scot-free and Tate's stuck holding the bag."

"And we also already know the product has its limits." Sadie continued with her argument. "Even if they get a few million so far off of investors, it's all Tate's loan money to begin with. Where's the real cash coming from?"

"Not everyone needs funding from Capital X," Kiely said. "Some of it came from people with genuine money to burn."

"That's it!" Sadie sat forward, the next layer of the scam they were about to create coming to life in her mind. "That's how we get them both."

"Both?" Kiely pressed her.

"Wes and Tate. Keep going with the honeypot because it's obviously a powerful lure. But we need to turn the two of them against each other, too. There's only so much money at play because a lot of it was Tate's to begin with. He's going to want even more than his criminal interest rates to get out of this deal with a profit. Especially since it's blown his entire operation to hell and back."

"You don't think either of them has an exit strategy?" Vikki asked.

Sadie considered the question, even as she used what she already knew about Tate to form her opinion.

"I think each of them thinks he's smarter than the other. So they might have an exit strategy, but it's predicated on each thinking he has all the money in play. And that's where we come in."

Pippa stood to pace. "This is good, Sadie. Really good. If we can get them to turn on one another, we can tug all the loose threads. How it started in the first place. How they're finding their so-called investors. And where they've been hiding the funds they already have in hand."

"We can even get Brody's money back." Sadie sat back hard against the pillows, an image of Brody's dejected face in the front of her thoughts. Although she'd been hard on him at first, assuming he was too focused on money instead of making strong choices, she'd come out the other side of that line of thinking. Brody had unfortunately been duped, on a project he'd believed couldn't fail. As someone who'd been duped herself, through a "grand romance" with Tate Greer, she was hardly one to judge.

And maybe that was the bigger lesson anyway. Maybe it wasn't about judgment but about helping someone out of a tough spot. One they hadn't asked to be in, nor actively sought out, but one they'd ended up in despite their best efforts.

Kiely's phone dinged and she frowned, staring down

at it. "I need to go pick up Alfie from day care. He's got a fever."

She was out of the chair immediately, her sole focus on leaving. Sadie rose and walked to her sister, quietly excited to see Kiely's concern and obvious love for her soon-to-be stepson. And, if recent discussions were any indication, *actual* son once she and Cooper were married and she could adopt Alfie as her own.

Wrapping her in a soft hug, Sadie pressed a kiss to Kiely's cheek. "Text me and let me know how he's doing."

"I will." Kiely hugged back—hard—before stepping away. "I'm sorry to rush out."

"Go." Sadie smiled. "Now."

In a matter of minutes, Kiely was gone and Pippa was up and readying to leave, too. "I'd rather stay and talk, but I've got a judge I still need to see to get a case on the docket before the holidays."

Sadie hugged Pippa before her sister could talk herself out of leaving. "You get out of here, too."

With no one left but her twin, Sadie turned to Vikki. "You're holding out on me."

"When have I ever done that?"

"A lot the past six months. Before that…" Sadie made a scrunched-up face before lightly scratching her temple in a mock gesture of thinking really hard. "Never."

"I'm not holding out on you."

"You are and I'd like to know why."

Vikki patted the bed, a clear invitation for Sadie to sit. "I'm worried about you."

"Now? But I'm safe."

"At this moment, yeah, sure. For good?" Vikki took her hand once Sadie sat. "I'm not so sure."

"Vik—"

Vikki squeezed her hand, the motion enough to stop Sadie from saying more. "Hear me out."

"Okay."

"I love you and I know you've been through a lot. Way more than anyone should ever have to go through."

"I hear a *but* in there."

"I told you to hear me out."

Sadie blew out a harried breath but shut up. Vikki had her "older sister" voice on and she knew she needed to listen.

"I did hold out on you. I did it a lot while you were dating Tate. I never liked him and it's not because I didn't want you to be happy."

"So why are you telling me now?"

"Because I couldn't say all I wanted to. I know I told you to be careful and I was hesitant about the engagement, but it was more than that. I never liked him. But—" Vikki broke off, her voice choked with tears. "I never thought he'd be such a monster. Or that he'd try to hurt you like this. If I'd had any clue, I'd have said something. Hell, I'd have run him out of town on a rail myself."

"None of us knew."

"Yeah, but my twin sense never stopped tingling around him. And I held back on you. I'm sorry."

Vikki pulled her into a tight hug and Sadie held on just as strong. She'd held back her own tears up to that point but let them fall as the heavy emotion of the moment finally caught up to her.

"I'm sorry, Vik. So sorry I was so blinded by him."

Vikki squeezed her once more before pulling back.

"You really need to stop apologizing for him. For your feelings. For all of it."

"But—"

"Nope." Vikki shook her head and wiped away tears. When she finally spoke, her voice rang strong and true. "I'm not holding back now, either. Not now, not anymore, and *not* about this."

"Not about what?"

"You didn't do this, Sadie. You didn't bring it on yourself and it didn't happen because you didn't have a lot of dating experience."

"But I—"

Vikki shut her down, barreling through the conversation like a GRPD cop hot on a chase. "Experience has nothing to do with a manipulative bastard like Tate Greer. He saw a way into our lives and he took it. I hate to break it to you, but it could have just as easily happened to Pippa or Kiely or me. You were the one he somehow flagged as his mark."

"I don't think the three of you would be so stupid to fall for him."

"Then you sorely overestimate a woman's power to overlook an attractive man who shows her attention."

"What's that supposed to mean? If he was ugly, I'd have ignored him?"

"No, no. What I meant was that I remember those first few weeks the two of you were dating. You talked about your conversations and the way he made you laugh. How kind he was and how much thought he put into each date. I was jealous."

"Of me?"

Although Sadie had built some level of confidence, she'd always seen Vikki as the glamourous one of the two of them. She had the blond hair and more slender figure, taking after their mother, while Sadie had thicker curves and the less flashy strawberry version of blond.

And until this moment, she'd never had reason to think any other way.

"Yes, of you. So were Pippa and Kiely."

"What? No way."

"Yes. We all did."

"So when did you stop feeling that way?"

"When I saw how he spoke to you. It was like after he'd done the work to get you to fall for him, he'd stopped trying. And the real him began to peek out from the edges."

"I know."

And she did know. Hadn't that been the most puzzling part of the relationship? Those early, halcyon days had been so much fun. Tate had been sweet and attentive, kind and considerate. But the veneer had eventually begun to crack. She'd told herself it was because they'd moved into a new phase of their relationship. One where things weren't quite so new and where they'd begun to settle into life without the bright, shiny haze of new love.

But it had bothered her all the same.

Only she'd ignored it. She'd convinced herself that it was inexperience. That she had no reason to be discontent. Or to complain.

Or to feel she deserved something more.

"Which is why I like Tripp so much," Vikki said.

The change in topic was swift and, if Sadie knew her twin, deliberate. "This has nothing to do with Tripp."

"It does if you let Tate Greer stand in the way of something amazing with Lieutenant Hottie."

"Stop calling him that."

Vikki reached out and brushed Sadie's hair over her ear. "Okay then. I'll call him something else."

"What's that?"

"A shot at happy-ever-after."

Chapter 11

Sadie thought about Vikki's words long after her sister had left. Long after the afternoon light had faded into a dark winter night. And long after the scent of dinner had drifted up the stairs.

Tripp had left her alone and, somewhere deep down, Sadie knew she needed to be a decent houseguest and go talk to him. Yet still, she'd stayed put in her room.

Part of her felt slightly childish, but a bigger part of her needed the time alone. The discussion with her sisters had been good for her. The time together and the comfort that always came from being with them had given her a chance to see things in a new light.

But with that light, she'd been forced to examine some of the things she would've preferred to keep buried. For the past month, every thought of Tate had been equated with personal inexperience. How odd then, to have Vikki suggest something else. A new view Sadie hadn't considered before.

Up until now, she'd taken the situation fully on herself. And while she suspected she would never be entirely free of the sentiment—and the embarrassment seemingly intertwined within—her sisters had also helped her look at what had happened with fresh eyes.

Tate had done her wrong. And rather than allow that battering litany to run in her head that she'd somehow allowed it, or somehow asked for it, Vikki and Pippa and Kiely had helped her to see things differently.

The knock on her door pulled her from her thoughts. "Come in."

Tripp poked his head into the room and as she caught sight of his face—that firm jaw and serious blue gaze—Sadie was surprised to realize she had missed seeing him. Oh sure, they'd talked about him all day, but it wasn't the same as seeing him again.

That took her right back to the morning and how it had felt to be wrapped in his arms.

To have that firm chest pressed against hers.

To have those lips caress her own.

"I just wanted to check on you. I made some dinner."

"Thank you. I'm sorry I didn't come down, but I—"

"It's okay. I'm glad your sisters were here. That the four of you had a chance to spend some time together."

"Me, too. Their visit gave me a chance to, um, process a few things."

"That's good." His brow furrowed. "Right?"

"Yes, very good. It also gave me time to work my way up to that apology I owe you."

Tripp opened the door more fully, leaning a shoulder

against the door frame. "I think I'm the one that probably owes you an apology."

"Nope. I think this one's all on me. And I need to say a few things."

He considered her for a moment but said nothing.

Just as she had earlier, Sadie felt so completely *seen* by him. The way his gaze drifted over her. The way his attention was fully on her. It was heady. And it was real, somehow. But it also reinforced all the reasons why she really did owe him an apology.

"I didn't want to listen to what you were saying earlier. But you were right."

"About what?"

"About Tate. About what happened with him, *because* of him."

"No, Sadie, I overstepped."

"For the record, I don't think you did. But I am curious why you tried to convince me otherwise."

He never moved off the door frame, but the casual nature of his pose belied the fierce light that leaped into his eyes. "Because I think you're pretty great. I always have. And it galls me to see how somebody who isn't worth your time could make you feel so badly."

"Thank you for that."

"You're welcome."

Tripp looked about to say something but held back. Instead of speaking, the two of them continued to stare at each other, the pulsing need that had arced between them in the kitchen this morning filling the air once again.

A part of her wondered if she should turn away, yet another part of her—a much bigger, deeper part—knew she couldn't.

This was Tripp. A man she had feelings for. And, if their kiss in the kitchen was any indication, feelings that weren't entirely unreciprocated.

But what to do about it?

With all the other stresses in her life, it would be so easy to simply reach out for it. To take the physical comfort she knew she would find in his arms.

Only, she was scared of what she'd find on the other side. The part that came after they got through this battle with Tate Greer and Wes Matthews and the whole RevitaYou mess. When life went back to normal and he went back to being Lieutenant Tripp McKellar and she went back to being CSI expert Sadie Colton.

When they had to see each other at work and handle cases together and find a way to live a normal life again.

The danger that was so awful right now had also created a fake intimacy. One that hadn't had a place in the real world before and likely wouldn't again.

Because how did you make a go of a relationship that started in the midst of a crisis? Sure, her siblings might be walking proof that you could come out the other side happily in love, but she just didn't see that for herself. She'd known Tripp a long time and it hadn't happened for them. She'd be a fool to think that would change after the danger died down.

"I do still have dinner downstairs. I can heat up a burger for you. Throw some frozen french fries in the oven."

"You don't need to go to any trouble."

"It's no trouble. Besides, I have a few things I want to show you. I've been digging through files all day, and I want to get your opinion on a few theories I've put together."

She sensed it was a bit of an excuse to get her out of the room, but Sadie didn't care. A burger and fries and Tripp sounded like a nice way to finish out her evening.

She was strong enough to handle it. More, she could remember that the situation was temporary and enjoy it anyway.

As she got off the bed to follow Tripp downstairs, Sadie decided she would do just that.

Tate stood in the shadow of Tripp's house, the cold air that swirled around him sharpening his senses. The scent of gasoline rose from the container by his feet. The night was cold, bitterly so, and the snow that had been predicted on the day before hadn't disappointed.

He'd likely do better to wait but he was running out of time. He needed to do this *now*.

It was time to end this.

Everything he had built, worked for, planned for; all of it had vanished in a matter of days. And the bitch sitting inside was at the root of it all.

It was shocking on some level. He'd run his business for a long time. He recruited carefully and he knew how to get around the cops and the Feds in equal measure.

And in a matter of weeks it had unraveled so badly, he'd be lucky to get out of Grand Rapids with nothing more than the money he'd stowed down in the Caymans.

Damn Matthews.

Tate huffed out a harsh breath, the air in front of him steaming with it. The bastard had been so slick and sure of himself. So convinced they'd make a good long go of this RevitaYou crap. And the results had been impressive. Hell, he'd looked at the users himself. Some of them actually *looked* ten years younger. The transformation had happened quickly and before they were even done with the first bottle, people were lining up for more.

As that line grew, Wes Matthews had spun quite a tale of profit beyond anyone's wildest imaginings.

Tate had spent most of his life convinced the straight and narrow path wasn't for him, but even he had thought about going legit on the product. It was too good and too effective not to think about actually putting it out to market and running a business to widely distribute it. The money would print itself.

Until it started killing people.

Because, as it turned out, you can't turn back time, no matter how hard you try to engineer it.

Now Matthews was gone, Gunther Johnson and Landon Street were in jail, and his traitorous little ex-fiancée was spilling her guts to the cops. And while the Caymans were looking better and better, he wasn't going anywhere until he dealt with all those damned loose ends.

Tate patted the box of matches safely tucked away in his pocket before he bent to pick up the gasoline can.

It was time to start recouping his investment.

Tripp knew something had changed, even if he couldn't fully put his finger on what it was. The tension that had hovered between him and Sadie this morning had vanished. Instead, what had replaced it was a spirit of collaboration from his partner, who seemed to have turned an emotional corner.

It was the only way he could characterize the "something" in his mind.

Even as he had to admit to himself that Sadie wasn't the only one who'd changed.

Her stormy exit from the kitchen that morning had left him with a lot to think about. More than a lot, if he were honest with himself.

And he didn't entirely care for some of his conclusions.

She'd said many things that made him think, but her parting shot had been the most effective.

In the end, you'll realize that they're just words. Safety. Security. Sanctuary. It's all an illusion anyway.

Was that the case?

He made his life under the working assumption that his job was to keep people safe. Yet her words had made him reconsider that and all he'd believed about himself.

If safety was an illusion, then maybe his job wasn't about keeping people safe at all. Maybe it was about holding back the dark so they remained just safe enough.

And so the dark remained just far enough away.

The exact opposite of Tate Greer, Capital X and the entire RevitaYou case that had consumed them all for the better part of six months. As the case had grown deeper, its secrets unfurling lead by lead, the dark had crept closer.

The capture of cop Joe McRath.

Followed by the uncovering of Capital X.

And then Sadie's kidnapping.

He'd believed he was doing his job, but was this all a lesson in dealing with the dark? In learning how to handle it when it inevitably came?

He'd been there before. Lila's death had decimated him, from the sheer violence of the act, the loss of their unborn child, and the unrelenting knowledge that it had happened because of him. A man he'd put in prison had gotten out and exacted the worst revenge anyone could imagine.

Tripp had borne its consequence every minute of every day since.

Yet even with that experience, he had never seen his role as defender and protector a useless act. He'd always believed in his ability to do his job and keep others safe.

And Sadie had upended that with a few well-placed jabs.

Only they hadn't been jabs. They'd been the serious assessment of a woman in the midst of a crisis. But they were also the words of someone who'd given her professional vow to serve and protect.

She wasn't a civilian, untrained in the world of criminal minds and the violent acts that stemmed from those places. She also wasn't ignorant of what went into his life day by day. The TV cop shows had it wrong. What looked like a life of swift action on a screen resembled that far less often in real life. Instead, he made his life on the tiresome reality of repeat offenders, avoidable crimes and endless reams of paperwork.

All while praying like crazy he'd avoid too many experiences like the rescue at the lake and the subsequent attack at the hospital.

The oven timer dinged and Sadie pulled out the cookie sheet of french fries. "These smell delicious." She smiled. "A most excellent idea for dinner."

"I have a few every now and again."

Sadie had already fixed her burger and, after scooping some fries into a bowl, met him at the kitchen table. He was pleased to see her navigate her way around his home, comfortable even if she didn't fully realize it.

He snatched a fry, happy that she'd salted them perfectly.

"So what did you want to show me?" she asked.

"Don't you want to eat?"

"I can eat and listen at the same time." She dipped a fry in ketchup. "I want to hear your theories. See if they match any of my own."

"Okay." He pulled his empty plate from earlier closer and grabbed a further handful of fries for himself. "I feel like catching Matthews is the key to all this."

"Abigail's father is the linchpin."

"You think so, too?"

"I do." Sadie set down her burger and wiped her fingers on her napkin before continuing. "I talked to my sisters about it. Vikki in particular, who's the closest to Brody and knows how scared he is, is putting a lot of hope in the scheme Riley and Ashanti have cooked up."

"It's good. They know what's needed to both reel him in and do it in a way that makes sure Matthews can't get off on a technicality later."

"My brother does good work."

"He does."

Tripp considered the man he'd come to know since joining the GRPD. Riley Colton was rock-solid. He'd started Colton Investigations after Graham Colton's murder and, like many others in local law enforcement, Tripp had carried a bit of skepticism the job choice was fully altruistic. The trauma of one's parents' murders would leave anyone raw, wounded, and seeking a path for vengeance.

Only, Colton had done the opposite. He'd built a strong business, steeped in preparation, an ability to follow procedure, and exceedingly good instincts.

Tripp had seen it firsthand—and had been forced to eat a rather large serving of crow—on one of the first cases Riley had helped GRPD with, about four months after founding CI. They'd had a low-level drug trafficker who'd suddenly increased business a thousand-fold. The entire PD, out en masse, had been trying to figure out where the thug secured his access and his supply. It was Colton who'd traced the details back to a dealer in Chicago who'd set Grand Rapids in his sights as part of an expansion effort.

And it was Riley Colton who'd uncovered the information in a careful and methodical way. One that had allowed the GRPD and the Feds to put the trafficker and the dealer in Chicago in prison for life.

"Colton Investigations is a top-notch organization," Tripp added. "I've always thought so, but the respect he commands from the rest of the GRPD as well as the FBI is all further proof of that."

"As the oldest, Riley remembers more of my father's stories than the rest of us. He knew the cases that made our dad so mad. The ones where a criminal got off on a technicality or a lapse in procedure."

"That'll shape a person."

"It certainly did shape Riley."

Without knowing where the question came from, Tripp pressed her. "And what about you? What shaped you and made you want to join the GRPD?"

Sadie stared down at her plate, toying with a fry before looking back up at him. "My parents were still alive when I went into the academy. So I can't say it's their deaths that gave me any sort of calling to law enforcement."

"What did give the calling?"

"I'm not sure." Her gaze dropped back to the fry, which she swirled in ketchup. Although Tripp could only see a partial view of her face, he didn't miss the emotions that furrowed her brow. And when she finally looked back up, he sensed a change in her.

Just like earlier, he felt it once more. As if she'd come to some sort of decision and was ready to share it with him.

"That's not entirely true. I do know. I was a bit aimless after high school. I was a good student. One of the best, actually. But I was mousy and my head was always buried in a book. I was sort of your classic nerd."

"I'm struggling to believe that."

"Well, believe it. I had a glamourous twin and I was the proverbial ugly duckling."

Tripp couldn't see it, but he knew he had no place to argue with her. He also knew the ideas she carried contributed to who she was. How she saw herself. And while she might no longer look like that forlorn teenager, the experience was no less real to her.

While he simply waited for her to continue, those emotions continued to play over her face. For as open and caring as Sadie was, Tripp realized that he very rarely saw her emotions. She had a surprisingly strong poker face, easily conveying her concerns for others while keeping her own emotions firmly locked down.

"Anyway, I was a nerdy kid and I wasn't ready to go to college. I wanted to, but something kept holding me back."

When she didn't elaborate, Tripp sensed it wasn't his place to ask. But he wanted to. And in the wanting, he realized just how badly he wanted to know *her*. All of her.

That was why, once again, he kept his thoughts to himself. He didn't share the intimate details of his life and he had no right to pry into hers.

But that didn't make the wanting less intense. Or make the interest fade away.

"Vikki was all excited about going into the Army and I wanted to share that excitement, only I didn't have it. I had the grades, but not the gumption."

"Gumption for what?"

"To leave Grand Rapids. To go out in the world. Even if it were just a few hours away at a state school. So I stayed. I took community college courses on subjects I really didn't care about and all the while wondered when I'd finally find something I did care about."

"What flipped the switch?"

"I started working out at the community college. I had a three-hour stretch between two of my classes. It didn't make sense to come home, and the classes weren't hard enough to bother with studying in the library. So I went to the gym. I started on the treadmill and worked my way up to weights. And the whole time, there was this woman there who was about my age. And she was always working really hard and seemed really focused. We struck up a conversation one day and she mentioned that she was applying to the academy."

"Who was it?"

"Rosie Archer. Now Rosie Santorini."

Tripp knew Rosie. She was one of his best detectives. She'd fast-tracked into her role as detective, a product of that hard work and determination Sadie mentioned. "That's an outstanding role model if I've ever seen one."

"She was. And she introduced me to a new career path. Every time I'd thought about college, it was through the lens of accounting or finance or something in the legal field. It never crossed my mind that I could make a go of things on the other side, focused on law enforcement."

"So you applied to the academy?"

"I did, but not at first. First, I was determined to get the education I needed. Now that I had a different purpose, I shifted into civics classes. If I was going to catch bad guys for a living, I wanted to make sure I understood the legal reasons why. And after I did that, I applied to the academy."

"Yet you ended up in CSI."

Sadie smiled at that, the first real smile he'd seen since they'd started their discussion. "Just one more tumbler in the lock."

"How so?"

"So I mentioned I was a reader…"

"Sure." He nodded, not sure where she was going but also recognizing what might appear aimless to others was all part of a definitive path for Sadie Colton.

"Once I realized that there was a way to use my love of mysteries and clues in my job. I was a goner."

"Nancy Drew's got nothing on you?"

"Something like that."

Sadie's smile fell, her expression changing so fast that Tripp's pulse kicked up several notches. "What is it?"

"Do you smell it?"

She was already on her feet, moving toward the sliding glass doors that led to the back patio, when Tripp scented the mix of fire and gasoline. But it was the bright flicker through the window, visible over her shoulder, that had Tripp standing, as well.

"Tripp!" Sadie turned from the window. "The house is on fire!"

Chapter 12

Sadie struggled to get her bearings, the scents of gas and smoke so overwhelming she fought off a wave of dizziness. How had it happened so fast? One moment she and Tripp were talking and the next, they were simply overpowered. Tripp had already moved, his chair overturned where he'd pushed back from the kitchen table. After assessing the situation out the kitchen window, he'd gone to the front of the house to evaluate the damage.

All while she continued to stare out the window into the backyard.

There was something out there. Something more than fire. She knew it deep down in her bones.

Tate was out there.

"The fire's surrounding the house." Tripp raced back into the kitchen, the vivid flames outside the window tossing an odd glow over his features. "Sadie. Did you hear me?"

"Tate is outside."

"What?"

"Tate. He did that. That's why the fire is everywhere. Front and back in equal measure. He set it, Tripp."

She'd barely finished the words when Tripp's hand closed over hers, pulling her toward the front door. "We have to get out of here. Wrap up in a blanket and I'll carry our coats."

Sadie felt herself being led, the firm grip of his fingers like a vise over hers. He barreled through the living room toward the front foyer, pulling a blanket off the couch as they moved before stopping at the closet to drag out their jackets. With deft movements, he wrapped a thick scarf over his hand to open the front door.

Thoughts swimming, Sadie heard a voice almost outside of herself. "Tripp! No!"

With a force she had no idea she possessed, she clamped her free hand down over his wrist, dragging on their joined hands to keep him from opening the front door.

"Sadie! We have to get out of here."

"You can't go that way."

Smoke already filled the room and Tripp's gaze darted from her to the door and back again. "We have to get out."

"That's what Tate wants. There's no way he's letting us out of here. Either we burn inside or he'll smoke us out and take us down in plain sight. That's why the flames are all over. We can't go that way."

"Then we'll go out the back."

"How do we know his goons aren't with him?"

It was a factor they had to consider. Although the takedown at Sand Springs Lake had also secured several of Tate's goons, they had to assume he had more.

And if he had more, they had to assume those men were also waiting outside the ring of fire consuming the house.

"The basement."

Tripp shook his head. "We don't have time."

With the smoke already impossibly thickening, they'd have to crawl into the center of the house to reach the basement door.

"It's our only way. You've got storm doors to get outside, right?"

It was a silly fact but one she'd thank herself for later if they got out of this alive. Sadie had always been intrigued by the idea of storm cellar doors that closed into the ground. The houses in this neighborhood were known for that feature.

"Yeah."

"We'll get outside that way. They won't expect us and you can get a better lay of the land."

"And if the fire's outside the perimeter of the cellar's storm doors?"

"We'll take our chances."

He looked about to argue but Sadie rolled right over any objection, screaming to be heard over the roar of the fire, "Get your weapon."

Tripp turned back to the closet and pulled out his service revolver before reaching deeper inside. He pulled out an extra gun and handed it over. "You still know how to use one of these?" he screamed.

She avoided the eye roll—well aware it would be

barely visible through the smoke anyway—and took the gun. "I'm all set."

It was only then that the lights in the house flickered before going fully dark.

Tripp's hand on her wrist shifted, his fingers lacing with hers. "Get on the floor and stay close to me."

In the thick, dark smoke, they began to crawl for the interior of the house. It was the exact opposite choice of every instinct she possessed to get outside.

But, in her gut, Sadie knew it was their only shot at survival.

Tripp mentally counted off the distance from the foyer to the basement door. It was off the hallway to a downstairs bedroom and, while it likely wasn't more than twenty feet, it felt like a mile. Smoke billowed so thick above them, he could only marvel at the fire's deadly speed.

But he took comfort from the steady presence of Sadie by his side where her arm brushed against his calf as they crawled toward their goal.

The noise and heat of the flames whirled around them, the blaze angry and shockingly loud. Along with the furious lap of the flames, the sounds of his house breaking and burning around him echoed in his ears like a raging nightmare. Still, he moved forward, determinedly onward toward the basement door and what he hoped was safety.

His shoulder hit the corner of the wall, but Tripp ignored the pain. That corner meant they'd turned the last few feet into the correct hallway. Reaching back, he felt for Sadie's shoulder so he could lean in as close as possible.

"We're at the door. I don't know how long the frame will hold, so you have to move across the basement as fast as you can." He shouted the words and still wasn't sure she'd heard them all through the rushing and whirling of flame. But he had to hope she understood. And what she'd missed, he'd manage himself, weaving a path through his basement.

With the scarf wrapped around his hand, he turned the knob. Darkness yawned beneath him but he had the sense of fresh, albeit musty, air. "Hold the handrail."

He felt Sadie brush past him in the dark before he reached out and closed the door behind them. The fire was gaining and it was only a matter of a few minutes before the house collapsed in on itself. Tripp was determined not to focus on that. The air was cleaner here and they'd make it.

They had to.

"I'm at the bottom." Sadie's voice floated over him, a disembodied sound that echoed off the thick concrete of the basement. Tripp took the last step, his feet touching the reassuring strength of the concrete. He grabbed her hand once more, his fingers tightening over hers just as a loud crash echoed above them.

The floorboards above their heads groaned with the weight and Tripp tightened his grip. "Let's go."

"Can we follow a wall?"

"We have to walk straight through the center. The stairs leading up and outside are directly opposite. It's the quickest way."

As if to punctuate his point, the floorboards groaned again, the wood above them coming to life with fire. It wasn't much—and the flames only added to the danger—but they also added the slightest bit of light.

"Come on!"

Tripp navigated them through the dark, desperately trying to picture the items he had scattered around the basement. There was a weight bench, which he remembered only as his shin connected with a rack of hand weights. Ignoring the throbbing pain, he moved Sadie deftly around the object and toward the stairs.

That terrible groaning continued above them and as the fire spread, the flames added light to their way. Tripp could finally see the stairs in front of them, the concrete at their feet devoid of any further obstacles.

"There, Sadie!"

"I see it."

With the way visible, Tripp ran them toward the stairs, the heavy creaking finally growing too much. He heard the cracking house above him, shuddering as the structural damage finally caused the wood frame to give way.

Sadie screamed and he practically threw her into the stairwell as the burning house fell into the basement around them.

Smoke rushed into their alcove along with an intense heat Tripp had never felt before. It was like being inside an oven, and he knew they wouldn't be able to withstand it for much longer. Pushing past Sadie up the concrete steps, his hand hit the underside of the storm door and he felt around for the latch to unlock it.

"Tripp!" Sadie shouted from behind him as the flames leaped further into the stairwell, lapping at them with hungry hands.

Tripp dropped the coats he still carried onto the top stair. He fumbled with the metal lock that kept the storm doors barred from external intruders, working it with frantic fingers when the bolt didn't want to budge. The frigid temperatures outside had made it hard to move and the lock seemed impervious to the heat steadily climbing behind them.

"Tripp!"

As Sadie's panicked scream washed over him once more, Tripp felt the latch give way. On a thick, heavy squeak, the door lifted in his hands. The snow that had lay more than a foot deep on the ground added to the weight, but Tripp ignored it all as sweet, fresh air swept into the ever-widening opening.

"Here. Let me help." Sadie came up beside him, her arms stretching beside his to push the door up. "But we have to do it slowly. We don't know who's out there."

"Yeah, but we do know what's in here. And we have to take our chances."

Tripp used the opening to look out into his backyard. Although little had gone as he'd hoped, the one thing in their favor was that the fire was lapping against the frame of the house. The path out of the basement was free and clear of flames.

Bastard knew he couldn't keep that blaze going in the snow, Tripp thought grimly as his eyes tried to adjust to the dim light in the backyard. Sadie's warning still echoed through his mind, nearly as loud as the fire, that Tate and his goons would be standing guard wherever they chose to flee.

While that danger might be real, they had to get *out*. Much of the house had fallen inward, but a few walls were still standing. He and Sadie weren't safe where they were and, worse, they risked being locked in if one of those walls fell the wrong way.

"We have to move," Tripp whispered urgently.

"What if he's out there?"

"Then we take our chances. They're still better than where we are. Do you have the gun?"

"Yes."

"Here." Tripp fumbled for the coats on the step. "Put this on. I know it doesn't feel like it now, but the moment you get beyond the blaze, you're going to be freezing."

"From a frozen lake to a fiery inferno." Sadie's laughter came out slightly manic. "The man is a lunatic."

"Yeah, but we've got the element of surprise on our side. It's possible he's thought we didn't make it out since the moment the roof fell in."

It was a small hope, but Tripp decided he'd take it anyway. Even the smallest advantage of surprise was something and since his house was blazing like the fires of hell, there was no way his neighbors hadn't called it in already.

The danger might be real, but he'd bet his life Tate and his goons wouldn't stick around once the fire company arrived.

That meant he had only a few more precious minutes to take the bastard down. With a burst of strength against the heavy door, Tripp used the momentum of his body to walk up the last few concrete steps, pushing the door high and wide. He was going to take down Tate Greer.

Finally.

One minute she was bracing herself against absurdly misplaced laughter and the next Tripp was on the move. The basement door creaked and groaned on its metal hinges as Tripp lifted it wide and high before running up the last few steps and out into the yard. She called after him but it did nothing to slow him down.

Nor did he even acknowledge he'd heard her.

Instead he just kept moving, farther away from the house and into what could only be Tate's crosshairs.

"Damn fool man," she muttered before adding one of her favorite curses for good measure. And then she focused on her own situation, the increasing collapse of the house a steady reminder she needed to move, too.

Sadie checked the gun, the piece familiar to her, as it matched the one she'd carried as a rookie, and followed Tripp into the cold. The house kept making those horrible wrenching noises, its remnants' continuing fight to stay upright rapidly waning in the bitter night air.

Deep snow sucked at her feet, cold against the sneakers she'd had on all day. The temperature was a shock against the oven-like warmth she'd experienced in the basement, but she didn't have time to analyze the changes. All she could do was move.

The urge to get away from the house was strong, but her gaze swung like an arc over the property. Outside lights were on at the neighbors' on both sides but she saw no lights reflecting from windows or people coming out onto the street. She vaguely remembered a few comments Tripp mentioned about the people who lived on either side of him. An elderly couple, who were in Florida this time of year, flanked one side, and a young couple without children, who were rarely home in the evenings, the other.

That meant no one would be observing through windows, watching the flames engulf the house. Nor would they have any sense of intruders sneaking around the grounds.

While she wouldn't expect someone to risk themselves for her—and as a law enforcement professional she sorely wanted them to remain inside—an extra pair of eyes or a shout from a window that they'd called 911 would be more than welcome at this time. Since she'd get neither, she moved on, trying to get a sense of where Tripp had gone.

The footprints she'd seen in the snow faded at the edge of the house, the heat of the fire melting the ground cover. So instead, she moved back and away, sweeping in steady arcs just as she'd learned at the academy.

Tripp's backyard was long and deep, the snow-covered grass ending as it ran into a stretch of woods. As she stilled, considering those woods on her next sweep, she realized how easy it had been for Tate to hide there and lie in wait.

A shiver went through her that had nothing to do with the cold.

And everything to do with the knife she felt pressed against the thin and tender skin behind her ear.

Tripp saw it all play out before him. He'd made a full perimeter around the house and it was only as he made the final turn into the backyard—giving the collapsing house a wide berth—that he saw his mistake.

The large, hulking form of Tate Greer had come up behind Sadie, one arm wrapping around her neck while the other held a wicked hunting knife up to the sensitive area just beneath her ear. The shout had already risen in his throat when Tripp pulled it back by sheer force of will.

Greer had played them.

There was no one else waiting with him. He'd done this all on his own. Tripp knew there were any number of clinical terms for it. Escalation. Psychopathy. Violent tendencies. But to his mind, the situation was far simpler.

Tate Greer was determined to finish what he'd started.

The first whirl of fire engine sirens echoed in the distance and Tripp knew there was no room to wait.

Greer was no doubt counting down, as well, and it would be the closing bell to whatever horror the man had in mind.

Sadie had stilled the moment the knife touched her body and Tripp knew they were at a collective disadvantage. She couldn't see him and he had no way of knowing how her own rush of adrenaline was affecting her.

Could she react with the speed he needed?

Would she fall or fumble?

And could Tripp line up a shot in a way that had Tate's reflexes moving the knife *away* from Sadie's body instead of into it?

He considered himself a good marksman, but he was no sniper. So aiming for Greer's head was out of the question. The risk was too damn great.

And as the sound of sirens bore down, there was no more time to think about it.

Resetting the safety and placing the gun in the back waistband of his jeans, Tripp moved forward. The snow-covered ground had a layer of ice and the only thing keeping him from sounding an alert was the continued shriek and whine of fire behind him. That, coupled with the wail of sirens, did enough to hide the steady crunch of his boots on icy snow.

Despite the surrounding noise, Tate's voice rose over the din. "You were supposed to be so easy. You were my ticket into every damn database I needed. To the police. To Colton Investigations. I had it all planned and you ruined it."

"Go to hell."

Tripp smiled in spite of himself, Sadie's swift retort affirming that the empty laughter that had concerned him while they were still in the basement had given way to pragmatic disdain.

It was the first glimmer of hope they'd get out of this.

She just had to stay strong.

And he needed to make sure Greer had no idea he was closing in.

With careful steps to ensure the snow didn't make any additional noise, Tripp moved closer. An idea formed and he dug the gun from his waistband, turning the butt side out. As soon as he was in range, Tripp raised his left arm and slammed the butt of the weapon on Tate's head while using his dominant hand to hold his knife arm still.

"Sadie! Drop and move!"

Sadie did as she was told, falling to her knees in the snow.

The force of Tripp's revolver hit its mark, but only served to anger Greer further. The man whirled, using some fancy footwork of his own as he spun around to face Tripp, the knife blade glinting sharply in the light of the flames. Even with the solid blow to the head, the man never lost his balance. An excessively neat maneuver that left Greer on his feet and still in full, controlled possession of the knife.

Tripp had learned early on in his rookie year never to underestimate an opponent. Some of the smallest men he'd taken down had near superhuman strength and a larger criminal often lost ground to the inevitable inertia that kicked in once a body started moving in the wrong direction.

Tate Greer fit neither description. He was a big man, with the large proportions of a heavyweight fighter. And he had the quickness and speed of a lightweight.

A lethal combination.

Tripp reared back as Greer's knife arm shot out, slicing through the air nanoseconds before Tripp got out of the way. While the force of the movement would have put any normal person off balance, Greer retained his, bouncing on the balls of his feet. "She's not getting out of here alive, man. And neither are you."

He slammed forward again, an angry grizzly with sharp claws, his arm waving that blade through the crisp night air.

The very tip of the blade sliced through the thick sleeve of Tripp's coat. Fire shot up his arm at what would no doubt be a deep cut, but he ignored it, instead channeling the pain toward his foe.

Tate Greer was the enemy.

He and his thugs had terrorized the good people of Grand Rapids for years. Long before RevitaYou had even been a glimmer of an idea, Greer had been harming people by lending money illegally and then siccing his thugs on them.

And then he'd turned his sights on Sadie.

Using her. Manipulating her. And then kidnapping and trying to kill her.

Whatever vows Tripp had made to serve and protect seemed inadequate for the moment.

Greer was his prey.

And any and all pretense of capturing the man, through proper channels as a leader in the GRPD, had vanished. Tripp wanted vengeance and had no illusion it would be sanctioned by his employer.

Greer slashed out with the knife once more and Tripp leaped away from the blade before going on the offensive. He still had his gun and wanted to use it, but the brutal, near hand-to-hand-combat style of his opponent meant the weapon could either work for him or just as easily be turned against him.

As the wail of the sirens grew louder, Tripp knew he only had another minute at most. He feinted to the side before pivoting and bringing the butt of the gun down once more on Greer's body. He'd aimed for the head but the gun grazed just off of the guy's shoulder. Despite missing his target, the blow did finally dislodge Greer's footing. Only, instead of stumbling back from the force of Tripp's strike, the man windmilled his arms, the knife once more flashing in the light of the flames.

Greer used the change in momentum to his advantage, thrusting forward. His knife struck the heavy padding of Tripp's coat before plunging through the thick wool and into his waist. The jab was quick, the pain a piercing nuisance, before Greer pulled back, still trying to regain his balance in the still-fresh snow.

Tripp saw the knife rise, streaked with blood this time and ready to strike again, when blue and red lights flashed from the street, the sirens keening into the night.

Sadie shouted, racing closer to them, her gun extended and pointed directly at Greer. The man seemed to hover for an endless moment in indecision until she shot off a round, the bullet going just wide of him. It was enough to push Greer into motion. He turned tail and ran for the woods.

Orange flames still sparked into the sky behind them but Tripp ignored them and gave chase, Sadie's heavy footsteps audible behind him while the thick snow dragged on his feet. He saw Greer stumble with it, too, but the man had a large enough head start that Tripp wasn't able to reach him. Registering once more that he had a gun in his hand, he stopped and took aim.

Pain ran a searing path from his arm to his elbow where Greer's blade had sliced him, but Tripp held his position, lining up his shot. Without giving himself another moment to think—or to reconsider aiming at another's back—he fired off his shots.

Six in a row, all directed at the weaving figure heading for the woods.

On the fifth shot, he saw Greer jerk and stumble, but still, the man never lost his balance. Or his momentum. He just kept moving into the woods.

"Tripp!" Sadie moved up behind him, hanging on his arm and holding him still.

"I have to go after him." Tripp tried to run but she seemed surprisingly strong, her hold able to root him to the spot.

"Tripp! You're hurt."

Her words registered dimly in his mind as he looked down to where she held tight to his forearm. He stared at her hand and the vise grip she had on his body, curious as to why her hand felt so heavy where it lay. And then his gaze drifted to the drops of red coloring the snow at his feet.

As the blood registered as his own, the adrenaline that had carried him through his backyard gave out. Along with the dizzying drop in blood pressure, a searing pain lit up his side. He saw the ground rise up, swift and immediate, before he felt Sadie's arms wrap tight around his chest, slowing his momentum.

And then the world went black.

Chapter 13

Sadie glanced around the emergency waiting room, her siblings assembled in the various chairs nearest her. They were all there. Riley and Griffin held court at the doorway, refusing entry to anyone who didn't pass muster. Pippa and Kiely took point on conferring with the hospital staff and getting updates on Tripp's condition while also peppering the GRPD with questions every time an officer came in to pay respects.

Vikki sat by her side, her hands clutching Sadie's as she crooned over and over that they'd find Tate and put him away forever.

"That bastard is going to pay."

Vikki had said the same thing, in a variety of ways, with a variety of colorful descriptions, for the past hour. Sadie was grateful for the comfort but all she wanted was to see Tripp.

"Hey, Vik. Why don't you let me take over for a minute?"

Vikki stared up at Riley hovering in front of them. Sadie felt her twin's hesitation in the clutch of her hands before Vikki nodded. "I guess I could use some disgusting coffee out of a machine that's nearly as old as I am."

"That's my girl." Riley dug some change out of his pocket. "Would you mind getting me one, too?"

"Sure."

Sadie saw the subtle communication pass between Riley and Vikki. Under normal circumstances, she'd be annoyed they were communicating about her when she was right there. But, all things considered, she could hardly say she wouldn't be doing the same right now if the roles were reversed.

Riley took Vikki's seat, his arm going around Sadie's shoulders. She took the moment to snuggle into her brother, amazed to realize how good it felt to let down her guard.

To ease the burden that had hung over her for more than a month now.

She'd believed herself moving past the pain of Tate's betrayal, especially after the time she'd spent with her sisters, but now she had a new agony to deal with. One that went far deeper, even if she'd only spent a few days with Tripp.

What if he'd died?

Tate's stealth attack had caught them both off guard and they'd both inhaled a lot of ash and smoke. Now Tripp was dealing with a deep knife wound on top of it.

The fire had left her throat raw and scratchy but it had nothing on the tight ball of pain that lodged there as tears welled up at the thought of losing Tripp.

On her hard sob, Riley pulled her close. "Hey now."

"I can't—" She broke off, another sob shaking her body.

"Shhh." Riley let her cry it out, all the fear and tension, layered over the helpless uncertainty of whether or not Tripp would be okay.

"This is getting to be a habit with us," Riley said once her storm of tears had passed.

"A habit that's, once again, my fault."

"We're back to that?"

"Yes, we're back to that. Because the man I nearly married tried to kill me and the good lieutenant tonight. Because he damn near succeeded and even right now Tripp is in an OR and his house is in ashes."

"He's getting a blood transfusion, a serious shot of meds, and a round of stitches. No one's operating on him."

"It's all my fault."

"No, actually it's not."

Another set of tears welled, quieter and hotter than the first. While she wanted to regain some control, Sadie knew the key was letting it all out.

Something she hadn't done in the sheer rush of events. Instead, she'd watched as the paramedics transferred Tripp from the freezing cold ground onto a stretcher. She'd protested when they'd wanted to strap her onto one, too, but had finally relented when one of them forced oxygen on her. The pure air had felt too good in her battered lungs and suddenly she'd been too tired to argue.

Even if she hadn't been too tired to watch the still-leaping flames from the back window of the ambulance as they'd rushed her—for the second time in a week—to county hospital.

She'd been checked out and, despite being offered a chance to be monitored overnight, she'd refused. She had no interest in being hooked up to monitors and an IV, and confined to a bed again. Tate was still out there and he'd already proved a hospital entrance wasn't enough to deter him.

She'd be damned if she was going to put herself in danger again.

Because, once more, he'd escaped. Like a cat with nine lives. Every time they were close to taking him down, the man vanished. While Sadie understood she and Tripp had been at a disadvantage this evening with Tate's surprise attack, they'd still been serious opponents. Two trained cops, both armed.

Yet Tate had still escaped.

Riley spoke once more, his voice strong and firm and full of conviction. "It's not your fault, Sadie."

"I brought this. On all of us."

"Like Dad brought his and Mom's murders on himself? Like Abigail brought on her father's crimes when she came into Griffin's life? Or maybe it's like Flynn's being responsible for his half brother Landon's bad choices?"

Riley kept going before she could even get a word in. "The RevitaYou case has blown wide open and every one of us has been doing our level best to fight it with all we've got. Don't you dare go taking this on yourself."

"Real nice to use our parents on me."

Riley smiled down at her. "I'll use whatever it takes. You're not at fault here. None of us is. But we are all in control of what we do about it."

"When did you get so smart, big brother?"

"I've always been smart. It's just that no one wants to give me any credit for it. And that includes a very pregnant Charlize, who's been texting me nonstop for the past hour for updates."

She wrapped her arms around his waist, hugging him tight. "Consider it a public service."

"How's that?"

"As your siblings, we're honor-bound to make sure your head doesn't get too big."

The laughter started down low and deep and Sadie could feel her brother shaking against her. It was only as she pulled back and looked up at him that she saw the mischief filling his eyes. "Consider it a family condition."

"Oh, there's no doubt about that. Now go call Charlize," Sadie ordered.

A doctor came into the waiting room. "Is there a Sadie Colton here?"

She stood abruptly, smoothing her shirt against her hips. "That's me."

"Lieutenant McKellar has asked to see you. He's been quite insistent, as a matter of fact."

Riley, still holding her hand, gave it a tight squeeze before releasing it. "Go on. We'll all be right here."

"Thank you." Sadie bent to kiss Riley on the cheek. "For everything."

Tripp reached for the small cup of water on the rolling table that fit across his hospital bed and winced at the sharp pain that radiated down his side. He knew he was more than lucky to be alive with nothing more than some stitches and enough antibiotics to fell an elephant, but the pain irritated him all the same.

Greer had vanished. And the shooting pain lancing through Tripp's side seemed like one more mocking example of how he'd let the man get away.

Again.

He was well acquainted with slippery criminals. Hell, the majority of police work was hunting them down and doing your level best to catch them. But Greer's ongoing vanishing act had reduced Tripp to the level of a keystone cop. He'd had the man in his hands, for Pete's sake.

You also nearly took a stomach full of hunting knife, the more reasonable part of him chided through the self-recrimination. A fair argument that gave little comfort.

Or none at all.

"Tripp." Sadie appeared at the door, her voice gravelly and still layered with smoke when she spoke again. "You up for a bit of company?"

She'd changed clothes, the oversize sweatshirt rolled up several times at her wrists drowning her in the heavy material. The soot that had marred her skin—the last thing he remembered seeing before he'd passed out—had been washed off and, somewhere over the past few hours, she'd taken a shower. Her strawberry-blond hair shone under the recessed lighting of his room.

She was beautiful. And perfect. Something clenched hard and tight deep inside him at the realization that she was okay. And at the even bigger realization that she might have been killed tonight.

Sadie took a few steps into the room but remained near the door. "How are you feeling?"

"I'm fine."

A small frown marred her lips, matched by the slight furrowing of the brow he'd come to adore. "I don't believe you."

"I am fine. But I can admit that I've also felt better."

"You were stabbed. And you inhaled so much smoke." She took a few steps closer. "When you fell down in the snow, I didn't know if you'd be okay. Or if—" She broke off, a hard sob escaping from her throat.

"Sadie, I'm fine." His heart broke as sobs racked her shoulders, dwarfed beneath the thick cotton of her sweatshirt. "Come here. Talk to me. I promise you, I'm okay."

She continued crying, the tears she seemed unable to control continuing to quake through her body. But she did move closer, coming to stand beside the bed. He ignored the pain that seared through his side as he sat up, readjusting so there was room beside him on the bed. He pulled her close, into the spot he'd made, before wrapping his arms around her. "Shh, now. It's fine."

She nestled into his arms, her body slowly calming. They both faced the doorway and he fitted his chin just over her head, holding her through the storm of tears. Even the pain in his side seemed to fade as he sank into the quiet with her, content to simply hold her.

To assure himself she was safe.

They'd made it through together. That was some sort of miracle, if he were honest with himself. Between the fire and the fight, the fact they were both here and relatively whole was…well, it really was a miracle.

That was a concept he hadn't thought about in a long time. Miracles. Wonder. Maybe even divine intervention. He'd stopped believing in all of it a long time ago, the reality of losing Lila and the baby too much to bear.

Or to continue to hope.

Yet, somehow, in the midst of all he'd experienced over the past few weeks, Sadie Colton had returned that to him. He did have hope that they'd get out of this. That Tate Greer and Wes Matthews would get their due. And that Capital X would, once and for all, be vanquished right along with the pure evil that was the RevitaYou supplement.

A fountain of youth that killed people. Vanity might be a sin, but Tripp was determined that no one else was going to die for it. And the people who had brought the drug to life would go down with the ship.

"Am I hurting you?" Sadie struggled to sit upright but he held on, holding her still.

"I'm fine."

"You just tightened up. I thought maybe you were in a lot of pain."

Tripp realized that he had tightened his hold as he'd thought about Capital X and RevitaYou, and relaxed a bit. "Sorry. Occupational hazard."

"Of what?"

He breathed in deep, the light, fresh scent of her adding to that unfurling hope in his heart. "Thinking about the day this whole RevitaYou thing is behind us all."

She laid a hand over his. "Do you think that will happen?"

"I do. We're close and getting closer every day. Make no mistake about it, today's incident was *because* of how close we are to arresting Matthews and Greer."

"Maybe."

Tripp heard the hesitation and let it go for a minute, curious if she'd continue. When she didn't, he prodded her for more. "Maybe? That's all you've got?"

She shifted then, gently moving out of his arms. He wanted her to stay—nearly asked her to—but it was only because he realized that he wanted her in the same place forever that he held back.

Had he really gone *there*?

What right did he have to even think that way? Sadie had her entire future in front of her. She would heal from the pain Tate Greer had caused and she'd move on. She would and she deserved to.

And she deserved it with someone who wasn't damaged and broken. Like him.

He might have found a few vestiges of hope these past few days, but he knew who he was and he knew his lot in life. Marriage and a family weren't a part of that.

Sadie Colton was designed for marriage and a family. It was written in every pore. Seemed to halo her, shimmering as clear as if he could reach out and touch that future himself.

"I say maybe because Tate is still out there. So's Wes Matthews. My family hasn't found Brody yet, no matter how many text messages my sisters have sent him. I'd have added to their number if I hadn't just lost my second cell phone this week."

She sighed heavily, the hair framing her face blowing in the light gust. "All I'm saying is that while I hear you, I'm not sure we're going to get a neat bow wrapped around this one."

"Who said anything about bows?"

"You were getting dangerously close."

Tripp wasn't sure if he was offended or ready to laugh. In light of all they'd been through, maybe that was a good thing. It meant that they could still *feel* something. Could still render emotion and find topics to argue about. To learn from one another and debate the facts.

For now, it would have to be enough.

His body might want more, but his mind knew better. He needed to stay strong and resist these inconvenient feelings for Sadie. Because no matter what she thought, he knew in his bones that this would end. Sooner rather than later, in fact.

Greer's days of running free were numbered.

And once that monster and his fellow villains were off the streets, life would go back to normal.

It would.

Because it had to.

Sadie felt the exhaustion down to her very marrow, yet sleep still eluded her as she struggled to get comfortable in the guest chair in his room. Tripp had finally dozed off about an hour before. She'd wanted to go say goodbye to her family, still hanging out in the waiting room, and send them home, and knew it would be an acceptable excuse to leave Tripp for a few minutes. As she'd hoped, by the time she'd returned to his room, his eyes were closed and he was snoring.

It was a sweet sound, which really meant she'd gone around the bend for this guy. She'd groused at her brothers for years for snoring like grizzlies, yet here was Tripp, likely just as loud, and she thought it was a symphony.

Because you've got it bad, Colton. B-A-D bad.

A fact she'd struggled with earlier when she'd left his arms. It had felt so good to lay there with him, practically intertwined on the small bed. She'd felt safe and secure, and in the cocoon of his arms she could let her fantasies go. There, with the masculine, woodsy scent of him surrounding her, she could pretend this wasn't temporary. More, she could believe that somehow they would find their way.

Together.

That was why she'd had to step away. Pull herself from that warm embrace and take the seat opposite his hospital bed. She'd stared at the beeping machines, the confirmation that his heart was still beating and blood still flowed in his veins. And she took heart that they'd survived yet again.

Because she'd rather be in a world with Tripp alive.

Beyond that truth, not much else mattered. Not her feelings for him or the increasingly urgent need she had to tell him—which was the path to disaster.

Yes, they'd grown close over the past week.

And yes, the feelings she'd always had for him had reawakened with the close proximity and intense experiences.

But it couldn't be anything else. And it was up to her to find acceptance in that.

"Sadie." Vikki whispered her name from the doorway and Sadie turned to find her twin standing there, her expression inscrutable. That was odd since she and Vikki always knew what the other was thinking.

Yet Vik's expression gave nothing away, even as Sadie sensed her sister had quite a lot to say.

She gave one last look at the monitor, then at Tripp, before standing and following Vikki out into the hall-way. "What is it, Vik? I thought you and Flynn were heading home with everyone else?"

"We were. But—" Vikki stilled, her green eyes

clouding. Their eyes were the one match they shared as twins.

"What is it, Vikki?"

"We were already in the car and Flynn was almost out of the parking lot when I asked him to come back." Vikki's arms went wide before pulling Sadie close. "I almost lost you tonight and I just—" Vikki let out a long, hard sigh. "And I love you and I needed to see you again. Hold you again."

Sadie clung to her sister, the bond they'd shared their entire lives even stronger than the tight grip that held them in place now. It felt good to hold her sister. To feel the solid lines of her body and know that she was alive and well and whole.

"First the kidnapping from the safe house and now tonight." Vikki sighed again as a shudder seemed to echo through her body. "I can't lose you, Sadie. I just can't."

"You didn't, Vik. I'm okay. Really, I'm fine."

"I know." Vikki took a step back and shook her head. "I know. I'm looking at you and I know you're fine. And I keep telling myself that. And then I think about what might have happened and it washes through me once more."

Flynn let out a discreet cough before moving down the hallway. The GRPD had put two guards on the ward this time. They'd been apprised of who could come in and out, and allowed Flynn to pass. He moved up beside Vikki and wrapped an arm around her. "We're both so glad you're all right, Sadie."

"I know."

Although she hadn't spent much time with Flynn since her sister had fallen in love with the Army MP while Sadie had been in the GRPD safe house, she knew he was a good man. He had the ringing endorsement of her family and she'd never seen Vikki so blissfully happy.

But seeing them now—their mutual support and affection for each other so obvious—made Sadie's heart happy. She *knew* the love Flynn felt for her sister—saw it in Vikki's love in return—and was beyond grateful.

It was proof that love could find its way in the darkest of times.

"You having a party out there?" Tripp's normally deep voice was still tinged with the husky aftereffects of smoke inhalation.

Sadie turned back toward his room. "Are you okay?"

He stared at her from the bed. "Sounded more interesting out there than in here."

Sadie walked into the room, gesturing Vikki and Flynn with her. "Do you need anything?"

"I'd like an opinion, actually."

"An opinion about what?" Sadie asked.

Vikki had already moved into motion, pouring Tripp a fresh glass of water from a pitcher on the counter. She brought it over, removing the older one that had likely grown warm.

"Thank you." Tripp used the controller on his bed to sit up and take the water from Vikki. After drinking deep, he eyed Flynn before setting the glass down. "I've got an idea."

"Something we can help you with?" Flynn asked.

"I think so. I need a few days to heal and Greer has already proved he can move around undetected. I'd feel a lot better if Sadie and I got out of town."

"I can't go anywhere—" Sadie started to protest.

But Vikki had already moved closer to Tripp. "You had me at 'out of town,' Lieutenant."

"I've got a private place. A small cabin. Hell—" Tripp laughed, the sound hoarse "—I usually have to use my GPS to find it. It'll be a great spot to lay low for a few days. Give us some time to analyze Greer's moves and what he might do next."

"I think it's a great idea. Inspired." Vikki was already turning to Sadie, her excitement crushing whatever it was Sadie wanted to say.

A few days out of touch from everyone…but *with* Tripp?

Sly fingers of need beckoned her forward, willing her to say yes to the idea, while the more pragmatic side of her was convinced she should say no.

A cabin so remote he needed GPS to find it?

"I can't just run away again. That's what I've been doing for more than a month now and it hasn't gotten me anywhere. I'm no safer now than I was before all this started." Sadie heard the arguments coming from her own lips and knew them for the lies they were.

Sure, on principle, she didn't want to turn tail and run from Tate Greer. But Tate had little to do with the silky voice that continued to keep her company in her head, suggesting that she'd actually like nothing more than *to* run away with Tripp for a few days.

Forever, really.

"It's a great idea, McKellar." Flynn nodded. "We can feed you any information you need out of Colton Investigations' HQ. And I'm sure Emmanuel can keep you apprised of whatever GRPD data you need."

"I've got full digital capabilities at my place," Tripp

added, reinforcing that the transition would be both easy and seamless.

"But I—" Sadie stopped as Vikki appealed to her once more.

"Sadie, please. Go away for a little while. Help Tripp get better, and get off the grid for a few days. You've both been through so much. You need time away from this mess. From the fear and the sense that there's another shoe waiting to drop."

She knew she should argue. Or stall. Or demand a few days to think it over, but really, what was the point?

Tripp McKellar had just invited her to run away with him. He might not understand what that meant to her, but really, how often was a woman offered a chance to make her dreams come true?

Chapter 14

Tripp watched Sadie putter around his cabin's kitchen from the comfort of his well-worn couch and wondered what he'd possibly been thinking inviting her up there. Sure, there'd been copious amounts of painkillers involved, but really, the drugs hadn't clouded his thoughts that much.

No, instead they'd blunted his ability to think three steps ahead of himself.

That was where he now found himself, healing with all the comfort of a riled grizzly while sporting a near constant erection.

It hadn't been this bad at his house. Maybe because she'd hid out much of the time in the guest room? Or maybe because her family had dropped in several times, effectively diminishing his more lustful thoughts about their baby sister?

Who knew?

All he did know was that after three days his side hurt like a beast, the stitches itchy as they healed, and Sadie Colton flitted around his cabin like his own personal angel of mercy.

She made his breakfast.

She refilled his coffee.

She plumped his pillows.

And all he wanted to do was wrap his arms around her, drag her down onto the old lumpy couch and make love to her until both of their eyes crossed. His desire was so great he'd even gotten over feeling embarrassed he had condoms in his gym bag. It was an oddly hopeful purchase he'd had no reason to make doing last month's shopping, yet had anyway.

Hopeful and now a taunting reminder from his worn-out GRPD duffel.

Tripp groaned at the injustice of it all.

"Tripp? Are you okay?" Sadie turned from where she stood at the kitchen counter, concern written across her face.

"I'm fine."

"You sounded like you were in pain."

"No." Unclenching his teeth, he tried to come up with something plausible. "I just moved the wrong way."

"Are your stitches okay?"

"I'm fine, Sadie."

The words came out sharper than he'd intended, but really, what was a man to do? Her light and sweetness and, hell, just *her*, was slowly driving him mad.

The computer Tripp had settled on the coffee table rang, an incoming video call lighting up the screen. He tapped the button to answer it. Literally saved by the bell. "McKellar here."

As the video came up, he saw several of his team members in one of the GRPD meeting rooms. Riley was also visible in the shot, along with Ashanti Silver.

"Looks like a full house," Tripp drawled.

"You better believe it, McKellar." His chief started right in. "We've got a lead on Matthews."

Sadie entered the living room, coming fully into view on screen. "Chief Fox. How are you?"

"Sadie. Good to see you."

"You, as well. Please tell us you're calling with some good news."

"You bet we are, little sister," Riley told her. "Matthews took the bait."

Although Tripp wouldn't go all the way to admitting to skepticism, he had definitely had his concerns that the honeypot plan to capture Wes Matthews wasn't going to pay dividends. Not because it was a bad idea, but because the notion that Matthews could still think about sex in the midst of his pyramid scheme going bad seemed like an impossible stretch.

Clearly, he'd underestimated the male libido.

Not that his was doing him any favors.

"Tell us what you've got."

Ashanti took over the video call, using the sharing feature to run through the most recent emails her "character" had shared with Matthews. A few of the images were quite graphic and Tripp couldn't help but side-eye Sadie.

To her credit, she was completely focused on the discussion. A true professional, all while that very libido

Tripp was so busy condemning in Matthews was distracting him with Sadie.

"But the best was the conversation we had last night." The images on the screen fell off as the GRPD meeting room once again came into view. And then Ashanti played the recording of her call with Matthews.

Tripp listened as they talked of deals and investments and some money Ashanti's "character" wanted to invest. She purred a little, letting off the throttle when the discussion of investments shifted toward a face-to-face meeting.

"I don't believe he fell for this," Sadie said to Tripp, but added under her breath and low enough it didn't interrupt the replay, "But Abigail said it would work and she was right. She even suggested they pepper in big words and reference a few old movies that he loves. Listen to how smoothly Ashanti slid all of that in there. He's putty in her hands."

Matthews certainly was, Tripp thought to himself. He remained quiet, listening to the rest of the recording before interjecting. "Has he committed to a meeting yet?"

"Not yet," Ashanti said. "I think I'll get him on the next call, though."

"Do we still think he's in the Bahamas?" Tripp asked.

"That's still the latest intel from the Bureau," Chief Fox affirmed. "They've worked well with us on this and Agent Winston has played more than fair with me."

Tripp suspected that might have something to do with how well Kiely was working with her new fiancé, but who wanted to quibble? While he understood the situations that often dictated one side or the other to behave territorially, they were all after the same end goal. And Tripp had had little time or acceptance in his career for the politics that often existed between the Feds and the local government.

Part of why he'd always respected Cooper Winston was his willingness to do the same.

Taking down Capital X and Wes Matthews needed to be priority number one. It was good to know that everyone collectively felt that way.

As if reading his thoughts, Fox added, "Sadie, your sister Kiely has been a huge help on this, too."

"Thank you, sir. She wants to see this wrapped up, just like we all do."

"Without question." Fox changed gears, his next question deftly shining a spotlight directly on Tripp. "How are you feeling, McKellar? Healing up well?"

"Yes, sir. Feeling good as new."

"You keep telling yourself that," Chief Fox chuckled.

In minutes, the call had ended, Tripp's computer screen once again dark.

"That is encouraging news," Sadie said. "I really wasn't sure this was going to work. But it's so weird, it's just like Abigail said. Her father is highly susceptible to this approach." She shook her head before gesturing in the direction of the now dark computer screen. "I didn't want to believe it but it's hard to deny that sort of response."

"It's hardly a surprise."

Sadie stood and had only taken a few steps toward the kitchen when she stopped, cocking a hand on her hip. "What's not a surprise?"

"Men. Their egos. And body parts farther south. It's a cliché for a reason."

"Maybe," she said and shrugged. "I guess I wanted to give him a little more credit, though. I may hate his criminal line of work, but the guy did work hard to build up his pyramid scheme. Seems like an awful big waste to lose it all just because he couldn't keep it in his pants."

"That's still to be seen."

"I suppose."

Tripp continued, all that lingering frustration still roiling in his gut. "Besides, guys like him? Like Greer? They all think they're above getting caught."

"Are you okay? Your voice sounds strange."

Was he okay? Up until a few days ago, he would've said he was fine. More than fine. And then Sadie Colton had come into his life like a hurricane.

Yes, he had been attracted to her before. But it was hard to believe how quickly that slow burn had turned into an inferno.

"I'm fine."

"You keep saying that, and yet each time you do, I'm finding I believe you less and less."

"What do you want me to tell you?"

"The truth."

What *did* she want him to tell her? That he cared about her? That he suspected he felt more strongly toward her than he should or than he ever wanted to feel for another human being ever again?

Or maybe she wanted him to tell her how she decimated his willpower with the barest glance.

Perhaps what she *really* wanted to know was that she was in his blood and, no matter how much distance he put between them or how many times he told himself he couldn't touch her, they were racing toward some sort of inevitable cliff.

And it would take barely a glance to push him straight over the edge.

"At the risk of paraphrasing a movie line, I'm not sure you can handle this truth."

Whatever patience she was hanging on to vanished in an instant. "You have some nerve, treating me like my ideas have no place here, with this surly dismissal. This was your idea, may I remind you. *Your* idea to come sit here and hide out from Tate Greer."

"I know."

"So why are you acting like this? We just got some good news. Hell, great news." She heaved out a heavy breath. "And all you can do is sit there being an ass about it all."

"I'm not—" He got to his feet, the tug of pain in his side nothing compared to the desperate need that twisted and churned inside him. "You know what, I'm not doing this."

"Doing *what*, Tripp?"

He was nearly out of the room when her question stopped him. The confusion, yes, but something else.

The hurt.

And with that small note of hurt something inside him broke wide open. His resistance vanished and, with it, any and all ability to stay away from her.

He pivoted, marched straight back to her and pulled her into his arms. One minute they were on opposite sides and the next she was right in the moment with him, her mouth fused to his, kissing him back like her very life depended on it.

It was what he'd wanted. What he'd yearned for.

And as his hand slid down her back to settle on her hip, Tripp finally quit fighting it.

* * *

Finally.

That lone word rang over and over in her mind as Sadie held on to Tripp.

How long had she wanted this? Wanted *him*?

There had been times when it had felt like forever. She knew she'd been someone before the day, as a rookie, that she'd been introduced to Tripp. But so often she'd forgotten what life had been like before she'd met him. Before she'd lived with the reassuring knowledge that there was someone in the world as good and decent and honorable as Tripp McKellar.

And hot, her subconscious reminded her as Tripp deepened the kiss further. *Never forget wildly attractive and hot.* Because to her, Tripp was the perfect man.

"Sadie," he whispered against her lips.

She ignored it, especially since most of what had come out of that lush frame in the form of words over the past hour had only served to annoy her. She much preferred what they were doing now.

Maybe if they stayed like this, mouths fused, they could get past whatever irritation had somehow found its way beneath his skin.

"Sadie." He said her name more firmly before matching the words with a fixed hold on her shoulder, stilling her.

"What?"

"We shouldn't—"

She lifted a finger and pressed it against the lips that had so recently ravaged her own.

"If you say we shouldn't do this, I'm going to slug you. And I have two brothers, so don't think I don't know how to deliver a rock-solid punch. Both because they taught me how and because I've used it on each of them with considerable effectiveness."

"But we—"

She pressed harder. "No. I'm sick of excuses for why this is a bad idea."

He shifted one hand from her shoulder, capturing her finger in his. "Would you listen to me?"

"Why?"

"Because I'm trying to be responsible here. You're here in my home at my insistence. And I'm your boss. And less than five minutes ago we were on a work call with the chief of the Grand Rapids Police Department. *And* your brother," he added in what felt like a low-blow afterthought.

"I'm not sure what my brother or, come to think of it, the chief, has to do with us having sex."

"Who said we're having sex?"

"I did. And I want to. Unless you don't want to."

"Sadie—"

"Yes or no, Tripp. I'm not interested in any other answer you can possibly come up with. That goes for excuses, too. Or any other half-baked reason that comes out of those impressively creative lips of yours. It's a question with a binary answer."

"'Impressively creative'?" A lone eyebrow quirked over those endless pools of blue.

"Yes."

"We shouldn't do this. And those reasons you're brushing off so easily are actually real reasons."

The light of battle was no longer reflected in his eyes. Instead, all Sadie saw was a very real, impossible-to-ignore vulnerability. And she understood it, because in that blue gaze she saw herself.

"I want you, Tripp. Right here, right now. I don't care what comes after this time. Or what might happen once we're back in the office. We're two adults. And I've known you long enough to know that if we make love, you won't hold it against me at work."

"But I—" He stopped, his gaze never leaving hers. "Yes or no, right?"

"That's it, Tripp. Yes or no." She kept her hands on his shoulders, but otherwise remained still. And in the waiting, recognized he needed the same from her. "My answer is yes."

He looked down at her for one inscrutable minute and she waited, not even daring to breathe. He wanted her. She knew that. Recognized the same need she felt in herself for him.

But still, she waited.

Because whatever held him back went far deeper than worrying about work. Or a boss/employee relationship that barely held water as an argument since Tripp had minimal, if any, sway over the CSI team.

No. This was something more. Something that went far deeper than desire between a man and a woman. Something she'd sensed in him for so long. Something deeply felt that held him back.

"Yes."

That word was practically a growl, guttural with need, as he pulled her close. His mouth closed over hers and Sadie thrilled to the heat that rose once more between them. Pressing herself against him, delighting in the hard lines of his body and how they complemented the far softer lines of hers, she put everything she was into the kiss.

Into her *yes*.

The couch that had been his work space for the past few days suddenly seemed as good a choice as any, the two bedrooms they'd each been occupying down the hall much too far to walk.

She was done with waiting.

She wanted him here. Now. And there was no more time to lose.

The clothes they wore—his well-used gym gear sporting GRPD labels from a bag in his trunk and hers, more loaners from her sisters—vanished in moments, falling to the side of the couch with gentle thuds as one piece followed the next. With a soft sigh, she pressed her now naked chest to his, the heat of his skin warming her despite the cold that howled outside the door.

Her breasts ached for his touch, her nipples sensitive points where they rubbed against the coarse hair of his chest. Sadie ran her hands over it, that male covering tapering to a narrow line just below his stomach. She was careful to avoid the bandage that covered his healing stitches, instead following that line of hair where it trailed to something even more male, more impressive. And as her hand closed over the firm length of him, Tripp exhaled heavily against her lips.

"Sadie."

The heat of him branded her, hot and hard and pulsing with life in her palm. She moved then, tentative stroking motions from base to tip, growing bolder when his breath grew more ragged, his hold on her tighter.

Without breaking that steady pressure, Sadie continued the sweet battle between them. His hands roamed over her body, drawing sensations as his thumbs brushed her nipples before both hands fully cupped her breasts. She stilled briefly, her chest arching into his hands as her head fell back, his ministrations shooting molten need to her core. It was only as he grew bolder, the press of his own hands more urgent, that she resumed those steady strokes.

"Wait."

He nearly stumbled as he stepped away, cursing as he crossed the room. Although she immediately missed his touch, she could hardly argue with the sight of his taut butt and muscled back and thighs as he crossed the room to his gym bag. "What are you—" She stopped as she recognized the box he came up with after digging deeply in the bag, another round of curses bulleting from his lips.

A giggle started deep in her belly, rumbling to life as he stomped back to her. His face still bore the unmistakable signs of sexual tension, which only served to make her laugh harder.

"What's so funny?"

"You." His mouth dropped as he caught sight of her, but she rushed on. "The cursing and that petulant little frown is too cute for words."

"Cute wasn't quite the look I was going for."

She reached for the box, digging out a condom and tossing the container onto the coffee table as he continued to stare down at her. She tore the foil before looking up at him from beneath her lashes. "Ruggedly handsome work better?"

"Much."

"Then sit that ruggedly handsome yet still-healing body down on that couch and let me get to work."

The surly look vanished as he took a seat. "Yes, ma'am."

Sadie settled herself over his lap, straddling his thighs with her own. "Did you just 'ma'am' me?"

"I'm afraid I did." He rubbed his thumbs over her nipples once more as he nipped kisses along her jaw. "Ma'am."

"You're going to pay, McKellar." She unrolled the condom over him, with deliberate, agonizing slowness, amazed that sex could be as much about laughter and fun as it was about pleasure.

And as she centered herself over his sheathed body and began to move, Sadie realized something else.

Sex was also about joy. And fun. And, as her pleasure crested, unleashing wave after wave of sensation through her body, she knew it for love.

Tripp held Sadie in his arms, his breathing still harsh and ragged against her neck. He'd buried his face there as he'd poured himself into her, holding her body tight against his.

They'd just had sex on his old, lumpy couch that had likely been constructed during the Kennedy administration and it was the best sex of his life.

No bed had ever been as comfortable and no woman had ever been as sweet. Or as utterly all-consuming as Sadie Colton.

She'd decimated him.

As he struggled to regain his breath, he was already thinking about when they could do it again. Because one taste of Sadie wasn't enough. A lifetime of Sadie wouldn't be enough.

And that was a sobering enough thought that he lifted his head from her neck and dropped it back against the couch.

He'd given in.

On some level, he supposed it was inevitable, but he'd believed himself strong enough to withstand her. Or, if not her, his maddening feelings for her, which he knew were misplaced. Because despite all evidence to the contrary, he and Sadie didn't have a future.

Even if he could see past the lessons he'd learned with Lila's death, he was still Sadie's boss. She might not directly report to him but he was still a superior in the department.

And besides, he wasn't past Lila.

He'd made a vow never to put another person's life at risk for his job. If Sadie was harmed because of him…

He'd never survive.

Sadie still straddled his lap but she shot him a warm, satisfied smile—clearly oblivious to his thoughts—as she slipped off to sit beside him. Reaching behind them, she dragged a blanket off the back of the couch and covered them both.

"How are your stitches?"

"Fine."

She gave him a dark side-eye as she settled the blanket into place. "Back to 'fine' again?"

Unwilling to pick a fight with the taste of her still on his tongue, he added, "Really, I'm good. The stitches are fine and I actually forgot they were there." Tripp patted the bandage, pleased to find the area tender but no worse for wear.

"Good."

He leaned over and pressed a kiss to her forehead, absurdly pleased when she snuggled into his side.

That, considering the direction of his thoughts, was the last thing he should be thinking. Yet there he went, lifting his arm to cradle her shoulders, snuggling her more tightly into the crook of his body. He felt himself fading lightly, the quiet rhythm of her breathing steadying his into the same cadence. His head nearly fell forward in sleep when she spoke once again.

"I'm glad we did that. And I'm counting the minutes until we can do it again."

Tripp's eyes popped open, his body immediately on full alert at the bold declaration. "You think we're going to do that again?"

"I sure as hell hope so, because one time is most certainly not enough."

He wanted to argue. Knew, really, that he *should* argue. But he felt too damn good to do anything but agree with her. "No, one time isn't nearly enough."

"Since I'm still smarting from the 'ma'am,' I'll do you one better and tell you I told you so."

Amused at the fact that sex had unleashed "chatty Sadie," he shifted so he could look down at her. "When did you tell me so?"

"How about every day since the day you rescued me? I can't believe you haven't seen the come-here-big-boy looks I've been throwing or felt the longing glances that bore into your back every time you turned around."

Come here, big boy? Maybe "chatty" wasn't quite the right term.

"For the record, I felt no longing glances and I'm not dignifying the 'big boy' comment with an answer."

"That doesn't make it any less true."

He supposed she was right, but he still wasn't going there. That made her abrupt leap off the couch, fully naked as the blanket fell away, enough to steal his breath away. But it was when she turned, giving him a full view of her gorgeous body, that he knew he was lost.

He'd made love to Sadie Colton. And it had been better and even more amazing than he'd imagined. And he'd imagined often and in great detail.

So yes, he couldn't wait to do it again.

Even if, somewhere in the recesses of his brain, he registered that she was talking to him.

"I'm glad we're on the same page. I'll make us a snack and then we can get to doing it again."

A snack?

The same page?

What page?

She continued, oblivious to his confusion at the rapid change in direction. "After all, once we get back to Grand Rapids, we have to give all this up. So I plan on getting my fill every possible moment until we do."

Chapter 15

Tripp hefted the ax and slammed it against the block of wood, Sadie's words still rattling around in his mind like loose marbles.

After all, once we get back to Grand Rapids, we have to give all this up.

Give it up?

Hell, they'd barely started and she was already talking about giving it up? Not that it had stopped him from making love to her once again after their quick snack of peanut butter on crackers. Nor had it stopped him from taking full advantage of that lush body in the shower, either.

But now, out here in the freezing cold an hour later with a few split logs beside him, Tripp brought her words back in vivid detail.

I plan on getting my fill every possible moment until we do.

Get her fill? What was he, some stud pony here to do her bidding?

Even if you've been exactly that all afternoon, Mc-Kellar, an exceedingly *un*helpful voice volleyed right back in his mind, *you were the one who told her this couldn't be real. Why are you so upset she recognizes that?*

Because, damn it.

Because she matters.

"Damn it," he muttered, sick of the circular argument.

And even more sick of arguing with himself.

"Tripp McKellar!" Sadie shouted his name as she marched toward him. She'd dragged on a pair of large fishing waders he kept in the cabin's closet and the oversize boots had her high-stepping because they were made to fit him, not her. "What in the hell are you doing out here?"

"Isn't it obvious?" He hefted the ax once more, banging it down on a fresh, unsuspecting piece of wood.

"You've got stitches in your side, you jackass. You want to rip them all out?"

"I'm fine," he muttered, well aware his use of that phrase had reached monumentally ridiculous proportions. He reached for another small log but she had already moved up beside him and kicked it out of range.

"You really are a jackass. And that's plenty of wood. Especially since there's already more than enough in the metal stand beside the fireplace. Get inside."

"You've got no right to order me around."

"And you've got even less right to test my crappy nursing skills when those stitches come loose."

It was the hitch in her voice as she said that last part that stilled him.

He was being that exact jackass she accused him of being and there was no logic for it. But for some reason, three epic sessions of sex had left him emotionally raw instead of satiated and practically comatose.

That made even less sense than the anger that continued to roil and seethe at her dismissal of anything between them once they left the cabin.

Wasn't that what he'd wanted? No strings attached. Someone who recognized and understood he wasn't meant for a relationship.

Right?

Tripp tossed the ax back into the small shed alongside the house and followed Sadie back inside. His gaze alighted on the stack of wood beside the fireplace before quickly bumping away to stare at something else—anything else—that wouldn't make a liar out of him.

Only, his gaze caught on Sadie's lush body and the rounded curve of her ass and, once again, he was trapped.

Trapped with all these *thoughts* and *feelings* he had no business possessing. Worse, that he'd sworn would never be for him.

She whirled on him, unaware of his perusal. "Do you want to tell me why you were out there putting your health at risk?"

"My health is fine."

"You know, I saw a nearly full bottle of whiskey in the pantry. I think I'm going to start a drinking game. Every time Tripp McKellar says the word *fine*, I'm going to take a shot." She moved up right in his face, hers set in dark, dangerous lines. "I should be good and drunk by noon."

"I am fine. And you sure as hell weren't worrying about my stitches in the shower."

Those gorgeous green eyes went wide about a half second before flames shot through them, lighting her up like the winning screen on a video game. "Don't flatter yourself, baby cakes."

Tripp had no idea where it came from. He'd never been one to even mention sex to a woman before and here he was taunting Sadie with what had transpired between them. And then had to stand there while she shot it all straight back at him like a little firecracker, more than able to hold her own.

That flickering anger that had gnawed at him every time she'd mentioned Tate Greer over the past week flamed to life, white-hot and pure. It had broken his heart to see how Greer had left her feeling less than.

But looking at her now, Tripp saw a new truth. The woman standing before him was empowered. Bold. And he still wanted her more than he'd ever thought possible.

Without knowing who shifted first—and in the end, maybe it never mattered anyway—they moved into each other. The light of battle winked out, floating away like a wisp of smoke as they came together. Nothing in the world but the two of them.

She welcomed him with her mouth, opening beneath him as his tongue sought hers. As his hands molded her skin, a masterpiece coming to life beneath his fingers. As their breaths met and mingled, growing heavy with need.

"I want you," she whispered, half challenge, half

plea, and he felt an answering response rise up deep from within. "Now."

"Yes." He reached for her, walking backward toward the bedroom as he held her against him. His hands were already at the hem of her sweatshirt, his fingers plying the warm skin at her waist. They'd barely reached the doorway when Sadie stumbled into him. His tight hold was the only reason they remained upright and he suddenly had an armful of woman as something cold and heavy brushed against his foot.

"Whoa." Tripp steadied her, his mind still hazy from her kisses. "Are you—"

He never got the question out as laughter shook her shoulders. Even as he tried to catch up, she nearly doubled over with it, one hand reaching out for balance on the bedroom door frame.

He had a momentary flash of good, old-fashioned, red-blooded male fear that she was laughing at him.

And then he saw it.

The huge fishing waders still clung to her feet, the thick soles planted against the floor, extending her feet to nearly double their size.

"Where did you even find those?"

His question only had her laughing harder. "Hall closet."

The catch-all box in the base of the closet drifted through his mind's eye. "It's a sexy look."

Tripp bent to remove them, his hands roaming over one firm thigh as he dislodged the boot. He did the same with her other leg, lingering longer than absolutely necessary, his pinky finger flicking against the sensitive skin at the very top of her thigh. He heard her quick rush of breath, the laughter fading away as if it had never been.

And once the boots had been removed, kicked and discarded into the hall, Tripp returned his hands to her waist, his mouth lingering over hers. "Now. Where were we, baby cakes?"

He felt her lips widen into a broad smile against his own as her arms wrapped around his neck. The storm of one battle ended just as a new, more delicious one took its place.

Sadie contemplated the cool air against her naked backside and realized that, for as generous a lover as Tripp McKellar was, the man was a serious blanket hog. Like a conquer-and-gather-up-all-the-covers sort of guy. But since the large body that shielded her front was practically a heater, she snuggled in closer and decided in the moment that it didn't matter.

Her thoughts were as lazy as the first rays of dawn filtering through the window, flitting from subject to subject with little effort. It wasn't a time of day she usually saw and it was a novel idea to simply lie there for a bit, enjoying the moment. And being wrapped up in Tripp.

How had this happened?

Well, she knew *how* it had happened. But the bigger question was why? And an even bigger one than that—why now?

They'd gone from colleagues to friends to lovers in the span of a week. And while she was wildly happy with the outcome, she knew it couldn't last.

Hadn't that been the real root of their fight?

The pitched battle they'd waged from the wood

stump outside, through the living room and on into the bedroom, may have changed tone and tenor along with location, but she was smart enough to know its cause.

This couldn't last.

Hadn't she tried to acknowledge that? To be mature and open and honest, proving to Tripp she didn't have expectations about what was happening between them beyond these few days locked away from the world?

It had been rather broad-minded of me, really, she thought with no small measure of disgust. Until he'd picked a fight with her. And that only added to her confusion because wasn't that what he'd wanted?

So how had saying it somehow pissed him off?

Much as she wanted to lean back on her inexperience and blame it for their argument, she knew his reaction had had nothing to do with how many men she'd slept with. Instead, it'd had everything to do with putting a timeline on how long she'd sleep with *him.*

He'd even used that stupid excuse about being her boss.

Suddenly restless, Sadie slipped out of bed. Tripp never moved, the thick covers still clenched in his arms as he slept. She found her clothes in a pile near the door and silently pulled them on before closing the bedroom door behind her and heading out to the living room.

The cabin wasn't large but it had a spacious feel, with high beamed ceilings that gave a sense of openness in the main gathering area. She curled up on the couch, still restless with her thoughts as her gaze darted around the room. She could watch TV but she wasn't in the mood for news or any of the old reruns to be found this early in the morning. It was only when her gaze alighted on the various computers Tripp had set up that she decided to email Kiely.

Her older sister was a badass private investigator, full of what her twin, Pippa, had always classified as vim, vigor and a solid dash of vixen. Kiely had never been a shy, retiring sort of woman and she'd be the perfect person to talk to about Tripp's out-of-line response to Sadie's magnanimous declaration of sexual freedom without strings.

Sadie loaded up her email, doing a quick scan of what had come in overnight. Pippa had sent the sisters a silly meme about Michigan winters and Sadie replied with a smile and a snowman emoji before opening a new window to type her note to Kiely. That made it all the more surprising when her video chat kicked in two minutes later, Kiely on the other side.

Her sister's face came to light on the screen, a small boy wrapped in her arms. Similar to the big man Sadie had left sleeping in the bedroom, the little guy had his arms wrapped around a blanket, only his eyes were wide-open and blinking in that sweet, chubby little face.

Alfie.

"Hey there." Sadie gave the camera a little wave. "Hi, Alfie." She didn't quite get a smile but she saw interest light in that little face.

"I saw you were online," Kiely said. "And since we were up, I thought we'd give our aunt Sadie a call."

Something clenched in her heart at the use of the word *aunt*. It was still so new, her sister's romance with Cooper bringing Alfie into their lives. She felt the same about Abigail and Griffin's baby, Maya. In a matter of months, Sadie had gone from not even being an aunt to having two little ones in her life with Riley and Charlize's baby on the way in the new year.

"I'm glad you did."

They talked for a few minutes, Alfie growing more animated and involved in the conversation. He was already talking and, while she missed a few things, Sadie managed to get most of what he was saying. And what she'd missed, Kiely easily filled in.

"You're getting good at this," Sadie said, her heart full.

"Good at what?"

"Toddler speak. You understand everything he says."

Kiely looked down at the baby as Alfie looked up and in that quiet glance, Sadie saw the truth. Her sister had, in a matter of a few short months, become a mother. She was changed—transformed, really—and it was beautiful to see.

Kiely beamed back, kissing the baby on the crown of his head. "That's because Alfie's so smart."

The small boy settled in Kiely's arms, his eyes blinking with tiredness.

"I can let you go."

Kiely shook her head. "He's a good sleeper and once he's out, noise doesn't bother him. Talk to me. I know something's going on, especially since you're never up at this hour unless you haven't gone to bed."

"That's not true."

"It's completely true and you know it. Spill."

Sadie let out a small sniff at being nailed so easily, but it was for show only. She desperately needed to talk and was beyond grateful Kiely was there to listen. And, just as her sister had promised, Alfie's eyes had already closed, his little head nestled against her sister.

"I slept with Tripp."

Kiely's answering grin was immediate and tinged with those solid hints of the vixen Pippa had always accused her of being. "I knew it wouldn't take long."

"Kiely!"

Part of her wanted to be shocked but really, how could she be when her sister was right.

So very right.

She and Tripp hadn't lasted that many days in confinement before giving in to the attraction between them. The three days had felt like an eternity but really wasn't.

"He's an attractive man and you're a beautiful woman. And the air practically combusts around you. How could I have been wrong?"

"The air combusts?"

"Yeah, it does. Which is yet another reason Tate Greer was never right for you."

"I thought it was because he was a killer and a criminal."

Kiely waved a hand. "That, too, of course. But if I suspend all that for the briefest moment—"

Sadie tried to stop her—how did you just *suspend* criminal activity?—but Kiely steamrolled over it. "Seriously. If you hold that part of it for just a minute, you'll understand what I'm saying. None of us knew who or what he was and, really, how could we? But we all knew there wasn't a spark between you. That was what we all kept pushing up against when we tried to talk to you about him. We wanted to know if you were happy."

"I still say him being a criminal makes sparks a moot point."

Kiely eyed her through the video chat camera before

cutting to the chase once more. "If you're having what I presume is amazing sex with Lieutenant Hottie, what are you doing emailing me so early in the morning?"

"We had a fight last night."

"Did you get makeup sex?" When Sadie said nothing, Kiely only smiled again. "I'll take that as a yes."

"I'm still mad at him."

"Why?"

"Because I gave him a no-strings out to this whole thing. The world is upside down and this place is like a cocoon. But the real world is still outside. Tate's still not caught and neither is Wes Matthews. I'm a big girl and I know the score."

"And you told him all that?"

"I was much more eloquent."

"No wonder you pissed him off."

The solidarity and support she was so convinced she'd find from her sister was nowhere in evidence. Instead, Sadie's mouth dropped and she nearly shouted into the screen before she remembered the sleeping baby as well as the sleeping man in the next room.

"What is that supposed to mean?" she hissed instead.

"It means he wants to think he has no strings. But he sure as hell doesn't want you to actually tell him that."

"Why not?"

"Because it's not what he really wants."

Sadie flopped back on the couch, utterly confused and rapidly losing the thread of the conversation. "This is stupid. And not the regular sort of stupid but the multiple-O *stooooopid*." She elongated the middle of the word, pleased when her sister finally seemed to agree.

"Totally. But that's men for you." Kiely kissed the top of Alfie's head again before looking down at him.

"I have no idea how they start out this way but end up that way. But somehow they do."

"Tripp is a grown man. He knows what he wants and I'm trying to respect that. He had that awful thing that happened to him with his fiancée dying…" Sadie searched her sister's face. "I have to be okay with it if he doesn't want a relationship."

"For him?"

Sadie shook her head, the truth crystal clear. "For me. Or it'll decimate me."

Kiely's gaze softened, her tone quiet. "Only you can decide that. But I will tell you one thing. Don't let him off the hook too easily."

Sadie heard the stirring from the other room and stared at the closed door before turning her eyes back to her sister. "What's that supposed to mean?"

"It means your feelings matter, too. What you want matters, too. You need to believe that, Sadie."

The clear sound of another human moving around came from the bedroom. "I've got to go."

"Think about what I said?" Kiely added.

"I will."

Then the screen went dark and Sadie shut down her email just as Tripp came into the living room.

"Morning."

"Good morning."

"Everything okay?" His eyes were alert, even through the lingering vestiges of sleep.

"Yeah. Fine. My sister Kiely called me. The baby was up, so it gave them something to do."

Tripp nodded. "I thought I heard voices."

Before she could respond with some sort of excuse, he headed for the kitchen, seemingly unconcerned she was already up or that she'd talked to her sister. She heard him open the fridge and the light scrape of a tin can against the countertop when he set it down to prep the coffee maker. Then she caught the sounds of water being added and coffee grounds hitting the filter.

How was it all so normal?

She got off the couch, not sure what she wanted to say yet deeply aware of the need to say it. And as she came upon him in the kitchen—his shoulders broad beneath a navy GRPD T-shirt, gray sweatpants riding low on his hips and his hair mussed from sleep—her sister's parting words rang loud and clear.

Your feelings matter, too. What you want matters, too.

"I'd like to know about before."

Tripp's gaze lifted off the coffee maker, the sleep fading a bit more. "Before what?"

"I'd like to know about your fiancée."

Tripp wanted to be angry. Somewhere down low and deep, he wanted to find some ire to blunt the pain and surprise of Sadie's words.

Only nothing came.

Not fury or frustration, or even the smallest rub of irritation.

Funny, how he'd felt all of those emotions yesterday during their argument and now he couldn't find a bit of them. Couldn't conjure them up, no matter how hard he tried.

"You know about Lila?"

"Yes, Tripp. I'm sorry, but I've lived in Grand Rapids my whole life. Even if I hadn't joined the force, I'd have heard the story."

"But you did join the force."

"Everyone there knows what happened to you. To her." Sadie's voice was gentle, but there was something insistent there, too.

Or maybe it was something insistent inside him.

A driving need to get it all out. Maybe, by finally speaking the words, he'd remove the ashy taste from his tongue and the bitter remorse that always steamrolled him when he thought about Lila and the baby.

Maybe.

"I had a girlfriend named Lila. We'd been dating about six months when we found out she was pregnant."

Sadie's eyes went wide at the news of the baby but she remained silent. It was the proof he needed, though, that he had managed to keep that part of the story as his own. The entire GRPD might have known what happened to him but no one had known about the baby.

That seemed monumental, somehow. Like there actually was still *something* completely private about his grief.

"I'd already made detective a few years by then and had several cases under my belt. I made enemies. And one decided to enact his vengeance when he got out of jail on a technicality."

"Tripp." She laid a hand on his arm but he slipped away, moving to the cabinet to pull down a few mugs. Her touch felt good—too good—and there was no way he'd get through this if he let her touch him. So he made himself busy with the mugs and taking spoons from a drawer and even moving to the fridge to get milk.

All while telling her about the day that changed his life.

"We got engaged after we found out about the baby. Lila had a checkup that day and I was going straight to the doctor to meet her."

He paused, images of the day still so fresh in his mind. The hints of spring in the breeze. The sun that beat down, warming the still cool air. And the dark, nondescript car that rattled without its muffler, moving through the medical center's parking lot like a shark preying the waves.

He'd seen it, of course. Heard it first, really. But he'd had no idea what evil lay inside. Or the desperate heart that beat for revenge.

Tripp told Sadie those things as he leaned back against the counter sipping his coffee.

"We were at a medical center and I kept hoping that would be enough to save her. I rationalized it to myself. That by having doctors close by, she'd have to be okay." He stopped then, the images that were never too far away seeming to fill all the open kitchen space, pushing out the air so that his breath came hard and fast. "But I was wrong."

"I'm sorry."

"Of course you are. Everyone's sorry." Tripp finally glanced up, surfacing from the depths of his memories. "Everyone always is. But no one is sorrier than me."

With that, he set down his mug and walked out of the kitchen. He didn't really care if she had any questions or if there were any other details she needed to know. None of it really mattered anyway.

Tate extended a hand, issuing a series of commands to Snake as he took a deep breath of the bracing cold air. They hadn't had any more snow, but it had remained frigid. The freezing temperatures seemed to hone the dog's reactions, his movements swift and immediate.

Which was exactly the response Tate needed right now.

Sadie and her police officer had vanished again. He'd called in every favor he'd had and no one had seen them or known where they'd gone. The two of them had basically disappeared four days ago and Tate had no idea where.

After three fruitless days spent trying to hunt them down, he'd had a vision overnight. An inspiration, really.

Snake returned when called, his back ramrod straight as he stared up at his master.

Tate flicked his gaze down to the dog, curious how a creature not nearly as smart as a human could be both tool and companion. He'd thought it before, until he'd had an epiphany while training Snake so many years before.

Discipline was nothing more than training with purpose.

All he needed to do was to use what the dog wanted as the reward to keep him in line. Praise. Food. Shelter. Pack. Whatever it was, identify that carrot and then dangle it at the end of a very long stick.

Each and every time, the dog responded in kind. It was time to do the same with Sadie.

She could hide, but all he really needed was the proper point of leverage. A lone carrot to immediately pull her out of hiding.

He issued another command to Snake. And as he

watched the dog bound over the cold ground as instructed, Tate considered the perfect place to snatch Sergeant Victoria Colton.

Chapter 16

Tripp avoided the wood-chopping routine again, even as he knew there was nowhere inside the cabin that would put him far enough from Sadie.

But he tried.

After he left her unceremoniously in the kitchen, he'd walked off to the bedroom, taking a shower and adding plenty of time to shave, too. Even with meticulous swipes of his razor, he was still done too quickly, so he'd finally opted to sit quietly on the couch and focus on his computer.

Sadie had obviously sensed his reticence to talk further, keeping to herself and focusing on the other department laptop he had with him.

Somehow they made it through most of the morning before she finally spoke. "We should probably start thinking about how to get out of here."

Tripp glanced up from the report he was reading. "Greer's still out there."

"Yeah. And we're stuck in here. I read Riley's report this morning and Ashanti's getting closer on the work with Matthews."

"So we stay put until it's done. Until we know you're safe."

She ignored his point and kept on pressing hers. "I still keep going back to the bigger idea that the only way we end this is to pit Tate and Wes Matthews against each other."

"Tate's trying to kill you."

"So we make sure he doesn't succeed."

He'd spent enough time with Sadie now to know that she wasn't nearly as flippant as the comment suggested. But still, he couldn't understand how she could be so blasé. Tate Greer was a threat. Tripp had several GRPD team members hunting for the man even now, trying to find him in any possible location anyone had ever placed him. All to no avail.

He'd ghosted them once again.

And Tripp didn't want Sadie anywhere near him when the man decided to reappear.

"It's not like we set you up as bait in the hospital or at my house. You were hidden away and that didn't stop him."

"I need to go back to living my life. Between a month in the safe house and now another week of running, I need something different."

Or she needed away from him.

Underneath, Tripp wondered if that was the real truth here and it drew a harsh stab of pain low in his gut.

He'd believed himself unable—and, more to the

point, unwilling—to care for anyone again. But some-how, some way, Sadie had gotten to him. Having sex with her had made it all more real, more tangible, somehow.

But it was being with her. Spending time with her and seeing her at her most personal and intimate that had allowed him to really see her.

Yes, he'd been fascinated before. And he'd even been smitten. But now?

The word *love* played through his mind, consuming him with all the impact of an avalanche.

He couldn't be in love with Sadie. Not now, not ever.

"You can go back to living your life after Greer's caught."

"That's not your decision to make."

Although the declaration was pointed, there wasn't a trace of anger in her tone. Yet it was as effective as waving red before a bull. "Don't brush me off or dis-miss me like I don't matter, Sadie. It's my job to keep you safe and I'm going to do it."

"It's my job to keep myself safe. I got myself into this and, while I appreciate all you've done, it's time to go home."

"And what if something happens to you?"

"Then I'll face the consequences." She set the com-puter down on the coffee table and turned to him, eyes pleading. "I've spent the past five weeks hiding from my life. I haven't worked. Haven't seen my family for much of that. I haven't even been inside my own home."

You were with me, that small, traitorous inner voice taunted, before going in for the kill. *Where you should be, always*.

Only, to hear her now, that time away hadn't been

enough. What was between them wasn't enough to make her stay. That was rich, coming from a man who refused to admit he cared for her. Maybe even loved her.

But, like always, he fell back on what he knew. What was tangible to him. "You said something to me the other day. About safety being an illusion. Do you believe that?"

"Yes."

"Then you make my life's work and the work of everyone else at the GRPD a lie."

"That's wildly unfair."

"Why? Isn't that what you're saying? If there's no such thing as safety and security, why does any of the work we do matter?"

Although she'd remained calm and measured up to now, Tripp saw her fight for composure. "My parents were murdered. Your fiancée and child were murdered. I almost married a man who wants to kill me. What safety is there in a world where any of those things can happen?"

Once again, a brick wall of disagreement seemed to have sprung up between them. "So you acknowledge it. Work with it. You don't go putting yourself in the crosshairs of a killer."

"No, Tripp. Instead, you deny any and all happiness in life. You deny yourself love and someone who cares for you because something may happen. You're accusing me of wanting to get back to my life but you refuse to live one."

Tripp's phone went off, the heavy ring interrupting the still rippling waves of her accusation. He saw Emmanuel's name on the caller ID screen at the same time a text came in from Cooper Winston.

"McKellar," he answered.

"Is Sadie with you?" Iglesias's question was out without preamble.

"Yeah. She has been for several days."

"Is Vikki with you?"

Ice pitted in the center of his stomach as Tripp shot a glance at Sadie. "No. Why?"

"She hasn't been seen since this morning."

Tripp glanced at the sun filtering through the window. "It's barely noon."

"Flynn is going out of his mind. They were supposed to meet for an early lunch and when she didn't show, he got worried. She hasn't been to work all morning."

"What's going on?" Sadie moved beside him, her gaze intent.

"Put me on speaker," Iglesias ordered.

Tripp did as asked, setting his phone on the table. He reached for Sadie's hand, not caring about the argument or their philosophical differences on life and love. She was going to need every bit of support he could give her.

"Tell her," Tripp ordered, willing everything he felt—and all he couldn't say—into their joined hands.

"Vikki's gone."

Sadie heard the disembodied voice of her future brother-in-law float off the coffee table and tried to process what Emmanuel was saying.

Vikki was gone? She'd never made it to work or a lunch date with Flynn. Nor was she answering her phone.

She wanted to ask questions—knew she should be asking questions—yet nothing came to mind.

Her sister was gone.

They were twins, damn it! Shouldn't she have felt something? Shouldn't she have known?

But she'd been here, hidden away. It was just like she'd told Tripp, only now, somehow, it seemed worse. She hadn't just run from her life, she'd put her sister in the crosshairs of a killer.

Because while she had no questions, she had plenty of self-recrimination.

"It's Tate Greer."

"That's what we think," Emmanuel affirmed.

"I know it is. He couldn't find me, so he's gone after the one person he knew could draw me out."

While the same would be true of any of her siblings, Sadie had no doubt it was deliberate and purposeful to take her twin.

"Are there any leads on where she is? Any traffic or street cams?" Tripp took over the conversation.

"The team's been scouring anything they can find," Emmanuel said. "But nothing's hit yet."

"We'll be there in an hour," Sadie interjected into the conversation. When Tripp did nothing more than look at her and nod, she pressed on. "There are going to be a limited number of places Tate can take her. Have Gunther Johnson brought up to Interview."

They ended the call, even as the face of Tripp's phone continued to light up with messages. Cooper texted again, followed by her brother. She made a quick call to Riley, assuring him they were headed back to the city. When he'd tried to argue with her to stay put, she'd hung up on him.

And in under a half hour they'd packed up and were on their way to Grand Rapids.

The sun was bright in the sky as they drove toward

the city. It was mid-December and it dawned on her as Tripp turned onto the interstate that it was coming on Christmas and she hadn't even thought about it. She'd spent so long locked in the safe house, whisked away from her life and her family, that when it had become too overwhelming to think about the holidays—and missing everyone—she'd shut it all out.

Only now, it all came flooding back.

"You've been quiet. How are you doing?" Tripp asked.

"Thinking about Christmas."

"It's so soon. Hard to believe it's here again."

"I made a deliberate effort to put it out of my mind in the safe house. And with all that's been going on, I continued to forget. But that doesn't mean it's not almost here." On a hard sigh, she remembered something else. "Oh, Tripp. Your poor house. What are you going to do?"

"Get a new one. It wasn't like I spent that much time in the old one."

She heard the flat assessment and recognized that he wasn't making up the casual response. Losing his house—his home—didn't seem to have that big an effect on him. "You don't sound that upset."

"It's a house."

She had no idea why she kept pressing the subject, but suddenly it seemed important. Huge, actually. "But you won't be in it for the holidays."

"I usually work through the holidays, so I don't bother with a tree or decorations."

Sadie thought about the small tree she put up each year in her apartment. She'd dubbed him Herman because he had a square, boxy shape that reminded her of

Herman Munster. It was silly and stupid, but she smiled each year when she pulled Herman out of the storage closet and set him up in her front window. And each January, when she carefully nestled him back in his box, she knew that she'd see him again.

Tripp had none of that. Whether by choice or now by habit, it didn't make things any less bleak. Or true.

But as she stared down the possibility that her sister would be hurt, or worse, Sadie understood it. She'd been so angry at Tripp's refusal to see all that could be, between them and, more broadly, in life. And then she'd been sad when he'd simply walked out of the kitchen this morning after sharing the details of Lila's death.

But now? Now she understood.

If something happened to her twin, Sadie had no idea what she'd do. It had been hard enough to lose her parents, but she and her siblings had found a way forward.

Yet Vikki's life being in danger was entirely different somehow.

The inability to believe in a world that contained light and love, and only risk if you tried for those things, suddenly made sense.

And with it, Tripp's determination to avoid it all.

Tripp stood outside the interview room, Sadie at his side. She'd been quiet since their odd diversion of a conversation in the car about the holidays and he wasn't sure what to make of it.

Sadie was strong enough for this, of that he had no doubt. Steely determination poured from her and he had no qualms about putting her in front of Johnson again.

It was the fact that she had to that still chewed him up.

How had it come to this?

And how had they never even considered the possibility that by leaving town, Tate would turn his sights on a new target.

The ever-petulant Gunther Johnson was brought into Interview and Tripp and Sadie entered shortly after him. One of the guards who'd escorted Johnson to the room fitted the handcuffs to the table locks and, in moments, the young man was seated, his careless sneer firmly in place.

"Look who's back."

Since Gunther had showed little but sullen attitude for the past few months, it was something of a surprise to see him initiate the conversation.

"We've got more questions for you."

"Why else would I be here?" Gunther said before turning his attention to Sadie. "That bruise has nearly faded away."

She touched her jaw. "How sweet of you to show you care."

Something dark and unexpected flashed across his face. "I don't go around beating women."

"Never said you did. But your boss certainly has no problem with it. Which is why we're here."

Although Tripp and Sadie hadn't overly prepped for the meeting, they had talked broad strategy. The idea was to put Johnson on the defensive and then pepper in how Greer and Matthews were going to take the score and run for the hills.

All part of Sadie's continued push to pit one of them against the other. So it was strange to see her employ such a risky tactic as empathy.

"You still haven't caught him yet?"

"You know we haven't, Gunther." Sadie leaned in.

"Because if we had, your life in here would've gotten a lot harder. Isn't that right?"

"Tate and I are square."

"Until he pegs you for the one who gave him up to the GRPD." She traced a small pattern on the table. "I can see to it that he finds out that little detail."

"You don't know jack, lady."

"I know plenty. And since I'm about to become the bait to get my sister back from the bastard, I'd say I know a hell of a lot more than you."

"What about your sister?"

"When he couldn't get to me, he took my twin sister. For revenge. To draw me out. His set of twisted reasoning really doesn't matter, does it? Because I'm here. And I need your help."

"Why should I help you?"

"Because I'm asking. Because an innocent woman's life is at stake. But if those aren't reason enough, I'll give you one more."

Gunther didn't respond though his interest was unmistakable.

"Wes and Tate don't deserve to get off scot-free in this whole thing, while you're stuck in here. I'm just a worker bee in CSI, but I've been around this place for a long time and I know how it works. The lawyers are going to go to town on what you know, who you know, and what you were part of. Especially if Tate and Wes get away and they don't have them to play with."

"That's B.S."

"No, it's not. It's truth. My father was a lawyer and my older sister followed in his footsteps. I know how hard she works to make sure guilty people pay." Sadie eyed him, never breaking her intensity. "And no one's going to cut you a break if they know you had an opportunity to help and didn't take it."

Just as in her first meeting with Gunther, Tripp was impressed with how smoothly Sadie handled the interview. And in her approach, he saw something else. For all her efforts to get answers and get through to Gunther, she never dismissed him. He'd observed a lot of interviewers through the years and knew it was unfortunately all too easy to forget the person sitting opposite you actually *was* a person. Instead, it was easier to create distance with labels like "perp" and "criminal" as a way to deal with sad wastes of life.

Only, Sadie didn't do that.

And it was fascinating to see how Gunther responded to her willingness to see his humanity.

"You're not playing me?"

"No, I'm not. I want my sister back and I need your help."

Tripp chose that moment to step in. He'd observed the young man for nearly three months now, unable to understand how Gunther would trade his life for such a dead-end choice as working for Capital X. What he hadn't done in all that time was see Gunther as anything other than a criminal.

It was time to change his approach.

"Gunther, this is your chance to step up."

"What's in it for me?" Gunther's ice-blue eyes assessed him, but for the first time they appeared to actually be considering the conversation instead of actively projecting contempt.

Tripp refused to drop into his historic default and assume the guy would make a poor choice. "You've got a chance to do the right thing."

Gunther stared down at the table and gave no indication one way or the other. Tripp shot a side-glance to Sadie and felt his heart stick in his throat at the desperate hope that lined her face.

She was depending on whatever possible shred of decency might still be in Gunther Johnson's heart. When they'd walked into the room, Tripp would have said that was impossible.

Now, after the guy had been exposed to a few rounds with Sadie Colton... Tripp wasn't so sure.

He reached out under the table, extending his fingers so they just brushed against hers. It was silent support, but as he touched her skin, Tripp recognized the comfort he was taking in return.

"Guy has a few old warehouses just outside of town."

"Where?" Tripp prompted before tossing out a few main thoroughfares that ran out of town toward the suburbs.

Gunther nodded on the last one. "You know it then. He's had 'em for years. Bought them on the cheap when they got all sad and abandoned. He..." Gunther hesitated before huffing out a low sigh. "He uses them when he needs to rough people up."

Tripp considered Gunther's description and the truth beneath it all. Greer, and by extension, Capital X, had been close all along.

Tripp glanced at Sadie but she was already rising, gratitude rolling off her in waves. "Thank you, Gunther. I won't forget this, and I will make sure my family doesn't forget it, too."

Tripp stood as the kid nodded, his eyes still that cool, calculating blue. Tripp didn't miss the way they followed Sadie as she rushed from the interview room. "I know I'm no prize, but women don't deserve that crap."

"What you did today, Gunther? It matters."

Although Tripp knew the young man's deeds wouldn't be erased by one act of decency, he also had hope that this could be the beginning of something new. Assuming the kid had played straight with them, Tripp would do what he could to ensure Gunther was treated fairly.

But for now he had to follow Sadie.

And this ridiculous idea she had to set herself up as bait.

"I'm not arguing with you." Sadie stared Tripp down before turning to her brother. The high, wide windows of the refurbished warehouse about a mile from Tate's hideout eclipsed Riley, the purple light of a winter afternoon filling the space behind him. "Either of you."

"You can't trade yourself for Vikki." Tripp had tried the argument several times and now Riley had started in. Despite his concern, Sadie steamrolled the argument.

"I'm the only one who can. Tate wants me. And he's using Vikki to get to me. His behavior keeps escalating and we know he's desperate. This will end it."

"What if we can't get to you?" Tripp asked.

It broke her heart a little to hear the hitch in his voice. But still, she remained strong.

"What do you think all these people are going to do?" Sadie pointed to the assembled police teams prepping and planning around them. The GRPD had commandeered the refurbished warehouse space, the home of a design firm that would be out all afternoon for its annual holiday party.

It had been sheer, blind luck that one of Tripp's detectives had known the owner of the warehouse and had asked to use the space, only to find out during the call the extra stroke of good luck that the place would be empty.

Sadie kept telling herself that stroke of good fortune was the proof that it would all work out.

That Vikki was okay.

And that she'd be okay, too.

"You don't have to do this, squirt." Riley pulled her close, wrapping her tightly in his arms. "You really don't."

"Yeah, I do."

Riley only hugged her harder before moving off to ask more questions of the two SWAT leads managing the op.

Once he was gone, Sadie was left alone with Tripp. Or mostly alone, if she ignored the fifty or so people milling around them, all preparing for the meet with Tate.

"Your brother's right." Tripp stepped closer but didn't touch her. "SWAT's here. We can get eyes in there and get Vikki out."

"This is quicker. And it's the easiest way to get what we want."

"And if Greer suspects you've got backup?"

"Tate's known for a while I've got backup. Part of me thinks that's what all this is about. He knows as well as I do that this needs to end, and he wants to show off how strong he is."

"That is why the professionals need to handle it."

"The professionals *are* handling it." Sadie strode closer and ran the tips of her fingers over his knuckles. The touch was light—as light as his had been in the interview room when they'd spoken with Gunther—and that made it all the more powerful.

"I can do this. And more to the point, I need to do this. I'm a trained cop and I know how to handle myself on an op. And my sister is inside that warehouse."

Sadie took some comfort from the fact that surveillance had confirmed Vikki was in the building and alive. But Sadie had grown impatient with waiting, ready to move in and get this done.

She'd let Tate into her life. And while she was coming to accept that she didn't need to emotionally flog herself over that fact for the rest of her life, she did need to act.

To save Vikki.

And, maybe, to save herself.

Chapter 17

Tripp ignored the unrelenting fear that gnawed at him with the sharpest of teeth and focused on the team. Everyone had fanned out into their prearranged spots, with SWAT taking point on another warehouse rooftop a building's width away. A sniper, two GRPD detectives and a K-9 trainer capable of handling Greer's dog were also positioned behind the warehouse, determined to catch Tate or his henchman should one of them run out the back.

The intel on the building was solid. Heat sensors had mapped out three people inside as well as the dog. What was presumably Tate and Vikki, based on how one body never moved while the other wove in and around it, were in the center of the building, the dog pacing in time. A third heat signature was positioned near the back entrance.

SWAT had tried to get eyes on that last individual to assess what they'd be up against, but the figure remained stubbornly in place, not moving or making rounds.

It was that third figure that scared Tripp. They were ready for Tate and had a properly trained handler focused on the dog. But the third person was a wild card.

"She's moving in." The comm device in his ear signaled that Sadie was on the move.

Tripp watched from his position, hidden at the edge of the same building SWAT had commandeered.

And prayed this wasn't the last time he'd see her alive.

Sadie had considered how she was going to play this meeting with Tate ever since she'd discovered Vikki had been taken. She'd downplayed the risk to Tripp and her brother and the rest of her family, but never once had she downplayed it to herself.

Tate Greer was dangerous. And there was no way he was going down without a fight.

He'd lost all he could lose and that made him even more deadly than he'd been before. As the head of Capital X, the risk in his life was matched only by all the pieces he controlled. His staff. The people he roughed up when they didn't pay. And all those under the thumb of his criminal enterprise.

But the RevitaYou scam had seen it all vanish, cracking his organization wide-open.

Now he had nothing left to protect. Except his pride.

It was for that reason Sadie had finally settled on her approach. Since she'd spent the past six weeks with her own pride in shambles, it turned out that *that* was the hill she was willing to die on.

The warehouse had a large, covered entrance and she stood there, laying hard on the doorbell that buzzed for after-hours visitors. The GRPD and the Feds had not been able to contact Tate, every call in to him going to voice mail. But he had allowed Vikki a tearful call out to Flynn. Sadie's future brother-in-law had nearly chewed through the phone. It was only through sheer dint of will and his extensive military training that he'd finally been talked into waiting in the SWAT van. If given the chance, he'd have fought Sadie to meet Tate himself, but it was SWAT who'd finally helped her win the argument.

The team leader's report on the interior layout, perimeter access and available sight lines, not to mention the minimal but still existent traffic in the warehouse district, meant they wanted as few extraneous people involved as possible. Anyone other than Sadie risked riling Tate up instead of getting Vikki out.

Sadie lifted her finger then laid it on the buzzer again. The distant sound of a dog barking registered and she nearly stopped the buzzing, having no interest in meeting Snake face-to-face again.

But then she thought better of it.

This was as much a mental game as a physical battle and she needed all the advantage she could get.

The door cracked open, a large gun pointing directly at her face spearing through it. The sound of the dog's whining filled the air, but at least the barking had stopped.

"About damn time you got here." Tate's hand snaked out and covered her wrist, dragging her inside. She'd barely cleared the door when he re-aimed the gun at her. "Take the coat off. Empty your pockets and your purse."

"I don't have a gun." She kept her tone flat and even, unwilling to rise to his bait no matter the subject.

"Yeah, right."

She held up her hands before moving them slowly to her coat to strip it off, letting it drop to the floor. She did the same with her bag, dumping it over first so the contents fell out—her wallet, a brush and a pack of gum.

The items had been deliberate choices, all designed to keep Tate thinking she'd subserviently come to save her sister. What he had no way of knowing was that the gum was a sweet little listening device Ashanti had cooked up about a year ago, or that a Taser had been neatly embedded in the material of the purse. A small switch in the handle would turn the purse into a lethal game changer the moment Sadie confirmed Vikki was okay and was within proper range of Tate.

She considered how easy it had been to enter as she bent to stuff the items back into the purse. It felt like the tide turning in their favor, but was it too easy?

The last briefing from SWAT ran through her mind. The only real identified unknown was the third person in the warehouse. No one had put eyes on the guy and a quick run of Tate's known associates hadn't turned up anyone not already captured. That didn't necessarily mean anything. Tate had eluded arrest for so long, there was no telling how many tentacles he had stuck in any number of places around Grand Rapids.

So she'd keep watch and stay aware. *He* didn't know she knew there was another goon in the place and she needed to keep it that way.

She stood and Tate moved behind her, pushing her

forward with the tip of the gun against her back. She stepped forward quickly, arching away from the gun as her gaze discreetly roamed the warehouse.

Where was Tate's henchman?

And then she saw Vikki and all thoughts of anyone else vanished. Her psycho ex, the gun and the dog were all forgotten as Sadie raced to where Vikki sat, strapped to a wooden chair, her green eyes wide pools of fear in her face.

"Vikki!" Sadie wrapped her arms around her twin, pulling her close and whispering as fast as she could, "It's going to be okay."

Vikki's hands and feet were bound but Tate hadn't gagged her and Sadie felt the press of lips against her cheek and a hard shudder when Vikki exhaled. "You're okay."

"You are, too." Sadie stepped back, concerned by her sister's pale face and fear-filled eyes. Vikki was terrified, which only served to give Sadie's anger a laser-sharp focus.

"He wouldn't tell me anything and I thought he had you."

"Shh, now." Sadie tried to pull Vikki close but Tate had already come between them, pushing Sadie out of the way.

"Aww, isn't this sweet?"

"I'm here now, so you can let her go." Sadie clutched the strap of her electrified bag and refused to cower. She wanted Vikki out of there and then she could distract Tate or subdue him until SWAT found an opening.

Tate pointed the gun at Sadie again, waving it in her face before using it as a pointer against her chest. "You aren't the one giving orders."

"I'm the one you wanted here. Let Vikki go."

Tate's lips curled, an evil mockery of a smile.

God, how had she ever thought herself in love with this man? The very idea of touching him made her skin crawl.

For the past six weeks, thoughts like that had dragged her down, making her feel less than. But in that moment, staring Tate down, Sadie felt the sands shift.

She knew what love was. Real, true love. For Tripp.

Funny how simple it all was now that she had the single-minded clarity to see it.

Tate had betrayed her. If it were simply a case of a romance gone bad, she'd have had to live with that. But it wasn't. He'd proved beyond any doubt that there was nothing good inside him. She could continue to wallow in that, or she could revel in the fact that she'd found this man's antithesis.

Thanks to Tripp McKellar, her faith in other people had been restored. He was good and decent and honest. And while she might think his theories on not forming attachments were stupid, in the end, it didn't matter.

Because she loved him.

And in the loving, she'd found herself again.

Tripp swore as he stared at the front of the warehouse, the quiet drone of comms humming in his ear. They'd cleared all unnecessary chatter off the line, leaving it mainly to SWAT and the department's hostage negotiator. And despite the fact Sadie had been in there for over ten minutes, no one could see her or even think about getting a shot off.

But they could hear her.

The GRPD's tech wizard had connected the interior

comm units to the small listening device Ashanti had created and planted in Sadie's bag, all while keeping the department's comms open and working so everyone had the same intel.

Right now, it was all they had.

Tate hadn't given them anything to work with when he'd opened the warehouse door. He'd handled it by the book, minimizing any exposure to himself as he kept Sadie firmly in front of him, effectively blocking himself.

No matter how well trained the sniper, some shots were still impossible.

The deep-seated desire to run in there was maddening and Tripp wondered how he'd let her do this. As lieutenant, he had a fair amount of say in the ops the GRPD ran and how they were executed. Yet he'd let her go barreling into this situation like John Wayne at her own personal *High Noon*.

Only…

Only it wasn't about *letting* her do anything. She was a grown woman with a strong mind and a high degree of capability. They hadn't sent a civilian in to manage this.

They'd sent a cop.

He'd do well to remember that.

And he'd damn near convinced himself she'd be okay when the voice of one of the SWAT leads came through his earpiece. "Third heat signature is moving. Out of the back of the warehouse and into the main. Moving slow but heading toward the cluster of people in the middle."

The wild card they didn't know what to do with.

Tripp's hands curled into fists and he stared at the warehouse door, willing the events inside to go Sadie's way.

He knew he should wait.

Knew that Sadie and Vikki's lives depended on it.

But he was a cop, too. They might have sent a cop, but there was no way he could let her do this alone.

Before anyone could stop him, Tripp raced toward the warehouse.

Sadie knew she couldn't use the Taser bag too quickly, but everything inside her screamed to get it done. *Get Tate and the dog. Deal with the third man. Get Vikki out.* Backup was so close, the moment she gave the shout, her little pack of gum would alert SWAT to move in.

But Tate's gaze was unrelenting, the gun never moving from where it targeted her chest.

For a split second, all the hope she'd carried inside and on into saving Vikki died. What was she doing there? She had no gun. No body armor. And she was staring down a madman.

Had she really thought she could do this?

Tate had outsmarted her at every step. From their first date on through to the house fire the other day. Did she honestly think she could win now?

"Why'd you do it?" She had no idea where the question came from, but once it was out, there was no holding it back. "Why me?"

That dark grin never faded, but Tate did cock his head, assessing her. "I thought you'd be an easy mark."

Thought?

"You thought wrong."

"Yeah, I did. You never gave me the intel I needed. You protected your family and the damn police department like their secrets were gold. And—" that grin grew darker even as the gun seemed to grow steadier "—I never wanted to be married anyway. I guess I'm really a lifetime bachelor, after all."

"Let my sister go. This is about you and me."

"I don't think I will."

"Then prepare for the full force of the US military to hunt your ass when you take one of their own. And you can put her sergeant fiancé at the front of that line."

Despite the truth of Sadie's words, Tate only laughed. "Keep dreaming, sweetheart."

"So this is the end?" Sadie's hand clenched tighter on her purse and she calculated how she could rush Tate with it and still prevent him from taking a shot.

And realized she couldn't.

Because she hadn't fully calculated the risk to Vikki. And, for all her planning, a man with a gun still trumped a woman with a Taser.

"It sure is, sweetheart. Good thing I still have the credit from our canceled honeymoon in Aruba. I think I may take that trip once this is all over."

Tate's hand never wavered and Sadie eyed her sister, desperate to communicate all her love. She wasn't going down without a fight, and there was no way she was leaving Vikki to Tate's sick and twisted goals. Because once she was gone, she had no doubt he'd turn the gun on Vikki before SWAT could get inside.

"You'll take that honeymoon over my dead body."

Tate nodded. "That's the whole idea."

Sadie moved then, flipping the small switch on the purse just as Ashanti had taught her. The bag hummed in her palm and she swung wide as she moved, determined to hit Tate with the broadside of the fabric.

As she moved, a gunshot rang out and, despite the

near deafening sound, her forward momentum never slowed with the bullet's impact. Instead, she connected with the large figure that raced toward them, even as her body continued onward. Tate seemed to disintegrate in front of her, his large frame crumpling to the floor as her own body tangled with Tripp.

Tripp who took the brunt of Tate's bullet, his heavy body slamming against hers from the force.

The dog moved, too, but Ashanti's invention was Sadie's saving grace. She swung the bag wide, hitting the full left side of the animal. An immediate whine went up as Snake stiffened before falling to the ground in convulsions.

Sadie dropped the bag, twisting to hold on to Tripp's shoulders, all while trying to assess where the shot that hit Tripp had come from.

And saw Brody twenty feet away, a gun in his out-stretched hands.

"Brody!" She shouted to him as the SWAT team rushed the warehouse.

But it was Vikki's warning that filled the room, intent on stemming the tide of firepower moving in.

"Don't shoot! That's our brother!"

Tripp registered the shouts of the sisters and put every bit of force and command he could into his voice from his position on the floor. His chest streamed with fire from where Greer's bullet had hit his vest, but he struggled to his feet. "Stand down! Do not shoot!"

He kept repeating himself, his voice echoing through the warehouse and on back into his ear via their comms.

As the adrenaline-fueled shouts of SWAT calmed, Tripp's gaze swung frantically. And found Sadie huddled over her sister as one of the snipers worked on removing the ties holding Vikki in place.

Brody Higgins stood beside them both, his hands in the air and his eyes wide in his face as they kept shifting to Tate Greer's lifeless form on the floor.

Flynn flew past Tripp into the warehouse, going straight to Vikki. The hostage negotiator working with SWAT was on his heels, moving to Brody. Tripp could do nothing but stand there, taking it all in even as the edges blurred so there was nothing to see but Sadie.

She'd done it.

She'd brought down Tate Greer and whatever was left of Capital X, and saved her sister. She'd known it was the right move and he'd doubted her.

Just like he'd doubted all along. Himself. His feelings. And all that was between them.

Sadie walked to him, moving in close but not touching. "It's finally over."

"All thanks to you."

"And to you." She tapped the vest. "I know a bullet to the vest isn't lethal, but it hurts like hell."

He laid a hand over hers. "I'm good."

"Tripp. It's over." She dropped her hand and turned to survey the room that, in a matter of minutes, had transformed with several teams from the GRPD as well as the FBI. And, mixed in with them all, was a bunch of Coltons. "Brody killed Tate."

"He did. And you were amazing." Tripp could only stare at her, all the things he wanted to say stuck somewhere in the middle of his chest. He loved her.

And he wanted to be with her.

But hadn't this showdown proved him right?

The world was dark and dangerous, and if he'd lost her, he would have been lost himself.

"I want to thank you, Tripp. For everything. You're the reason I got out of Tate's clutches at the lake. And you made sure I was safe after the hospital and the fire. Thank you." She moved in closer, rising on tiptoes to press a kiss to his lips.

It was more chaste than any they'd shared so far, but it packed a far greater punch.

Because in this kiss, he'd felt her goodbye.

Sadie was breaking apart inside as she stepped back, but she refused to give in. Refused to take it easy on Tripp and accept a relationship that was half measure. She loved him and she wanted a life with him. A whole life, not one loaded with strings or laden with fear.

They were strong and they were capable. And they channeled those qualities into doing a job that mattered. If there was danger tied to it, they'd both long accepted the personal risk. Each was entitled to *be* a person. To having a personal life.

And to finding and keeping love.

But she couldn't tell him that. He had to find it all on his own. Had to understand it in his bones.

Riley rushed up to them. Oblivious to the quiet moment, he pulled her into a bone-crushing hug before stepping back and turning to Tripp. "McKellar. Wes Matthews bit."

"Ashanti said she was close," Sadie interjected.

"Closer than we realized. Matthews is smitten and decided to surprise her. He's on a private plane landing in an hour in Florida. Ashanti's already on a plane with the FBI. Chief Fox has a team already coming together to watch the takedown. He wants you there if you're up for it."

Tripp nodded at her brother before turning to Sadie. "I'm sorry."

"Go. We're done here."

His gaze narrowed and she knew he'd heard exactly what she'd meant.

They were done.

Because she wasn't living half a life any longer. She deserved better.

And so did he.

Tripp stared at the large screen in the GRPD's biggest conference room, communications flowing fast and furious from the speakerphone in the center of the oversize table. Matthews's plane would arrive in Florida in ten minutes. Air traffic control had already granted permission to land and the small aircraft was in final descent now.

He should feel triumphant. Satisfied. The RevitaYou case was nearly closed.

We're done here.

Who knew Sadie's comment would be so prophetic? Or as much about them as the case?

"Ashanti's in position." The announcement flowed through his comm unit, Cooper's voice calm as he relayed directives from inside the private terminal.

The takedown was all mapped out. Matthews was on US soil but he had to willingly go with Ashanti. Any appearance of coercion wouldn't look good when this case finally went to trial.

Tripp had every confidence Ashanti could pull it off.

She looked the part of a wealthy investor, her pretty skin set off to perfection against a winter-white suit.

"Plane's on the ground." Cooper affirmed through the comms.

And then they let it all roll.

Tripp listened to Ashanti's smooth purr as she met Matthews for the first time. The lighthearted lines she drawled so effortlessly played to his ego and his intense love of old movies. She had a ready reference from *Casablanca* as they strolled from the terminal toward the waiting limousine outside.

And she was more than happy to channel *Citizen Kane* once she got him to the car.

But it was her last and final reference—to *The Wizard of Oz*—that put the Feds in motion. Just like they'd planned, the moment Ashanti confirmed they weren't in Kansas anymore, Cooper and his team moved in.

Tripp wanted to enjoy it. Wanted to revel in the reality that this was all finally behind them.

Come Monday, he'd go back to his old life.

One that didn't include spending his days with Sadie.

He heard the words flow through the speakerphone. Saw the video feed that matched up on the west wall. And cheered with the rest of the team when Cooper's boss held his badge at eye level in Matthews's face. "Wes Matthews, you're under arrest."

"Wh-what?" the man sputtered, his eyes shooting to Ashanti before swinging back to the large man standing much too close for comfort. "This is ridiculous. I'm here on a personal matter."

Ashanti smiled then stepped back a few feet. "Actually, you're here at the government's request. I'm just doing my patriotic duty."

Before Matthews could sputter out another word, Ashanti turned on one very fine heel and walked away.

Tripp knew her husband waited in another SUV a few feet beyond. A beloved Grand Rapids teacher, he was equally loved by his wife. And despite the thousand plus miles of distance, Tripp also knew what awaited Ashanti when she reached him.

Support.

Mutual respect.

The absolute certainty another had your back.

And, damn it, he'd had that. With Sadie. He'd had all of it and he'd thrown it away because...

Because of Lila?

The FBI read Matthews his rights and informed him of the charges.

Because of the baby?

The man spluttered and cursed the whole time as several FBI team members moved in and secured him in cuffs.

Because he was stupid.

It was the only answer left. Because he'd finally found forever and he would be the world's biggest fool to let it go.

Sadie looked around the small library of the home she'd grown up in and wondered how she'd ended up back here. Not the literal here, since she regularly visited her brother or came over on CI business.

But since she'd already been given one of the guest bedrooms for the night and even had a toothbrush set out on the sink, the proverbial "here" seemed pervasive.

The house doubled as CI headquarters and Riley had already pulled her aside to discuss how he wanted to further expand the business. Ashanti's successful work on the Wes Matthews situation had further confirmed Riley's instincts.

Colton Investigations frequently worked with law enforcement, and the more skilled individuals he carried on his payroll, the more cases the firm could work.

That was why he wanted Sadie to come work for him. As CI's first crime scene investigator.

Sadie rolled the idea around, more and more convinced it was the right choice. As an ex-FBI agent himself, her brother had vast resources, and she'd already told him that he'd need to invest in state-of-the-art equipment if she was going to even consider it. Riley had not only said yes, he'd given her a budget she could work with, and she was already dreaming of the great new tools she could buy.

But it also meant coming home.

She'd keep her apartment and continue living on her own, but making this choice meant she would be tying her life even more tightly to her siblings. And while part of her questioned if she lacked independence, a bigger part of her thought it sounded nice.

Better than nice, actually, especially with Vikki joining CI full time, too. To be part of the family business and use her knowledge doing a job she loved.

She and Vikki had spent about an hour together earlier, talking through what had happened and how happy they were to be back together. By the end, Sadie had known how badly Vik wanted to get to Flynn and she'd sent her off then wended her way through the house to a quiet room not full to bursting with Coltons.

She loved her family, but a bit of quiet was welcome. "Sadie."

Vikki was back and stood at the door. "Someone's here to see you."

Her twin slowly backed out of the entryway as Tripp filled it. And in that moment Sadie finally understood what she'd been feeling.

Like Vikki had wanted the comfort of being with Flynn, all Sadie wanted was Tripp. And she'd accepted that what she'd wanted wasn't possible.

Only, he was here. Now.

And that feeling of safety only intensified, wrapping her in its tight, warm arms. "Hi."

"Hey."

"I heard the FBI took down Matthews."

"It was textbook, thanks to Ashanti. And that is good, since we're going to need every advantage when this goes to trial. And Brody is home and safe."

Sadie nodded, well aware of the risks if things hadn't been handled to the letter. Namely, that Wes would get off and find some way to replicate the project elsewhere.

Tripp continued to stand there, discomfort riding his shoulders like a cloak. "So, um, look… You said something to me. After we talked last. About it all being over."

Hope fluttered once more in her chest but Sadie pushed it down. She couldn't go there. Couldn't let herself believe things might be different for them. "Because it is."

Tripp stepped into the room, carefully closing the French doors before turning back to face her. "Did you mean Greer and Matthews and RevitaYou? Or did you mean you and me?"

"Does it matter?"

"It does." He moved closer. "To me."

"Why?"

"Because I'm done hiding, Sadie. I'm done living half a life. And I'm done believing that having no one in my life is better than risking loving someone."

"I'm glad to hear it."

He stared at her, those steady blue eyes never leaving hers. "Does that mean you'll give me another chance?"

"At what, exactly?"

"At us. At being a couple. At making a life together."

She wanted nothing more, but she couldn't quite let him off that easily. "You're not still upset that it might be awkward at work?"

"No."

"And you need a place to live. You thinking of free-loading off of me for a while?"

A small smile twitched the corners of his lips. "If you'll have me."

"And what about a Christmas tree?"

"What about one?"

"I'm putting up Herman once I get home. I'm not living without a Christmas tree."

"Herman?" His eyebrows narrowed in confusion.

"The tree."

"Oh. Then I won't, either."

She opened her arms. "Come here, Tripp. Please."

It was only once he pulled her close that she let him off the hook. "Even if you feel weird at work or leave your clothes laying around my apartment or hate the Christmas tree, I'm going to love you anyway. I hope you know that."

"Good. Because I'm going to love you, too. Because

I do love you. I love you more than I ever thought possible."

"I love you, too." She pulled him in for a kiss, reveling in the fact that he was there and they were together.

It was only long moments later, when the kiss had faded and they had their heads pressed together, that she remembered her news.

"I do have one more thing to tell you."

"Oh?" Interest sparked in those blue depths. "What is it?"

"I quit. Consider this my two weeks' notice."

Epilogue

Christmas Eve

Alfie raced through Riley's living room as fast as his toddler's gait would carry him. He had speed but was still a bit wobbly on his feet. Sadie let out a quick sigh of relief as she saw Tripp put a steadying hand on an antique manger set that had been her grandmother's.

Now that there were small children in the house, it looked like they'd need to reconsider the placement of some of the holiday decorations. An idea that only made the smile she couldn't seem to stop grow wider.

Then she smiled even more broadly when Tripp reached down and plucked Alfie up, holding him high above his head. The little boy giggled. "Uncle Tip! Airplane, Uncle Tip!"

"Uncle Tip" obliged, moving the boy around in the

air before walking him to the tree so he could touch one of the more precious ornaments on a high branch.

"Watch out, Tripp," Kiely admonished as she walked into the living room with a large tray of desserts. "Those little fists are quick."

"Good thing I'm quicker," Tripp said, closing a hand over Alfie's just before his fingers made contact with crystal.

Tripp then leaned in and made raspberries against the boy's belly, sending Alfie into gales of laughter and effectively distracting him from the tree.

Cooper, following behind Kiely, extended his hands for his son. "Is this one making trouble?"

Tripp gave the boy a quick kiss on the head before he passed him over. "Only the best kind."

"There's a best kind?" Kiely asked.

"When you're two, it's all the best kind."

With his precious charge deposited in his father's arms, Tripp came and took the seat beside Sadie. Just like they always did now, his hand covered hers, their fingers linking. It felt so right—and so natural—Sadie couldn't believe how quickly that simple touch had become a necessity.

Just like Tripp.

The time had seemed to pass in a blur, the RevitaYou case wrapping up with record speed. With Tate Greer dead and Wes Matthews in federal custody, the work had shifted to the federal prosecutors who'd taken over.

It had also left the two of them some quiet time together to settle into their relationship. As part of that, they'd also spent time with her family. Tripp had settled in well to the "Colton Chaos" as she liked to think of it, taking all of them in stride. It helped that he knew so many of them through work, but Tripp had seamlessly moved into a more personal relationship with each of them. Riley, in particular, had warmed to Tripp, their already strong work friendship morphing into a more brotherly relationship.

As if she'd conjured him, Riley entered the room, his hand on Charlize's extended belly before he gently situated her in a chair by the fire. Once he was satisfied she was comfortable, he turned to face them all.

"I think he's going to make a speech," Sadie leaned over and said to Tripp. "Settle in."

Tripp pressed a quick kiss to her cheek. "I'm ready to be inspired."

Sadie couldn't resist sticking her tongue out at her brother before whispering back to Tripp, "You're a traitor to the cause."

Riley waited as everyone quieted, his gaze slowly moving around the living room. Sadie's eyes followed and, despite her teasing over Riley's assumption of de facto elder statesman, she understood his pride. It was an awesome sight to see them all there.

Griffin and Abigail sat on the floor, Maya nestled in Abigail's lap, a stuffed reindeer in her small hand. Vikki and Flynn sat beside Pippa and Emmanuel on one of the large couches that bookended the room, while Kiely and Cooper kept Alfie occupied between them on a matched love seat. And Brody had taken a seat on the end of the couch where Sadie and Tripp sat, opposite to Riley.

Sadie gave Tripp one last kiss before scooting over to sit beside her brother in spirit. Brody had saved her and Vikki. He'd finally decided to take things into his own hands, ending the threat Tate had posed, determined to keep them all safe.

"If I haven't said it lately, thank you." Sadie tucked her hand in the crook of his elbow. "For everything."

Brody blushed but nodded. "I did what I had to do for my family."

"You did."

Riley raised his glass. "As we approach the holiday, we're all here and all together. Our family has faced innumerable challenges this year, but as we come to the close of it, we're stronger than ever. All while growing quite a bit."

"Colton world domination!" Kiely shouted at her brother, eliciting a laugh all the way around. But she was the first to lift her glass in return, everyone else following suit.

"To family!" Riley said, his glass high.

"To family," they all responded in kind.

Sadie gave Brody a large hug before shifting back to extend her hand to Tripp. As his fingers closed over hers, she knew she'd found her place. She'd always had one as a Colton, but now she had another one.

With Tripp.

The man she loved.

As the lights of the tree shone down on all of them, Sadie settled into the joy and beauty of her present.

And knew the future had never been brighter.

* * * * *

Author's Note

For those of you familiar with the Grand Rapids area, you'll know that Sand Springs Lake won't be found on any map. While we tried to use many real areas in and around Grand Rapids in this series, I sought out a fictional location to place Sadie at the opening of the story. I hope you'll forgive the artistic license and agree with me that it would have been a lovely place to go to summer camp!

WE HOPE YOU ENJOYED
THIS BOOK FROM

HARLEQUIN
ROMANTIC SUSPENSE

Danger. Passion. Drama.

These heart-racing page-turners will keep you guessing to the very end. Experience the thrill of unexpected plot twists and irresistible chemistry.

4 NEW BOOKS AVAILABLE EVERY MONTH!

"Get down," he shouted. "It's a drone."

Eva had seen enough movies to know what drones
could do. Jumping aside, she dropped to the floor and
crawled toward the door, glad of her dark room. If the
thing was armed, she wanted to make herself the smallest
target possible. Luckily, her window was closed. She
figured if it crashed into the glass, the drone would come
apart.

By the time she reached her closed bedroom door, the
thing hovered right outside her window, its bright light
illuminating most of her room. She dived for the door
just as the drone tapped against the glass, lightly and
precisely enough to tell her whoever controlled it was
very good at the job.

She'd just turned the knob when the drone exploded,
blowing out her window and sending shards of glass like
deadly weapons into her room.

"Eva!" Jesse's voice, yelling out her name. She focused on that, despite the stabbing pain in her leg. Somehow, she managed to pull the door open and half fell into the hallway, one hand against her leg.

Heart pounding, she scrambled away from her doorway, dimly registering the trail of blood she left in her wake.

"Are you all right?" Reaching her, Jesse scooped her up in his muscular arms and hauled her farther down the hall. Outside, she could hear men yelling. One of the voices sounded like her father's.

"Is everyone else okay?" she asked, concerned.

"As far as I know," Jesse answered. "Though I haven't been outside yet to assess the situation. What happened?"

"It was a drone rigged with explosives." Briefly she closed her eyes. When she reopened them, she found his face mere inches from hers. "Someone aimed it right at my window."

Fury warred with concern in his dark eyes. He focused intently on her. "There's a lot of blood. Where are you hurt?"

Hurt. Odd how being with him made everything else fade into insignificance. In his arms, she finally felt safe.

Don't miss
The Widow's Bodyguard
by Karen Whiddon, available January 2021
wherever Harlequin Romantic Suspense books
and ebooks are sold.

Harlequin.com

Get 4 FREE REWARDS!

We'll send you 2 FREE Books <u>plus</u> 2 FREE Mystery Gifts.

Harlequin Romantic Suspense books are heart-racing page-turners with unexpected plot twists and irresistible chemistry that will keep you guessing to the very end.

FREE Value Over $20